DEFENDING MY BUNK

AGAINST ALL COMERS,

SIR!

DEFENDING MY BUNK
AGAINST ALL COMERS,
SIR!

GARRET MATHEWS

Like the main character in this book, I went to Fort Leonard Wood, Missouri, in 1971 for basic training after four free-and-easy years of college. I was sure the drill sergeants were going to kill me.

- Garret Mathews

ZONE PRESS
Denton, Texas

Defending My Bunk
Against All Comers,
Sir!

Garret Mathews

Published in the United States of America
By Zone Press

www.zonepress.com

an imprint of Rogers Publishing and Consulting, Inc.
201 North Austin
Denton, Texas 76201

Editing and Design: Randy Cummings

ISBN: 0-9777558-9-4

CHAPTER 1

March 1971

Night falls on the seven-story monolith known as a college residence hall, or a dormitory, or a place parents would board up if they knew half of what goes on.

I've lived in room 5065 for three years. Nothing gets past me.

I know who's getting any and who isn't.

I know who thought he could get even higher if he tried eating the incense.

I know who likes to sneak cartons of milk inside room heaters, turn it up 10 degrees and then pretend he has no idea what's causing the smell.

I know who finally landed got the job interview with the insurance company, only to find out all the guy had in mind was selling him a term-life policy.

I even know what's going on right now.

Newton, the psychology major, is scribbling furiously. He's trying to compose a letter that will not only fool Dear Abby, but make her nationally syndicated column.

He got nowhere pretending to be a mountain climber who lost a testicle in an avalanche, and wanting to know if it would hurt to watch a porn movie. This time, he's recovering from an industrial accident that required the complete removal of his asshole. He asks Abby if he should tell his girlfriend about the surgery, or let the chick find out for herself.

A dozen of us follow Osgood to the back door of the dorm. He stands motionless on the sidewalk, where he must remain for 10 minutes. This is the rule. He cannot jump up and down. He cannot wrap his arms around his body. He can give no outward indication that he's cold. The slightest violation means he forfeits his fee.

We watch through the fogged-up window, and wonder how he keeps from becoming a hunkahunka frostbite. He turns red, then sheet-metal white. His nipples could cut rock. The only way we know he's not unconscious is his frozen breath.

Osgood has absolutely no athletic ability, but in the sport of sidewalk-standing in Arctic weather, he's an overpaid superstar.

He stuffs the bills in the side of his jockstrap.

"Appreciate it, boys. Next show's at midnight."

I'm expecting an important visitor, as important as visitors get to a senior who faces the pointing finger of Uncle Sam come June.

Sixteen months ago, they had the first national draft lottery for men ages 19 to 26. Prime time TV. Little white balls with our birthdates on the front were put into this hopper and swirled around. Some guy with a suit said a few words, and then they started pulling up the balls at random. It looked like a giant game of bingo except this was war. Each local draft board has a certain amount of openings it must fill, but you could consider yourself relatively safe if your birthday was the 150th selected, and extremely safe if it was No. 200 or more. My ping-pong ball was the 71st to come up. I will almost certainly have a military experience. I can wait to be drafted, volunteer for the draft or sign up for the reserves or National Guard.

Everybody who gets inducted has eight weeks of basic training followed by another eight weeks of advanced individual training in whatever military specialty you signed up for. Active duty is a much shorter commitment - as little as two years - but Vietnam is likely to be in your destination. The guard and reserves are safer, but you must agree to two days of monthly drill and two weeks summer camp for six years.

Carl, a friend of my roommate's, joined the Army reserve last year after getting out of school. I'm planning the same draft dodge, end run, whatever you want to call it. Vietnam doesn't get most-favored nation status from me, or anyone else around this place.

It was different during World War 11. There was an enemy that wanted to take over the world - an enemy you could put an evil face on. If you couldn't get pissed at Hitler, there was something seriously wrong with your anger coefficient.

Vietnam isn't like that. The enemy is north of a line on the map that wants to take over the corrupt land mass south of the line on the map. There's no Hitler, just squirrelly VC who live in holes in the ground. If they want both sides of the line, what's it to us?

Not worth getting shot at. Not worth dying.

If we're going to praise the Lord and pass the ammunition, give us an Iwo Jima. Give us panzer divisions. Not a Hill 16-A.

Carl dates a girl who goes to school here. Tonight, he said he'd cut it short and give me a primer on what happens when the Army has its way with you.

I look around my dorm room.

Poster of Peter Fonda on a motorcycle and his buddy Dennis Hopper giving the finger. Poster of George Harrison and a dove, captioned "Work For Peace." Poster of Chicago's antiwar album that features group members in guerrilla-style uniforms. Self-help pamphlet on what to do if you're tear-gassed. A magazine article about two political science professors here who were arrested for disrupting field exercises by the Corps of Cadets. A notebook filled with jokes my 72-year-old industrial procurement teacher told in class. The most recent entry begins with a toilet-paper shortage at a boarding house, and ends with him pretending to wipe his ass with a lone sheet and saying, "What's par for this hole?"

And a poster of a poem by Frederick Parls:

I do my thing,
And you do your thing.
I am not in this world to live up to your expectations,
And you are not in this world to live up to mine.
You are you,
And I am I,
And if by chance we find each other,
It's beautiful.

Assorted roach clips. Assorted love beads. Assorted stolen Civil Defense signs.

I am freer than I've ever been in my life.

Go to bed when I want. Boycott cleanliness if I want. Pour Vitalis on our dicks and see who can scream the loudest if we want. Boycott the campus bookstore. Sneak packs of rubbers in books and watch the matronly librarian shriek in horror, remove all personnel within a 25-foot radius and otherwise treat the things like nuclear waste.

I can piss on the steps leading to the university president's mansion.

I can wear my jeans to the limits of the manufacturer's guarantee - 1,000 consecutive days or one machine-washing, whichever comes first.

I can pretend that when the door on room 5065 closes on Saturday night, I'm sending my girlfriend, Kathy, to orgasmic frenzy, even if all she wants to do is talk about how cute Neil Diamond is. That's why we put Vitalis on our dicks. Might as well use them for something.

The Army is the sworn enemy of this enlightenment, the coughing up of everything that is college.

Rumors constantly clock in.

That the drill sergeants will make it extra hard on us because we used the student deferment to delay going in the service, and spent four years getting high and doodling pictures of Nixon with a ponytail.

That they will march us day and night until our minds are right and we swear to God we no longer care who performed at Woodstock.

One guy on the dorm says he's heard from a reliable source that they threaten to shoot us.

I have to find out from someone who's been there. Someone who knows what a platoon looks like. Someone who knows the percentage of basic trainees who don't survive boot camp.

Suddenly, a loud "hut, two-three-four" from the hall followed by laughter.

I look out the door to see a shrimp of a guy in an Army uniform looking at room numbers. It would be impossible for a human being to be more out of place.

"It's a lone sentry," Wingfield hollers from his crow's nest.

"Tell him the front is that way," Newton hollers back, pointing to the duck pond.

"Disarm him," Gino shouts. "We've had enough civilian casualties this semester."

The little guy absorbs the insults and keeps walking and looking.

If Brick finds out what's going on in his sink, we probably will need protection. But who elected this castaway from the PX?

Then it hits me.

This must be Carl.

Except for his glasses and red face, he looks like a leafy vegetable.

"Had a drill," he explains. "Didn't have time to change out of my fatigues."

I try his cap on for size.

"So this is what I have to look forward to."

"Yeah," Carl says. "Steel helmet, pistol belt, bayonet - they dress you for success."

I pour him a Southern Comfort. It lasts as long as it takes Audie Murphy to draw a bead.

Clearly, Carl is bugged about something more substantial than showing up in a college dorm wearing OD green.

"The reserve meeting today," he explains. "I really blew it."

"How?" I ask.

"They're trying to make a truck driver out of me."

"And it's not taking?"

"Yeah, I'd call knocking the roof off the motor pool not taking."

"With dynamite?"

"No, with a truck. You ever been around a bunch of Army guys?"

I shake my head. And I don't want to either.

"Some'll tell you the truth. Some'll mess with you. You never know who's who."

I pour one of my own and sit back in the chair. This will be my first dose of military lore and I want to take it all in.

"I'm driving the dump truck, right?" Carl says. "There's a ton of shit in the back. Ropes, shovels, spools of cable. The sergeant of the motor pool tells me to back the truck in the bay.

"Here's where you gotta understand the military. The sergeant wanted to have a little fun, and I was the only channel on TV. He knew I had only driven the truck a time or two. There's maybe three inches of clearance on either side of the door. The Marquis de Sarge was positive I'd bang into the side and everybody would have a big laugh.

"Somehow I managed to get the truck inside the motor pool without hitting anything. They didn't get their har-de-har-har, so he told me to raise the bed and empty the load.

"Here's where the trust thing comes in. Some of the guys want to see you do good. If they see the truck bed getting near the ceiling, they holler at you to bring it down. Other guys get off on chaos and they lie out their ass. When the bed gets up to the ceiling, they scream out that you've got plenty of room and bring it up some more.

"So this is what we've got: The Amateur Night truck driver barely knows how to work the dump levers. He hears the advice from both sides, tries to process the information, can't, gets flustered and does nothing. With no one to tell it otherwise, the back end goes onward and upward and smashes through the roof.

"The ceiling came down in chunks. It was like being in an earthquake. Some guys were laughing and some were running for cover. I felt like a piece of insulation. All I wanted to do was get blown away."

I don't know what to say.

"So you want to find out how you'll do in the Army, is that right?"

I think I already know. That could easily have been me in the dump truck.

"This is the biggest thing right here: Do you have common sense?" Carl asks.

I've known this person less than 15 minutes, and already he's nailed me. As a child, I was told I didn't have any common sense. Time passed, and I proved it. More time passed, and I would put it on my business card if I had one.

"You know how it is when you have to figure something out on the spur of the moment, and you just stand there with your finger up your ass?"

I nod.

"The Army eats up guys like that."

Oh, God.

"Ever shoot a rifle?"

"No."

"Ever fold laundry well enough to please your Mom? In the Army, that ranks right up there with overrunning the enemy."

"No."

"Ever report to the commode first thing in the morning and clean someone else's shit stains with a toothbrush?"

"No."

"Prepare to be a casserole, my friend."

Oh, God.

But as bad as I feel, Carl is worse.

"Do you know where the battery is on a dump truck?" he asks.

"Under the hood?" I reply. "Isn't that a rule?"

"Not in the Army. It's two hours after the ceiling incident, and the word is out that I've become the company fuck-up. I'm supposed to be pulling maintenance on my truck. Captain hasn't had his afternoon chuckle, so he comes around and wants to know if I've checked the battery. I lie and say, sure, first thing every morning. Then he calls my bluff. Wants to see a demonstration.

"I'm cool because I know it's just a simple matter of looking under the hood. I swagger to the front of the truck and pop the top. I'm not a complete idiot. I know what a battery looks like. A square box with little covers over the water thingies. I look everywhere. By the engine. By the belt. By the radiator. Nothing.

"Out of sight, not in the truck, right? So I blurt out that it doesn't have one.

"The captain gets a load of that and hollers for everybody to come over.

"Officers, enlisted men, merchants from their stores, farmers from their fields - every living soul reports to my truck.

"Captain announces in loud voice that Carl here drives the only truck in the Army that magically starts itself without a battery.

"Thigh-slapping all around.

"Then dozens of people - probably all Teamsters - point to the step leading to the passenger-side door. I open it and there's the battery, bigger than life. I thought they'd never stop laughing. This has absolutely been the worst day of my life."

I didn't cry at "Love Story," but "Battery Ballad" rips my guts out.

"Assholes gave me a nickname. Wanna guess?"

I can't imagine.

"Jumper Cable."

Carl looks at his watch.

"Gotta be leaving pretty soon. Sky's gonna fall on me while I walk to my car. Wouldn't want to keep it waiting. You say you've got some questions for me?"

Have I got questions? Does Vitalis have sting?

"Will I die?"

"No, but you'll think you will. That's the part of boot camp the Army likes most of all."

"What do you mean?"

"Spreading a bunch of crap that isn't true. Getting you all worried. Like the time they told us we'd have to pair up with somebody and actually give mouth-to-mouth resuscitation. Refuse to do it, the DIs said, and you'll flunk first aid. Flunk first aid and get recycled."

"What's recycled?"

"Your worst nightmare. That's when they make you start basic training all over with another outfit. I'd hear that word and do anything they say. Bring on some fairy from New York City with canker sores, I don't care."

"Did you really have to put a lip lock on another guy?"

"Hell, no. We just had to look at a glossy photo and pretend. But that's what I mean about stressing you out. They see us all afraid and going from squad to squad trying to find a guy we can stand to kiss, and they get off big-time."

"What did it feel like when they cut your hair?"

"Like all of a sudden I had this big breezeway on top of my head. It bothered me for a day or two, but then I realized everybody at this god-forsaken place looks like he's got the mange. I fit right in."

"That's going to be weird," I say. "I've grown accustomed to my comb."

"Flush it when you get out there. One less thing to think about."

"I've been running a bunch of laps around the drill field," I say. "How important is being in shape?"

"It's not unimportant, but the physical part isn't the hardest thing. Ever get up at 4:30?"

"Roll over, yes. Become upright, no."

"Ever stay on the go for 16 hours a day?"

"No."

"Doing stuff you don't want to do?"

"No."

"With people you don't want to be with?"

Carl is wrong. I am going to die.

"Gotta go. Here are a few things to remember: Don't let them catch you with your hands in your pocket. Don't be first at anything or they'll expect it all the time. Don't be last for obvious reasons. Your best bet is to stay in the middle and be as anonymous as possible. Act sincere and you can get an hour off on Sundays. Tell them it's your religion. The Joint Chiefs don't want to take on the church. The DI would wave me off and I'd go back to the barracks and read Playboy. One last thing. Don't steal any ammo. Then they probably would kill you."

A mock salute and Carl is gone.

If I thought talking to a real soldier would reduce my anxiety, I thought wrong.

I'll get drawn and quartered during basic training. Then at reserve meetings, they'll run over my remains with dump trucks.

Why am I so scared?

I've never been what you could call decisive. I didn't get around to applying for college until it was almost too late, and I didn't care what I majored in. Dad stepped in - as he has learned to do - and suggested business. He thought if I studied moguls, I'd grow up to want to be one. That sounded no worse than anything else, so that's what I put on the form.

In college, I've been the shit shoveler in the Saddle Club's parade. Staying in the rear. Plugging along. Just going to class and doing my job. And it is a job. Not smart enough to nail the "A" and have my chest pinned by the parade marshal, but hard-working enough to get that "B" and earn the congratulations of the corral keeper. I only understand fragments of what the profs are talking about, and would flunk except for my ability to memorize reams of notes. I pack all the paragraphs in for the exam, spew it out on the test paper and completely forget it by supper.

Quotient curves, market baskets, standard deviation - I hate you. I'm not going to make my living selling something to somebody, and I'm not going to stand in some glass stall pulling inventory control on the crap that comes down the conveyor.

So why don't I change majors?

Silly, because I'd have to show some initiative. Find the right dean. Sign a bunch of papers. Buy yet another stack of expensive books I won't want to read.

My problem is that I have no passion for academics. English, history, sociology - whatever I changed to would just mean new and different notes to memorize. It would be like getting hitched to another plow.

Better to just ride it out until I graduate. Shake some formal-looking dude's hand, collect my diploma and then toss it in the trash for all the good it'll do me.

What I really want to do is write funny articles for newspapers. I've done a bunch the past two years, and several have been printed in the school paper. Socialites who hire hippies to punch up their parties. Bras that glow in the dark so lost souls can find their way. Congressmen getting so old they could get a quorum in the Mayo Clinic. I can go on and on about almost anything.

Slim and Gino are always on my case about joining the staff of the Collegiate Times. I lie and say I'm too tied up with macroeconomics for such a massive time commitment.

Truth is, I'm too shy.

I went to their office once with a folder of fresh stories. The busy guy behind the news desk shot me a "What do you want?" with a ferociousness that almost broke off the pencil he had in his mouth. I was already scared. Now I was petrified. Forget introducing myself to the features editor. I had to get out of there.

But it had to be without revealing my true purpose.

"Uh, I'm with work-study and we're going around cleaning offices and we're wanting to know what time to clean the newspaper office," I said.

"Midnight. That's deadline. Then we go to the Greek's for beer."

"Er, midnight. Right," I stammered. "Uh, ah, good. Very good."

I left faster than a vacuum cleaner sucks up a paper clip.

But a vital piece of information had been dispensed. Now I knew how to turn in my stories without having to encounter Pencil Man, or anyone else in authority. Folder in hand, I waited in the bushes outside the Student Union with eyes aimed on the second-story window of the newspaper office. 12:05. 12:10. 12:15. Lights out. I gave the last staff writer a few minutes to clear the hallway before sprinting up the stairs, slipping my material under the door and making my getaway into the night.

No muss, no fuss, and they don't know my face from Mister Clean.

I spend my spare time typing the cleaner stories and sending them to editors of large newspapers. I just know one of these guys will fall in love with my work and hire me.

So far I've gotten nothing but rejection letters.

"The articles are in very poor taste and I would not want to see them in our paper." - Cleveland Plain Dealer.

"We don't handle fiction here. As to the judgment you seek about your future, your best course is to continue as a business major." - Cincinnati Enquirer.

"I regret to say we have no openings that we think you could possibly qualify for." - Raleigh, N.C., News and Observer.

But I'm not discouraged, As soon as one batch comes back, I type a new cover letter and ship it out again. Some big-city editor will laugh himself silly over the glow-in-the-dark bra and beg me to work for him.

There's entirely too much stress in my life trying to get through labor economics, and getting enough stories ready so I can send off to *The Dallas Morning News* by the weekend.

I don't need the Pentagon, too.

And on top of everything else, I have to live with the fact that the Army came up on me and I did nothing about it. Other guys who don't want to become part of the war machine fled to Canada, or ate 317 bananas on the eve of the physical to make their blood pressure go into uncharted territory. The most I could muster was to pretend not to hear anything during the auditory exam. I passed with better marks than a listening device.

I just did what they said. Did nothing to influence the outcome. Pretended it was happening to someone else. Just plugged along.

Carl's visit reminds me to call Dad. The last time we talked, he said he might have a surprise for me.

We exchange pleasantries for about two seconds, and then he gets right to the point. My future.

"You just gonna sit there and let them draft you?"

"Uh, gee, Dad," I stammer, "I've been real busy with tests and everything."

"You wanna go to Vietnam, or get your service hitch over with stateside without being shot at?"

He's been after me for months to call Army Reserve and National Guard outfits to see if they have any openings. I've done what I've always done when faced with a stop along life's highway. Come to a gradual halt and stay in a fixed position for as long as possible. Don't dare be a participant. Be an observer instead. Even if it's my balls that are on the line.

Mom's in the background excitedly saying, "Tell him, tell him."

I'm thinking either peanut butter cookies are in the mail, or they're getting me designer headbands for my birthday.

Dad drops the news.

"The reserves. You're in."

"Really?"

"I knew you wouldn't do anything so I did. The fourth unit I called has a slot open. You come in Friday after your last class to sign up."

"Thanks, Dad. You're something."

You have to know my father. Yes, he did what he did so his firstborn won't have to ship out to Da Nang. But he also enjoys being the burr under the saddle - the guy who pesters and pesters until you finally give in. Go out to dinner with him and he adds the check five different times to make sure he isn't overcharged. He never fails to find something, even if it's just a dime. He walks out of the restaurant as proud as if he's solved the national debt. We were at a motel a few years ago and the air-conditioning wasn't working right. The family's on vacation, but he spends three hours fixing it. Got grease and oil all over him, and Mom threatened to leave him. Next morning, he gave the motel operator a bill for $110 labor plus parts. Guy paid every cent.

"Non-com answers the phone, right?" Dad says. "Probably an E-6. Know what that is?"

I think of Osgood. "Elvis to the sixth power?"

"No, a mid-ranking sergeant. Puts his pants on the same way you do."

"But his are starched."

"Never mind. I pretend I'm you. I tell the guy I'm graduating in June, and does he have any openings? He says no, they're full.

"Well, I'm not about to accept that. I tell him to check supply. They always need people to pass out ponchos. He pulls the file. Nothing.

"Then I have him check for mechanics. You can never have too many grease monkeys. He looks. Nothing.

"Then I remember what you're taking in school. Payroll, I tell the guy. Net income earned. F.I.C.A. taken out. Got to have a good man at the pay window. Persistence pays, son. He examines the records, and turns out the man in that slot gets out later this year. You're his replacement. You report to Fort Leonard Wood in Missouri for basic training on Sept. 3."

"But Dad, I despise that W-2 crap."

"Do you like Saigon better?"

"Friday afternoon, you say? I'll be there."

Sharp. Maybe even starched.

I should be out of my head with joy, but I'm not.

If I had been anywhere near a grownup, I would have taken care of this myself. Called the non-commie, or whoever he is, and told him I want to be in that number.

But I didn't, and had to depend on a dad of a motel repairman.

I just see what's in front of me. Shirts next door going at closeout prices. The leading candidate for student body president advocating locking the president of the university in the administration building and charging him with trespassing. Newton writing another letter to Dear Abby asking point-black if she wears corduroy drawers.

The dorm is a chaise lounge. I want to keep sitting until campus security comes to fold it up.

I don't do new well.

And that's the Army.

A wide-eyed stranger in buttons and brass.

Biding its time. Waiting to take me away.

I hear Osgood running down the hall and banging on doors.

"Jock time, boys. Special midnight show. Osgood's Famous Water Torture Test. Same jockstrap. Same 10 minutes standing outside in horrible weather. Only this time the fool takes a cold shower immediately before. Double the risk, double the fee."

The crowd files in the bathroom, and Wingfield sets the shower on stun. Osgood stands in like it's Acapulco in July, tilting his head from side to side and opening his mouth wide like the chicks in the shampoo commercials.

The guy hooks me again. I pay the two bills.

Osgood, the Pied Piper of freezer burn, leads the way to the back door. Water is still beading on his back as he steps outside.

Within 60 seconds, you could balance a dinette set on Osgood's nipples. He stands silently and unmoving. Give him a parka and an icepack and he could be one of Robert Peary's men at the North Pole.

I look around at my fellow students who can't find anything better to do on a Sunday night than watch frozen stilettos form on a guy's chest.

I'd keep it right here if I could.

Freeze-frame Osgood and his nipples.

Dutch and his sheep nuts.

Slim and Gino and their cookbook.

The performance is over. Calmly, as we've come to expect, the star flips a three-inch icicle off his jockstrap.

"Next show, 10 o'clock tomorrow night. Ice-cold pop cans taped to my ass. Triple the risk, triple the fee."

We walk back to our rooms and talk about what we've just seen. The consensus: If Osgood did half as well in his business courses as he did standing outside damn near naked, he'd be CEO of Coca-Cola.

Brick greets us in the hall. He is holding his dripping-wet underwear and beaming.

"Cleanest I've ever gotten them. Must be the pre-soak."

CHAPTER 2

The Greyhound lurches to a stop beside what looks like a large garbage can spread end to end with front and center doors and oversized ball bearings for tires. Two soldiers are standing watch.

"Cattle car, you ignorant peckerheads," the biggest screams. "Shake your pitiful little asses and get in."

The smaller man approaches his buddy with a look of concern. They confer.

"Uh, wait a minute, guys," Little Man says. He sounds almost polite, as if wanting to make amends for the insult to our asses. "Line up. Don't matter where."

Little Man reads from a training manual. He is more serious than a Holy Roller preacher.

"It says here that before any instructional situation, a joke will be told. Said joke will serve to prepare troops for positive learning environment. Said joke should be either funny, clever or, preferably, both. Failure to tell joke could result in disciplinary action."

He nods to Big Man who takes center stage.

"Anybody know why it takes two hours to get from Fort Leonard Wood to St. Louis, but only 10 minutes to get back?"

We have no idea.

"Because Fort Leonard Wood sucks."

Little Man puts his manual away. The Henny Youngman rule thus obeyed, he can get back to the business at hand.

"Stow your gear and get in the cattle car," Big Man hollers. "I don't give a fuck if it's crowded. Last one in bites dicks."

A pause to wipe the froth.

"What sorry pieces of shit they keep sending us. Makes me want to wipe my ass just looking at you."

It's after midnight. We're squeezed inside a rolling garbage can going God knows where to have God knows what done to us, and there's a guy I don't know sitting on my lap.

Seems a good time to review events of the day that have brought me to this moment.

Up at dawn. Parents drive me to airport. Plane is waiting. Only thing that can get me out of it now is a skyjacker. Shake hands with Dad, more or less manfully. Then Mom starts crying and goes on and on about how this is the last time she'll see me alive. She asks for a lock of my hair, "Just in case."

This is the last thing Dad wants to hear. He spent most of last night trying to convince me it's not in the Army's best interests to blow me away. If every basic trainee dies, Dad reasoned, how can the country possibly carry out an effective national defense policy?

Hugs all around, and I promise to call as soon as the sergeant of the dial tone lets me.

Three-hour flight to St. Louis. Then a lengthy wait at the terminal for Greyhound to saunter the 125 miles west on Interstate 40 to Fort Leonard Wood, Mo.

Go to bathroom. See guy in process of removing his Army clothes and putting on civvies. He feels the need to explain.

"Don't want to go walking around the airport in uniform. They give you the finger, spit on you, throw stuff at you. I don't need that."

Earlier, I heard a soldier talk about how much money you save on airfare if you take the military discount and wear your uniform.

"Not worth it, man," the bathroom guy explains. "I'd rather pay more than look like a freak."

"That bad?" I ask.

"Every bit," he replies as he stuffs the uniform in his garment bag and walks away.

The Fort Leonard Wood bus is announced. I fall in step with a guy who has a horrible limp. The rest of us fresh hires look like we need painkillers. This kid is smiling.

I wonder aloud how he can be in good humor.

" Because I ain't staying."

Say what?

" Because of this." He raises the bottoms of his jeans. Even in the dark I can see his left leg is at least two inches shorter than the right.

No offense, I say, but you're not exactly able-bodied.

"Of course I'm not."

Then you shouldn't be on this bus.

"Sure, I shouldn't."

I'm confused. If ever there's an excuse for getting out of the Army, it's dragging one leg after the other.

He pulls out his wallet and fans the bills.

"I went with my friend to the recruiter. My buddy got all signed up and we started to leave. Then the Army guy pulled me aside. Asked if I wanted to take a free plane ride. Asked if I wanted free meals for two days plus 20 bucks he'd kick in himself.

"I've never been more than 100 miles from my hometown. Never been anywhere near an airplane and this man's gonna give me spending money to boot? I said, hell, yeah, what do I have to do?

"The recruiter said he's short on his monthly quota and I can be one of his fudge factors. He puts my name on the list and gives me some other guy's paperwork.

"Here's the plan: I fly out to the camp. They see in about two seconds that somebody really screwed up. I get a bed for the night, a flight back home and a free adventure. Can't beat that."

The bus is a missile into the night. Slower than the real thing, but no less guided.

No toilet stop. No stop to check the tires. No stop to see if anybody tried to off himself.

Too soon, there's the sign. "Fort Leonard Wood, Exit 1 Mile."

Time for one last fantasy. Abbie Hoffman is driving. He doesn't want us to learn to kill our fellow man. He doesn't want Short Leg to defraud the federal government. So he hits the gas and doesn't slow down until we get to Springfield. When questioned by the press, he says he was just doing the Cambodia Shuffle.

But, no. The bus gets off at the St. Robert ramp. Three minutes later, we're at the front gate.

I'm expecting flashing lights, maybe even a floor show featuring helmeted go-go dancers spelling out, "Your Ass Is Mine."

But all we see is a single soldier with the white gloves of a traffic cop.

"Go to the same place as usual?" the Greyhound driver asks. "Where they park all the cattle cars?"

A bored White Gloves just nods. Clearly, he dances for no man.

I don't either.

The guy on my lap weighs a ton, smells like a wet sock and has a boil on the back of his neck that looks calcified.

But I can't be bothered with that right now. Where are we going? And what will they do to us when we get there?

We pass a row of square buildings. I'm looking for something, anything, to feel good about. They aren't adobe huts. That's a positive. They aren't making us pull the cattle car like we're a mule team. You gotta like that. The road is paved and I think I see a Pepsi machine. Maybe we'll survive with flesh wounds.

"Out, out, out," Little Man says.

"Line the fuck up," Big Man hollers.

"Reception center," Boil whispers.

I shake my head. "Penal colony."

"No, no, no, goddammit." Big Man is screaming at Short Leg. "Quit standing sideways."

The kid gives it his best shot, but he's like a grocery store cart with two wheels missing.

"What the hell's the matter with you?" Big Man wants to know.

Little Man, ever alert to matters of procedure, eyeballs Short Leg from top to bottom and consults his training manual. Then he whispers to his buddy.

"Uh, you, stand down," Big Man says, significantly lowering the volume, "or at least try to."

A soldier we haven't seen before comes up and says something to Short Leg. They leave together. And not for limb-lengthening school, I'll wager.

The temporary troop had it pegged. Here and gone without ever seeing a spent round.

But class is in session for the rest of us.

"I say 'Attention!' and you WILL stand like this," Big Man says, looking like a steel girder in boots with a fender for a forehead.

"I say 'Parade rest!' and you WILL stand like this," he goes on, striking a decidedly uncomfortable pose with hands held tightly behind his back. If I had to watch a parade like this, I wouldn't go. Especially not at 1 o'clock in the morning.

Our gear is in front of us. For most, it's suitcases and the occasional satchel. But one guy packed a pillow - a big, fluffy job straight from his bedroom.

Big Man is first to notice.

"If you can't shoot the enemy, you'll smother him to death in his sleep, is that right, troop?"

"No, actually it's because of my sinuses," the smallest of our bunch replies calmly in a New Jersey accent I hate already. "This one is thicker than most pillows and it seems to help the drainage. I know it looks a little strange for a grown man to carry his pillow to basic training, but it's really quite medicinal."

"Fuck medicinal," Big Man says, kicking the pillow.

"No, really, it's true," the kid replies instructionally, as if he's the one in charge. "You know what a placebo is?"

"Fuck, no."

"It's a mental thing, Mr. Sergeant. Something you think will work, even if it has no basis in science. They give you a pill, you believe it's a wonder drug and, bingo, you're cured. Same way with the pillow and my sinuses. My pillow is probably no different from any other, but I've come to believe in it."

"Fuck your pillow. Fuck your sinuses. Fuck the hospital you were born in."

"I know it's a tough concept. But if you're sufficiently attuned to your inner self, it's not difficult to understand."

Big Man lacks the upstairs equipment to win a reasoning competition with a septic tank. Wanting to hit the guy but wary of his buddy's rule book, he storms inside the nearest building and slams the door.

Clearly, no basic trainee fresh off the cattle car has ever given a lecture on sinus pressure. Little Man is unsure what to do next, so he adopts an old standard.

"Smoke 'em if you got 'em, boys."

Thanks to Fluffy Pillow, our tormenters are taking five.

Boil says what the rest of us are thinking.

"You really had 'em going back there, man. Bingo, ha. They didn't know whether to shoot you or just beat you to death. What's your name, anyway?"

"Kippler, Eric, with a 'c'." His pillow has suffered severe abdominal wounds, and he's performing emergency first aid. "They can't, you know."

"Can't what?" Boil asks.

"Beat even a little shit out of us. They can threaten to mutilate us. They can show us pictures of trainees they claim to have mutilated. They can even schedule us for mutilations. But they can't actually do it. Don't you morons know that?"

The points Kippler scored with "Bingo," he just threw out the window.

"I ain't no moron," Boil growls.

"Sure we are," Kippler says. "We're here, aren't we?"

I speak for the doubters in the group.

Big Man, I point out, is a fortress of a human being. If Little Man hadn't stepped in when he did, your guts would be on the ground.

Kippler's ears perk up at the slightest hint of an argument.

"A mere detail. I would have thought of something. I always do. The difference between me and the rest of you is that I know how to talk."

Now Boil is really pissed. Thinking may be beyond him, but he's been verbal since pre-K.

"What are you, some kind of fucking lawyer?"

"In three years, yes. You'll be paying money you don't have to get me to keep you out of jail."

Again, I speak for the doubters. Unless we're in front of a New Jersey tribunal, which at least in my case is highly unlikely, we'll hire a mouthpiece who doesn't think his clients are worthless pieces of shit.

Kippler reacts to an adversarial situation like a junkie to a hypo.

"Let's take a hypothetical situation here."

"This ain't no courtroom," Boil says.

Kippler shoots him a look of superiority in the manner of Robert Frost reading from his work to the guy who writes the Burma-Shave signs.

"I'm not exactly a hulk of a man, right?"

Everybody in Missouri could kick his ass and only be 30 percent on-task.

"And I probably won't be the greatest soldier."

Anybody who brings his pillow to basic training has fuck-up written all over him.

"Exactly. So how am I planning to get by?"

Bribe the guards, somebody says.

"No," Kippler says, "simply be smarter than everybody else. I got 1450 on my SATs. Anybody close?"

I made 980. I slink into the darkness.

Boil drops off the page.

Kippler is really starting to feel it now.

"Guy commits assault on my pillow, and then he confronts me, and I get him to walk away. How many of you could do that?"

Not me. The first time Big Man hollered at me to fuck something I'd hump it in front of the entire group. Be too scared to do anything else.

"You fight back without appearing to fight back," Kippler explains. "Sinuses and placebos were my counterpunches. He thought I'd just stand there and take it. When I didn't, he had no idea what to do. He ran inside the building so we wouldn't see him lose face."

Big Man opens the door to a classroom.

"Major wants to see you pricks. Take a seat."

The flight, the wait, the bus, getting screamed at, Kippler - we've had enough for one day. We file in like a bunch of 90-year-olds. If the room was a beachhead, we couldn't hold it against a squad of Brownie Scouts.

Unlike Big Man, the features of the reception center's head honcho are decidedly non-Cro-Magnon. Early 40s. Jaw only medium-thick granite. Touch of gray in the temple. Touch of mashed potatoes in the gut. Except for the perfectly pleated uniform and the insignia and the horrible haircut, he could work alongside your dad at the bank.

There's no anger in his voice. No intimidation. No this-is-your-last-night-on-Earth.

The man is even smiling. God, can we keep him?

He gives us the welcome to Fort Leonard Wood bit. These barracks will be your home for the next few days until we can get you processed. And there's a lot to be done. Take tests. Do paperwork. Get uniforms. Get nametags sewn on. Get shots. Get gear. Guys have been coming in all day and you're the last ones. Around 200 of you. Five platoons. One company.

He speaks firmly for the first time. You'll all be together - now and in basic - so get used to it. College guys, high school guys, guys who need to be led around by the hand. The Army doesn't care who you are.

One last thing, the major says. He walks to the back of the classroom and stands in front of a section of wall that has a gaping hole in it.

"Some of you brought weapons to the base. Some of you have pills, reefer, liquor, maybe even smack. That's OK. If I was your age I might be holding, too. But you have to get rid of it. This is your last chance. We catch you dirty from now on, you go to the stockade."

He makes a point of turning his head.

I don't have anything more deadly than a coin purse, but several guys mill around the wall. One drops something in and starts to leave. Then he pats himself down, realizes he's forgotten something and goes back to the hole. He lets fly with something that makes a thud when it hits bottom.

"A .44," Boil says as we file out of the classroom. "I saw the barrel."

Flashlight in hand, Little Man walks us across the road.

"This is where you sleep." He points to a two-story wooden structure where Eisenhower could have napped as a private. "This is the operations shack. That's where we'll be." He points to a building barely bigger than the loudspeaker overhead. It looks like a press box, except this is war. "All your information comes from here. When to get up. When to fall in. When to report for work detail. When to go to bed. You can shit on your own."

He leads us up the stairs. The scene is right out of "Cool Hand Luke." Rows of bunk beds. Rows of footlockers. Guys in all forms of underwear. Nobody is more than half asleep because they want to be ready when Big Man comes at them with a club in the middle of the night.

I put my suitcase under an empty bunk, kick off my shoes and start to curl up.

"Not so fast," Little Man says. "We need fire guards. You, then you, then you and then you." I feel a finger on my foot.

"Fire guard?" questions Kippler, also among the chosen.

"Yes, smart-ass," Little Man says. "You take one-hour shifts."

Little Man gives Kippler the same kind of paddle my fifth-grade math teacher pulled out of her desk to mete out punishment.

"Instructions in case of fire are on the back."

"What do I do?" Kippler asks. "Just hold it?"

"You walk up and down the barracks. For that hour, you're the eyes and ears."

"Just walk?"

"Yes."

"The whole time?"

"Yes."

"Can I sit down?"

"No."

"What if I have to No. 1? I'd have to sit down then."

"Well, yes, you can sit then."

"Can I lean against the wall while I review the instructions? If I walk and read at the same time, I might bump into a bed and wake somebody up."

Little Man is becoming exasperated.

"Well, yes."

"Can I stop to look at the bulletin board? Might be some information there that will help me in case of a fire."

"Well, yes."

"If I'm absolutely positive I don't smell smoke, can I use the last 10 minutes to write a letter home?"

Little Man has had enough. We hear him running down the stairs.

The last thing I see before falling asleep is Kippler grinning.

I dream a "Gilligan's Island" rerun. Mary Ann is walking along the beach. She gets sand in her top. Poor thing can't go around itching. So she takes it off. She gets sand in her bottom. Don't want to itch there either. So she takes it off. I watch from behind a coconut tree. She sees me, smiles and runs my way with her arms extended.

Just then my shoulder starts to hurt. Someone I don't know has hit me really hard.

"Sorry. Tried every other way to wake you up. It's your turn for fire guard."

He hands me the paddle. "Now you're the eyes and ears."

Dutifully, I begin to march back and forth. Then I look at the operations shack. No lights on. I look at the building where the major spoke. No lights. I survey the rest of the Missouri blackness. Nothing.

Unless the CIA has installed surveillance equipment in the butt cans, there's no way for them to know I'm lying down. I stretch out on the front step. To keep from nodding off, I read the paddle.

"Fire is defined as an act of combustion followed by burning. Fire can maim, cripple and even kill. Be suspicious of fire when you experience a rapid increase in room temperature. Flames, usually a bright yellow, accompany fire. If the fire has progressed to this level, DO NOT ATTEMPT TO PUT IT OUT YOURSELF. Evacuate all personnel. Should fire be on your person, immediately notify your commanding officer."

A guy gets out of bed. Scruffy. Sloppy. At least 50 pounds overweight. Dirty shirt. Dirty bandanna. Looks like he majored in rock concert.

I figure he has to go downstairs and piss, so I move my legs.

"Can't sleep," he says. "Want some company?"

"Sure, keeping the world safe for democracy is hard work."

"College?" he asks.

"Yeah. Business. Hated it, though. You?"

"Political science. Tried to go through on the five-year plan, but the

Army wouldn't let me."

"Let me guess. You went early in the draft lottery."

"Popped me some popcorn, rolled a number and sat back to watch the show," he says. "The second white ball that came up was my birthday. I hadn't even gotten the salt and already I was gone."

"God, that's awful. I was number 71. At least there was time to build up some suspense. What did you do?"

"Smoked four numbers," he goes on. "Couldn't even find the bed. Spend the night in the rec room. Did you protest the war?"

"Only in my head. Never marched."

"I did. Went to the Ellipse in Washington in May. They were going to arrest me, but they ran out of paddy wagons."

"How come you're here and not in Toronto?" I ask.

"Chickenshit."

"Me, too."

"Friend of mine tried every other way to get out of it and couldn't, so he shot off two toes," he says. "Right before he blacked out, he said he could hear them hit the floor. He was laid up for two months, but it worked. Didn't even have to go with us to the physical."

"That's a hell of a thing. We'll go down in history as the generation who had to aim at ourselves so we wouldn't have to aim at the bad guys. Did you try to flunk?"

"Told them I was queer. Even signed a paper saying I was queer. They just laughed. I guess you have to prove it."

"Didn't get your name."

"Martin, but everybody calls me Skebo."

"Skebo?"

"It was something my old man put on me right after I was born. Apparently, I wasn't the best-looking of babies. He got this shocked look on his face the first time he saw me and the word just blurted out."

Skebo has long blond hair almost down to his crack, by far the longest in the barracks. Parted in the middle. Straighter than a slide rule.

Mine looks more like silage. Thick and lumpy. His goes down. Mine goes out.

"Reserves?" I ask.

"Yeah, it's pretty sweet. Supply unit. Inventory stuff. Gonna drive a little Jeep around. Basic and advanced individual training is 16 weeks. I can do that. Go to Canada, and they'll always be chasing after me. Why screw up the rest of your life for 16 stupid weeks? That's what I tell myself when I try to rationalize being chickenshit. Anyway, then I can get back to living the way I want to live."

Which is what for a poli-sci major?

"Commune, man. About 300 of us. Singles, marrieds, grandmothers, cats, dogs, peace, love, ganja. We call it the Farm. You can work at the sawmill, or at the free store, or at the children's school. Or you can work outside the settlement. Me, I teach at the community college. Everything is pooled for the common good. If I want a pair of shoes, I turn in a voucher that's evaluated based on other financial requests. If I need brogans more than somebody else needs pants, the committee puts my paperwork through. Groovy way to be. At night, you get out the guitar and do a little James Taylor to the girl beside you and watch the stars squint, you know what I mean?"

"Probably can't have a guitar in the Army unless it's green."

"Aw, this ain't the Army," Skebo says, trying to sound sure of himself. "The Army is walking point at some shit hole near Da Nang. This is just dicking around."

We look around in time to see a troop clear out his nostrils. The wad hits the floor with a splat.

"But it's enough for me," I say.

"Me, too," my suddenly shaken companion admits.

"Chickenshit."

"Yeah."

A handful of hair gets in Skebo's eyes. He enjoys the view for a few seconds, and then flags it down.

"You're fixing to lose a good five pounds up top," I observe.

"Yeah, but not for long."

"Uh, you seem to be forgetting the monthly drills and the two-week summer camp. The Army's your barber for the next six years, buddy."

"Not from what I've been hearing."

"Which is?"

"That you can get a short-hair wig. There's like a lawsuit or something on whether the military can legally dictate what you look like for the other 29 days a month a reservist or National Guardsman isn't in the military."

"How does it work?"

"You slick down your hair with motor oil. And flatten it out with rubber bands until the back of your head looks like a wet paint brush. Then you put on the hair net. Then the wig. They say it takes 45 minutes to get ready for the day."

"I'll bet it feels like you've got a dead farm animal on top of your head," I tell him. "Be really bad on a hot day."

"Yeah, but think how good it would feel to buck the system. The Army bozos would look at your head and think you're getting with the program. What a laugh. I'll get one if it costs 50 bucks."

At that moment, I hear the loudest siren I've ever heard. It is followed by Reveille with the instrumental quality of a fourth-grade tonette band.

Guys get to half-mast in their bunks. What do they want us to do? Salute, duck for cover or nominate someone for human sacrifice?

A voice comes over the loudspeaker. It's Big Man.

"If you turds aren't out here in two minutes, I'll make bowties out of your balls."

This is the first time I've seen hot potato played with shirts and pants. We make a mad dash to the pavement where Big Man is spewing forth. He smacks his lips in the manner of a buzzard that's having lunch catered.

"The next time you fall out, you WILL do it right," he screams. "Get in five rows. Forty deep. Move, goddammit."

We scatter like little kids on an Easter egg hunt. Big Man yanks a few here, plants a few there and we're in place.

"A, B, C, D and E - that's the rows. You pricks got that?"

We murmur as one.

"OK, now spread down. If you're 5A, you stand beside 5B. If you're 32D, you line up next to 32E."

"Bra sizes," somebody says, chuckling.

"There's no laughing in my lines," Big Man hollers. "Get the fuck where you're supposed to be and shut up."

Even in the pre-dawn fog, I can tell I'm behind Boil. No amount of

22

neck hair can hide his calling card.

"Look ahead of you," Big Man bellows. "That's your guy. Memorize something about him. His ass. His hat. The back of his shoes."

I'm not worried. I could go 95 percent blind and find my spot.

"Everybody see where he's supposed to be?" Big Man is walking through the ranks. "You fuck this up and I don't want to be around when they give you a loaded M-16."

He makes us shout out our numbers. We get 20 in a row until some bee-brain says "10G."

"MIT was short one, and now they've found him," Kippler whispers.

We half-march, half-stumble to breakfast, putting divots in each other's heels with every step. We pass by barracks inhabited by troops who arrived earlier in the week. They already have their fatigues, a fact they loudly point out.

"Hey, civilians," they holler from the second floor, tugging on their shirts and sounding like apprentice Big Men. "Look up here at some real soldiers."

Just days ago, they were one of us. Now they've been turned into them. Please, God, I say silently, don't let me get beaten down like that.

Breakfast is wretched. Eggs, bacon, jelly - they're all playing run around the May Pole. Stir and the tray looks like a dirty river. It might be something I'd take in an IV, but not on a plate. I eat just enough for my stomach to remember what it's there for.

After throwing away more food than they had at Guadalcanal, we line up outside the mess hall.

Ever the teacher, Big Man wants to see if his lesson plan has taken hold.

"Fall in, you pussies."

It doesn't go well. I find Boil, but he can't locate the guy ahead of him. I look to my right and see a total stranger. The guy who's supposed to be at my left is two ranks back trying to pick bacon out of his teeth.

"You assholes would need a map-reading class to find your peckers. We're gonna start over. If you don't do better, I'll take you behind the building."

Big Man looks like a middle linebacker for the Raiders who's been bitten by a rabid dog. I don't want a personal briefing session and neither does anybody else.

This time, we get it pretty much right. Boil still needs to learn to play "X Marks the Ass," but the rest of us are more or less in the right place.

"Well, congratthefuckulations. Let's move out."

Silently at first, but then with cadence.

"Left, left, your military left," Big Man barks. We get maybe 50 yards and a street comes up. A question comes up that isn't in any of the drivers' ed books I've ever read: Who's got the right of way when a motor vehicle and a stumbling herd of men arrive at an intersection at the same time?

"Road guard, road guard," the DI screams.

We keep marching. In seconds, we face the very real possibility of becoming pedestrian casualties. But better that than incur Big Man's wrath by coming to an unauthorized halt.

"Goddammit, when I say 'Road guard,' that means the top man on the left flank and the top man on the right flank run out and stand in the street and give warning that we're about to pass."

Skebo sprints into the breach. Two feet of blond hair flapping in the breeze, he shoots a stiff-arm at vehicular traffic. Transfixed by fear, they obey. Today, hippies are taking over the crosswalks. Tomorrow, the world.

We reach the building where the medics will give us the once-over. Big Man checks his watch. We're early.

"Do what you want," he orders, "but don't move."

With darting eyes, I take my first inventory of my comrades in fear.

A full 25 percent of us are of color. About half wearing jeans. A couple dozen in ball caps. Two mohawks. Three ugly sets of muttonchop sideburns. One "Free The Chicago Eight" T-shirt. One "Vote for Allen Ginsberg" T-shirt. One "Neil Young Is God" T-shirt. Three troops wearing swim trunks. Four paperbacks hanging out of back pockets. Full assortment of Roman noses, pointy ears and acned chins.

I notice a too-thin black guy in bedroom slippers. Kippler sees that I see.

"Bought him a Coke at the airport," Kippler whispers. "Name's

Gaines. Son of a sharecropper. Those are the only shoes he has."

Big Man orders parade rest. We are to file inside the building where an assembly line of medical types will do everything from examining our tonsils to fingering our balls.

It is all diabolically efficient, although I don't understand why I have to drop my pants to have my blood pressure taken. Buck naked, I go from station-to-station carrying a jar of urine. I imagine being on guard duty. Someone tries to sneak up on me. The hell with a rifle, I'm holding a much more powerful weapon. "Halt," I shout, "or I'll throw this on you."

The shots are administered in air-gun fashion, my first experience with syringe-less vaccinations. The corpsman holds the thing against your skin and a surge of science delivers the goods. You're fine for about 30 seconds, and then everything settles in your lymph nodes and you feel like the baseball pitcher who can't lift his arm over his head.

The heat is stifling as I move from table to table. Central Missouri may be nowhere, but the sun has found its way.

The nurse, one of those yawning professionals who could hold your pecker, count the wrinkles and enter the total on a form, wraps the elastic thing around my upper arm. Then she gets out the longest needle I've ever seen. Put links on it and you could measure first-and-10 yardage. I'm thinking with a weapon like that she's bound by law to read my vein its constitutional rights. Or maybe there's paperwork to sign before my body is officially violated. Surely something to delay the proceedings until I can get mentally prepared.

But no. She thrusts like my arm is a 400-year-old maple and she's got to get deep enough to draw sap.

There's pain, sharp at first, but fading to bruising. Then for some reason I decide to watch the blood filling up the cylinder. Up, up, it shoots. Cranberry juice in color, with a touch of A1 Sauce.

I start to feel dizzy. Then dreamy. The stool is replaced by a bed. A nice soft bed. I float on a cushion of air. The ceiling is like a pulsating heart. Please make it stop. I catch a glimpse of the nurse who is using both hands to pull the needle out of my arm.

Then nothing. No fade to black. Just black.

So this is death. I've heard a lot about it, but this is my first time on the slab.

You think, but you don't feel, hear or see. Hot damn! I'm going to get out of basic training. But don't bury me out here. Put me on the slow freight home. Might take an extra two days, but it'll save Dad some money. I cost him plenty in life. The least I can do is cut him a break on the funeral expenses.

Suddenly, it's as if the contents of a swimming pool have been dumped on my face.

"Wake up, goddammit." It's Big Man. "You fainted. Lucky you didn't hurt somebody." He's holding a bucket. Indeed, why practice CPR when you can just draw two gallons from the tap?

"I'm not going to get in trouble, am I?" the nurse asks.

"Shit, no," Big Man replies. "Just tell them he needed a transfusion and you gave him one."

"That's cool," she says, holstering her needle and moving on to the next arm.

"How do you feel?" Big Man asks.

"Got to puke. Got to puke now."

He hauls me outside as he would a dog that ruined the carpet. I make yellow, orange and red all over the curb. My mouth feels like under the table at a cheap diner.

"Aw, quit worrying," Big Man says. "You ain't gonna be French-kissing nobody no how."

We fall in for the march to the barber shop. I don't feel so good.

"You gonna throw up again?" Big Man wants to know.

I'm afraid to open my mouth. I'm hoping he gets the message with the lake of sweat and the jerking of every muscle group in my body.

Big Man hands over the bucket he used to bring me back to life.

"Don't get nothing on nobody," he warns. "Don't wanna cause no plague."

We stampede down Caisson Drive. I'm the only one carrying an anti-digestive device.

"Your right, your right, your military right," Big Man shouts.

I think what I'd give for a shot of Lavoris, and what those around me would be willing to kick in. Meanwhile, Boil slows down for some reason and I run the bucket up his ass.

"Watch out, dickhead," Boil snarls.

Big Man steps in. "If anybody's gonna call somebody a dickhead, it's me." He tries to get in my face but can't advance because of the sustained fire coming from my mouth. "Be more careful next time," is all he can muster before being driven back.

The barber shop is beside a grove of trees. I look at Skebo and his locks that probably took four years to grow. Reviewing my military history, I think of all the old generals who always seemed to come to a grove of trees to die. In like manner, so has Skebo's hair.

Five chairs. Five barbers. Two orderly-types with large brooms.

I feel up top. Follicles of plenty. Standing tall. Standing proud. Prepared to fall as one.

"Now at least you'll at least look like soldiers," Big Man roars. His head looks like he applies Nair to it every 15 minutes. Probably does the same to his pubic hair. If we start getting inspected down there, I'll start blowing off some toes.

"You WILL report to the barber shop. You WILL not say smart-ass bullshit like 'Give me a trim' or 'Just take a little off the top.' You WILL NOT put your hands on top of your head trying to prevent the haircut. The barbers clip what they see. If it's hands, you'd better learn how to salute with your wrists. You WILL NOT make any attempt to save your hair for some goddamn scrapbook like those pricks from the last cycle."

The barbers are even more efficient than the medical staff. No "Where are you from?" No "Sure hope it doesn't rain." The guy simply presses the clippers against my scalp as hard as he can and goes 'round and 'round like he's peeling an apple. I'm deflowered in less than 20 seconds.

We're given a few minutes to ourselves after the mass shearing. Probably to see if we can still recognize each other in a sea of bald knobs.

Boil is easy. The barber didn't - or couldn't - lance it.

I find Kippler solely by size and accent. The absence of hair gives his thick-framed glasses no visible means of support. If he so much as breathes, they fall to the tip of his nose. He is telling anybody who wants to listen that the military-industrial complex owes him another set of eyewear.

Where's Skebo?

Can't tell. We all look like we just came out of a delousing ward. I try to remember what he was wearing. Blue shorts, I think, and flip-flops.

I go from cluster to cluster. No nature boy.

The lone troop is by the culvert where the trees fizzle out and everything becomes ditch.

He looks like the elderly Indian banished from the tribe. He's sitting on a rock and watching his flip-flops float in the stagnant water. The top of his head, which hasn't seen the light since LBJ was in the White House, could be a beacon for light aircraft.

"Want to talk?" I ask.

"I hope my shoes sink. Hair's dead, I'm dead, shoes might as well be dead, too."

I rescue the footwear. "Can't march barefoot, man. Remember the wig? We're just out here a few weeks, right?"

Skebo shakes his head. "It's all over. Flip-flops are for guys with hair. Guys who like Captain Beefheart and the Grateful Dead. If you don't have hair, you're Conway Twitty. One minute I'm part of the counterculture, the next I'm vice-president of the Young Republicans."

If he stoops any lower, he'll drown in the ditch.

"C'mon, it'll grow back."

"No, it won't. They probably sprayed some defoliant. Nine months from now and it'll still look like mahogany."

"They only beat you if you let them." I step back. I can't believe I said that after four years of college in which I didn't stand up for a damn thing. I've finally become an activist for something. Hair.

"You believe that?" Skebo asks.

"Yeah, I think so." I'm amazed at my new sense of conviction. "Will anybody you love or care about ever see you like this?"

"No."

"Do you plan on sending snapshots or other facsimiles of yourself back home?"

"Hell, no."

"Then why do you care what you look like out here? Look at it like this: Your hair will get some much-needed time off. Go on vacation or something. Then when it comes back, it'll be all refreshed and ready to grow."

Skebo gets to his feet. "Didn't work, but nice speech, man. Thanks."

"Forget it. You'll probably have to give me one tomorrow."

Big Man hollers that we're moving out.

"Now we get our jerseys," I hear some asshole troop say. I want to smack him. This isn't the baseball team. They aren't going to give out letter jackets.

Skebo looks like a zombie. His life's work, his hair, is heading for the Dumpster. Might as well take the rest of him.

Naturally, Big Man makes things worse.

"Whassamatter, Samson? Without your hair, you can't even pick up your pecker. Gimme 30 pushups. That'll help get your strength back."

I think back to the dorm about what Carl said. The Army senses weakness, any weakness at all, and they crawl all over it like fire ants.

We watch helplessly - and silently - as Skebo goes up and down. Don't want to pick up an illegal-use-of-mouth penalty out here.

They route us to a warehouse. One group gets fitted for uniforms and shoes, while the rest of us report to the supply bay where we load up on the staples of war.

Pistol belt. Helmet liner. Steel helmet. Field jacket. Stupid-looking winter cap like the one the county agent wore in "Green Acres." Poncho. Tent pegs. Tent stakes. Something called a shelter half that you match up with someone else's for the bivouac.

Over in menswear, we're issued khakis, fatigues, socks, an overcoat, two pairs of boots, one pair of parade shoes and galoshes like the ones our moms made us wear to elementary school that we took off on the bus because we were too embarrassed to let anyone see us in them.

And, finally, two duffel bags to put it all in.

I'm thinking, no way. You could miniaturize this stuff and we'd still need a cargo truck to haul it around.

But no. A cadre member spreads a schematic that shows the proper way to fold and place each item. Following the diagram, he fits everything inside the dufflebags with room to spare for at least part of Kippler. This guy should be a stocking stuffer when he grows up.

I'm fascinated by the pistol belt. Because I never watched "Combat," I assume you wrap the thing around your shoulders a la Pancho Villa.

But Kippler, an expert on everything, says it goes around your waist.

"Canteen, bayonet, bullets - I don't know how, but it all clips on," he explains. "Militarily speaking, it's like wearing room service."

Our Army crap is supposed to be in the duffel bags and our civilian clothes in the laundry bag. But because we squeeze every bit as bad as we make formation, stuff is dangling around necks and waists and stashed inside shirts.

I feel like a pack mule at the Grand Canyon. The gear weighs at least 50 pounds, it's 95 degrees and the only breeze comes from Big Man's throat.

"Double-time. March."

The Green Berets couldn't run with all this on their backs. The best we can do is take six paces and then pick up what's fallen out.

"Goddammit, get them ditty bags stowed," Big Man screams.

But it's no use. We're a constant stream of military issue all the way back to the barracks.

"Pitiful," Big Man says, kicking a canteen.

The wooden steps creak under the weight of dragged gear. We maneuver the bags to the side of our bunks and heave as we would a case of shot puts.

Siren.

Happy news from the operations shack, our window to the world. One hour of free time before supper. The PX is on-limits.

I fairly sprint down the hill. After a full day of doing the Army's business, I plan to reacquaint myself with the Information Age. Check out the pennant races. Catch up on Nixon. See if any more dominoes have tumbled overseas.

Never have I seen a sadder-looking merchandising establishment. The word "store" only applies because there's a cash register. All I see are brass, buttons, fake grenades, a box of Snickers from the 1960s and a giant bin full of "Property of the Army" T-shirts.

"Where's the newspaper rack?" I ask.

"Don't have one," the man behind the counter says. "By the time the truck gets way out here, they're usually at least a day late and the pages look like they've been put through a shredder. Besides, most of the men just want fuck books."

I'm instantly suspicious. It's like a "Twilight Zone" episode. World peace is declared. Weapons of destruction are blown up. Flower children blanket the Earth with petals.

But because there are no newspapers in Central Missouri, we keep training as if nothing has happened.

I get back to the second floor in time to see Big Man give a demonstration on the proper way to spit-shine boots.

He flicks his cigarette lighter and plays Mr. Wizard. "Gotta burn it in, boys. Makes it last longer."

I can't see exactly what he's doing. Something about bringing the polish to a warm glob, honking on it a couple of times and then spreading an everlasting glow.

But I can see the joy in his eyes. Like he's really accomplishing something. Like he's making the world a better place.

Too many of our guys are standing around him. They should be at their bunks asking how to join Skebo's commune. Or listening to Crosby, Stills and Nash. Or suggesting treatment centers for Boil.

It's like they're losing their allegiance. They've only been in this place overnight and already they've bought into it.

"How hot should the flame be?" someone asks, actually sounding like he wants to know.

"Is it OK to do the shoelaces, too, or will they catch fire?" another troop chimes in.

What are they thinking? They shouldn't care about having perfect shoes. They should be figuring out a way to draw a peace symbol on a tank.

After supper, we're confined to quarters where we arrange our footlockers and otherwise become as battle-ready as possible considering we don't know the military way to tie our laundry bags to our bunks.

Lights out at 8:45.

Guys holler out in the dark trying to prove they're the dominant male.

The first voice loudly proclaims he's going to climb inside his girlfriend's crawl space and hibernate. Another voice promises to bury his face in the next set of tits he sees, and it could be the cleaning lady for all he cares.

A lively discussion of pussy ensues, after which there is general agreement that "nooky" is a Southern expression, "poontang" is used most often in Northern circles and "She's got the rag on," has national understanding.

Not everybody seeks dominant status. Some just want to go to sleep.

"Y'aaaall shuuut uuuup."

This takes a full five seconds to come out. Every syllable gets its moment in the sun.

Got to be Mississippi or Alabama. You can hear the red clay commingling with the cotton patch.

"What the hell did you just get through saying?" asks the guy who moments before violated every privacy covenant he had with his girlfriend.

"I said y'all shut up."

"What's that one word? It didn't come clear."

Not only does this guy fink on Linda Lou, he's an outside agitator.

"You mean 'y'all'? Means you and you and you and the rest of you."

"Say it again," says his tormentor, who, judging by his accent, grew up well to the north of even Kippler.

"Y'all. Goddammit. Y'all. Y'all."

"What do you call yourself, man?" somebody shouts.

The Southerner starts to rattle it off, but he's interrupted.

"Ya," Hibernation says.

A nickname is born.

It's quiet except for the overhead fan and the moaning of women's names.

Then, loud and clear: "I eat lit cigarettes for money."

It's coming from three bunks over, one down. I can just barely see the guy, who is naked except for red socks.

"You're shitting," says Hibernation.

"You'd die," Cleaning Lady weighs in.

The guy is unmoved. "Half a pack. Five dollars."

In college, you freeze to death for money. In the Army, you torture your taste buds.

I kick in my 50 cents, ever the sucker for the show-stopping act. The one-ring circus is set up under the swinging light bulb at the top of the stairs. Hibernation furnishes the Marlboros.

"You gotta chew or you give the money back," Cleaning Lady stipulates.

The headliner yawns and agrees.

I've never seen anything like it. His teeth go down on the cigarette cracker-style until there's nothing left. Then he pops another one into his mouth without even taking a breath. He seems to find the burning end particularly succulent.

Clearly, this guy just had his favorite late-night snack and it was on the house.

"Thank you boys," he says in the manner of Lawrence Welk praising his accordion player after an especially rousing number.

I go to sleep wondering what I could do in front of a bunch of guys that they would pay to see. Some talent - bizarre or otherwise - that I alone possess.

Only one thing comes to mind. Typing.

I can get 65 words a minute on a timed writing if I don't have to do numbers. Let me plug in an electric and I'll approach 85. I can even bob and weave at the keyboard like Ray Charles.

But I know it's no good. Eating lit cigarettes is manly. Typing is queer. The troops would just try to look up my dress.

Our second daybreak in the Army is less frantic. The siren is as loud as ever, but we know they probably won't kill us unless we really deserve it. We take our places in front of the operations shack wearing our new fatigues and little green caps that fit over our hairless domes like sealant.

Today is like 200 men going on a bunch of errands. Little Man is like a station-wagon driver, except this is war. Get ID pictures taken. Mail civilian stuff home. Take eye exam. Get fingerprinted. Take IQ test. Take psychological test. Take personality-profile test. Take leadership-potential test. Fill out what-you-want-to-be-when-you-grow-up sheet. I go with "writer." It's the first time I've ever put that word on a form. I start to use block letters, but decide it looks more believable in cursive.

The last stop is an incredibly long wait inside an airless building where a platoon of Rosie the Riveter look-alikes sew on nametags.

We survey each one from pudgy fingers to teeth that look as if they were handed out randomly and in small lots. Not a looker in the bunch. Our attention immediately turns to Cleaning Lady, but he has crumpled up his tits manifesto of the night before and is standing as far away from the women as possible. So much for immersing oneself in one's subject.

We get back to the reception center in time for a few minutes to ourselves before the next siren blast.

Little Man tells us we're on schedule with the processing. Tomorrow, we'll take more tests, listen to the chaplain and get our dog tags. We move out to basic training the day after.

Collective gulp.

The reception center is here today, gone tomorrow. Basic training is growing roots.

He hands out a piece of paper that lists all the equipment we're supposed to have. We are to empty our dufflebags and take inventory. Last in, first out, I remember from production management class.

But never mind that. I'm a writer now. Says so in my file.

Some of the men finish early and decide to go to the Don Knotts flick down the street. But it's not like going to any movie I've ever attended. You have to wear fatigues and you have to march. Probably have to fall out of the theater before you can laugh. Sorry, Barn, I've got letters to write.

Sept. 5, 1971

Dear Mom and Dad,
Hate it here.
We haven't had a decent meal yet. The cooks make the stuff in giant caldrons and smoke cigarettes while they stir. They perspire something awful and you know that gets in the mix, too. I might not be getting my 100-percent-a-day adult requirement of

niacin and riboflavin, but I won't have to eat any more sweat and ashes the rest of my life.

We got paid today. Thirty-five whole dollars. One guy in the barracks is like you, Dad. He told us he has steel traps inside his footlocker and anybody trying to rip him off can expect to bleed.

I've been meaning to talk to you in person, but haven't gotten around to it yet. They have a place here called Phone City that has about 40 telephones, but only about half function. The lines have been real long and there's absolutely no privacy. After the second or third "I love you," the next guy says that's plenty and starts bugging you to hang up. I promise to call when I'm less depressed.

I've got to tell you about one of the drill sergeants.

This guy wasn't born. He was poured. The doctor slapped the cement truck on its rear and said, "Congratulations, you're the father of a brand new baby footer." When the other kids were going to day care, he was busy supporting a high-rise.

He could be asleep and still whip six of us. All he cares about is the Army. I'll bet he doesn't know who the vice-president is, but he can quote the regulation that states the maximum allowable inches socks can ride up on our ankles.

We didn't know what to call him, so we went with Big Man. Then somebody in the front row noticed the name tag on his shirt, Haddox, and passed it down. The weird thing is, he's never owned up to it. Never stood up in front of us and said, "The name is Haddox. Fear it." He's thinking, in that don't-know-the-VP brain of his, that we'll be even more intimidated if he bypasses the whole first-name, last-name bit.

Works with me. I start shaking when he gets anywhere near us and I don't calm down until 15 minutes after he leaves. If he ever chews me out, I'll be like the Wicked Witch at the end of the movie. Full meltdown.

My goal is for this man never to have a conscious thought about me. At the end of the cycle, I want my name to come up and he says, "Hmm, that sounds vaguely familiar." Then he mulls it over and says, "Nah, never heard of the guy."

The eight-hour sleep rule is strictly enforced, and sometimes it's too late to shower when we get back to the room. I absolutely cannot close my eyes with crud on my person. Sponge baths don't work. There's something inside me that knows the water didn't get turned on. Tonight I sneaked to another company's barracks across the quadrangle, found a floor where guys were still taking showers and went in like I'm one of them. Clean and thus eligible for sleep, I slipped back undetected. Or at least I think I did. Tomorrow, they'll probably court-martial me for having shampoo residue from an unauthorized soap-and-water facility.

Oh, by the way, I passed out and thought I was dead, but I

won't go into detail because I don't want you to worry.

I'd better sign off. Please send me all the letters I get from newspapers where I've applied for a job. Unopened, Dad. I'm letting my mustache grow, but don't expect much.

Love,
Me.

Sept. 5, 1971

Dear Kathy,
    Hate it here.
    Miss you. The guys talk about sex almost every minute. So far, out of respect for you, I haven't joined in. But I can't hold out much longer or they'll think I'm some kind of weirdo, or, even worse, an intellectual. I won't drag it out. Short sentences only. I'll only describe you in general terms, and that's a promise.
    Had my first detail today. Cleaned butt cans with this little black guy from Georgia. Son of dirt-poor parents. Came here in bedroom slippers, the only shoes he owns.
    This troop's only been out of his home county once before the Army, and that was to go to his grandmother's funeral. Quit school to help his dad on the farm.
    Boom. Here we are. Thrown together by the Army. Pampered college boy and a guy who's had everything against him since the day he was born.
    Gaines and I talked the whole time we were on detail. I told him about the dorm, and the dope, and comparative economics, and listening to Jethro Tull, and the students who took over the architecture building after the shootings at Kent State.
    He told me about living in three or four different shacks a year because his father had to move with the season. He told me about sleeping with five brothers in the same room. He told me about not seeing his first wooden floor until he went to school. Gaines makes me feel guilty. Nobody told him about the draft dodge that is the reserves or National Guard. He just signed up. The recruiter said infantry? Nobody told Gaines that's who dies. Nobody told him anything. So he said, yeah, sure, infantry. He'll be in Vietnam before his 19th birthday. It's not right.
    Vietnam is bad, Kathy, even if just what it does to turn sons against fathers.
    My dad's been pretty cool about this being a different deal from World War 11. He knows what he fought for at Palermo isn't the same thing we're doing at Fort Leonard Wood.
    But this one troop told me he hasn't had any contact with his father in more than two years and he hopes it stays that way.

Seems the senior was a big hero at D-Day. Saved two guys from bleeding to death on the beach until the medics got to them.

Mr. Gung Ho then. Mr. Gung Ho now.

The dad can't understand why his son doesn't want to go to Southeast Asia and gun down communists. He can't believe something that came out of his loins tried to flunk the physical by pretending to be a spastic, and when that didn't work, escaped to the National Guard as a file clerk.

The dad told his troop/son that he's a coward. The troop/son told his father to fuck off. That was 1969. The kid says he doesn't even know for sure where his dad is. Says he'd sooner look up a drill sergeant.

Don't tell anybody I said this, but I have found one good thing about this place. I never would have met anyone like Gaines. There is no system other than the Army that requires you to mix 'n' match with the rest of society. I learned more today cleaning butt cans that I did in a year of school. College doesn't offer a course in how the other half lives. It should. Or else send every hot-shot senior with a high lottery number to this shithole so they can see it firsthand.

Enough of that. I'm starting to sound like one of those kids who follows Eugene McCarthy around the country.

All I want to do is just get by. Stay in the touring lane. Serve out my sentence quietly cleaning butt cans.

That's about all I have.

Smoke 'em if you got 'em.

Love,
Guess who

Rumor of the night: There's a telescope in the operations shack and they keep it aimed at us.

I sleep soundly until 4 o'clock when the guy in the next bunk is informed he has fire guard. The 3 o'clock floorwalker tries to wake him in a civilized manner, but that doesn't work so he slaps him about the face. The 4 o'clock guy calls the 3 o'clock guy a cocksucker. The 3 o'clock guy responds in kind and they square off.

Hibernation hollers that he has a knife and if he has to get up, it's not going to be any fun for anybody.

I'm thinking, hey, if the cadre has a telescope, now might be a pretty good time to use it.

Nothing.

That proves it. The only thing they have mounted on a tripod is a fuck book.

Kippler jumps in to save the day.

"OK, 3 o'clock, what's the problem?"

"Dick here won't take his fire guard."

"Is this true?" Kippler wants to know.

"I don't know whose fire guard it is," 3 o'clock replies. "All I know is it's the middle of the night, my face hurts and this guy is why."

"Does anybody here want to pull fire guard?" Kippler wants to know, taking the issue to the people.

No one responds. We're either too tired or disappointed the two cocksuckers didn't duke it out.

"C'mon, who wants to do it?" Kippler goes on. "You can write letters, arrange your gear, toss pennies in your steel helmet. Whatever."

Ya raises his hand.

"I will," he drawls. "I like to watch the sun come up. Pretend I'm getting ready to go squirrel-hunting."

Kippler has 4 o'clock approach the bench.

"You owe Ya a favor. Agreed?"

He nods.

"The next time Ya gets a detail, you'll pull it for him. Agreed?"

He nods.

Kippler, the judge-advocate, orders the two troops to shake hands.

Never having been the central figures of a labor dispute before, they comply.

"Hip-hip-fucking-hooray," Hibernation calls out.

Case adjudicated, Kippler leads the way back to bed.

Where we moan for an hour before the siren goes off so loud it gets in your pores. It's like living next door to the whistle at the factory. Two hundred men slip into something less comfortable.

This is only our third military morning, but we're short-timers by reception center standards. Hundreds of fresh hires have arrived since that first night when Boil and my lap became intimate. They haven't had haircuts, haven't had half their blood drained, haven't tried to sleep in Cool Hand Luke's bed, haven't been told they fall in like a bunch of goddamn third-graders.

And here we are, wily veterans of the eye exam and supply depot. All-knowing sages of the AP news ticker that is the operations shack. The incoming can only guess for whom the siren screams. We know.

That first pre-dawn formation, biscuits burned in the oven while we tried to sound off from A-1 to E-40. Today, we call out the numbers in the time it takes to pass the sugar.

If we don't think about what we're wearing, we can almost forget where we are.

The chaplain talks about faith and belief. Give him a pulpit and it could be church.

The major talks about applying ourselves to the job at hand. Give him a stack of brochures and a card table and he could be the Army's representative at career day.

A historian-type who looks like Mr. Peepers tells us this place was activated in 1940 at a cost of $40 million and named after Major General Leonard Wood, who won the Medal of Honor in the campaign to capture the Indian chief, Geronimo. He rattles off the names of supposedly famous soldiers who took basic here. None of them click in my mind. It's like being in civics class and not knowing the material.

The pretend prof closes his notebook.

"Maybe one of you troops will follow in their footsteps."

Nah, we'd trip.

After lunch, we're issued our first real collector's items.

Dog tags.

Name and serial number only. Rank is missing. Good move. No sense putting a lot of pressure on us to achieve.

We flip the things in each other's faces like they're toys.

All except Boil.

"I'm not wearing mine," he says defiantly, taking the tags off and putting them in his pocket.

"Why not?" somebody asks. "It's the first thing they've given us that's cool."

Boil explodes.

"Cool? Do you know why dog tags are made like they are?"

We have no idea. Obviously, I wasn't the only one who didn't watch "Combat."

"Do you think they gave us dog tags so we could impress bitches?" Boil yells, his face reddening.

Hibernation gives a "yes" gesture with his private parts.

Boil tries to hit him, but is held back.

"Goddammit, it's in case we die."

We get quiet.

"You put the dog tags in the dead soldier's mouth, and then you kick them in so they'll stay. That's how the body is identified."

The story comes out in whispers, little by little. Boil's father was in Korea and died at Inchon with his face blown off. Nobody would have known who he was if his buddy hadn't put the dog tags in his teeth. And kicked.

We separate.

Which is what guys do when we don't know what to do.

Arrange ourselves in concentric circles. Leave the guy who caused it at the epicenter.

We quit playing with our dog tags and bury them under our shirts. Boil will never win Mr. Congeniality, but he takes the reality-check title going away.

All of us are desperate to know what boot camp is going to be like. How much running. How much shooting. How much getting in your face.

But it's like the entire reception center permanent party has taken a crash course in "no comment." The most detailed response is an uncivil, "You'll find out soon enough."

Even the chaplain is in on the plot. All we get out of him is, "The Lord sows, but basic training reaps."

Isolation is their primary weapon. No newspapers. No contact with civilians. No contact with troops on the other side of the base who have started the basic-training cycle. Like Indians on a reservation, we're restricted to the company area. If we start to wander off, there's a cadre member riding fence.

The Army should have a course outline like we had in college. This is what we'll cover this week. This is where you'll be sore. This is what you'll complain about the most.

But no. They let us create our own monster. Fuel our own fear.

We're lounging around waiting for lunch when an unscheduled 11:45 ear-splitter storms the barracks.

And with it a voice from our not-too-distant past.

"Fall out, you pussies."

Haddox. He's had two full days off and he's primed for action.

We respond with the same speed that suited the other cadre members. Yawn. Take a piss. Proceed in slow motion down the stairs. Stroll to the operations shack as if we're hand-in-hand with our girlfriends.

Thirty seconds pass and nobody is front and center.

Haddox blows his brains out on his whistle.

"Goddammit, you WILL move out faster than that. You WILL hit the ground running, or I'll take a lawn mower to your balls."

We race to our places, buttoning our pants as we run.

The DI holds a stopwatch, the most advanced piece of technology I've seen at this place.

"Too slow. Too fucking slow. Go back upstairs and try again."

This is a new concept. A track meet from the inside of a building to the outside.

We sit on the edge of our beds waiting for the starter's gun.

When it comes, 200 men charge toward stairs that might hold a dozen. It's assholes and elbows and fallen soldiers. We're a mob scene without the Molotov cocktails.

"No, no, no," Haddox screams, hurling his stopwatch like he's the coach of the Olympic 100-yard dash team and we just got beat by Barbados. "You're gonna learn how to get down a fucking flight of stairs if it takes all day."

This time we play it smart. Half of us stay on the first floor, standing 10 deep in front of the pissers and crappers. With fewer men to run down the stairs, we're bound to get out faster.

Which we do. Barbados is left in its tracks.

"Not good enough," Coach says. "Go again."

This time nobody goes upstairs. Two hundred men are pressed closer together than a stack of 45s. The walls are bulging. If we exhale, it's Jericho time.

Whistle.

Sprint.

We're at the operations shack faster than Robert McNamara can roll an eyebrow.

At least somewhat pleased, Haddox inspects the ranks.

"Arms down, soldier. Straighten out that hat. Get the head of your belt even with your buttons."

Chop 20 inches off him and this guy could be Napoleon.

A Napoleon with a memory.

"Where's that little dick with the pillow?"

If I'm Kippler, I keep quiet. Stay in the background. Blend in with the other 5-foot 5-inch guys who are soldiers in name only.

But ever the honest Injun, the troop raises his hand.

"Here, sir."

"I ain't no sir. I work for a living. Is that pillow of yours still in country?"

"Shipped out, Mr. Sergeant," Kippler replies.

"What about your fucking sinuses?"

"Much better, thank you for asking. This brisk Ozark air has done wonders for the congestion. My ears don't have that stuffy feeling any more. I just might settle out here."

"Well, isn't that just fucking dandy?"

"Yes, it is. I haven't had the opportunity to price any property yet, but I've spoken on the phone to a real estate agent and he's going to show me some lots. Of course, the extent of my investment will depend on the movement up and down of the prime rate."

He says all this bullshit with the sincerity of a Chase Manhattan senior executive. No member of the Barrymore family could equal the performance. And in a single take.

There's no smile, no hint of a smirk. That would give him away and Haddox would proceed with the dismemberment. Once again, the DI is left with nothing to say. He dispenses a little venom about needing a pillow in the first place, that a real soldier could sleep on a thorn bush.

But his presentation is ineffective. Once again he retreats, this time inside the operations shack.

Kippler 2, Haddox 0.

More tests. More marching practice. Another work detail.

I'm given a rake and told to clean out under the barracks. My partner is a guy from Chicago named Apperson.

The first thing I notice, other than this is the swarthiest individual I've ever seen, is the pair of dice tattooed on his left forearm. A "5" and a "2."

"Lucky 7?" I ask, trying to make conversation.

Decidedly not, I am to find out.

The guy's been in and out of Juvenile Hall. In and out of Cook County Jail.

"Armed robbery," he says casually, scooping up a half-rotted sock. "Sometimes I got caught."

Ah, yes, another fellow I never would have met except for the Defense Department and, like Gaines, quite open about his past.

"Usually I worked the parking lots outside the clubs on Rush Street. Get 'em while they're weaving in the dark trying to find their cars. Put a razor next to their throat. Get two, three wallets, and then move on.

"This one dude wet his pants. Tourist with one of them prissy little money belts. Wet on that, too. Took it off and held it out like I was still gonna to take it. Damn thing's dripping with piss. He gets it all over his fingers and shit. I said, man, you can keep it and walked off.

"Did you ever outsmart the law?" I wonder.

"All the time. When I was in junior high, I had a regular racket going. I was little for my age, and I made good use of it. Get me a box of Cracker Jack and walk down the street all innocent-like. I boost a purse, take the bills and throw the thing in the trash. Take a couple of side streets and then start gnawing on the Cracker Jack like an 11-year-old. And when the cops came, where'd I put the money? Right in the Cracker Jack box, man. I'd just eat around it. They ran by and never suspected a thing."

I cannot fathom such lawlessness. The worst thing I ever did at that age was put a tack on the preacher's toilet seat. I had to stack vestments for two months.

"Wanna hear about my last arrest?" Apperson says excitedly.

Certainly. Wouldn't want to miss another installment of True Crime.

"Six months ago, I'm walking around the Lincoln Park Zoo looking for somebody to stick up. Here's this guy over by the flamingos. Completely by himself. Everybody wants to see the elephants, not some stupid-ass pink birds.

"I sneak over and tell him to hand over the billfold. Then I flash the razor. Always worked before, right? But this motherfucker jumps six feet away from me. He puts his hands up like he knows karate, and starts shouting at the top of his lungs that I'm a son of a bitch of a thief. This never happened before. I take off running. Got to get away from this crazy person.

"You'd think he'd be glad he got to keep his money and didn't get hurt. But hell, no. He comes after me hollering shit. I'm hoofing as fast as I can, but he's gaining on me. I'm throwing out wallets, I'm throwing out razors. If I get caught, I wanna be clean. I hear this big noise behind me like a tornado. He tackles me and I fall over this bike rack. I swear I've been ruptured. He jumps on top of me and starts beating my head against the pavement.

"When I come to, I'm in the hospital with 20 layers of bandages. My head feels like it's not there. I don't know if it's Monday or Thursday.

"Then this cop serves me with a piece of paper. It wasn't enough that this track star almost killed me. Now he wants my ass in court for felonious assault. And I didn't even touch him. I'm thinking, shit, they've really got me this time. This is prison.

"I'm farting around a few days before the trial when my probation officer calls. He talked to the judge and the judge talked to the Army. They got this deal for me. I volunteer. I get through basic training. I get through wherever they send me for three years after that and my record's clean. It's like I never even saw them damn flamingos."

Thinking I might need an explanation, he provides one.

"Too many of you college boys are hopping the freight," Apperson says, pointing to a used rubber that somehow made it to these parts. "They gotta make their quota somehow. I might not be for shit, but I fill up a uniform."

Then I recall Short Leg back at the airport. They thought nothing of putting the handicapped on the midnight bus to Missouri. Why should it surprise me that they'd welcome the criminal element?

"I'm hip," Apperson goes on. "I said I'll join your Army. Beats pulling one-to-five."

I rake up the rubber, but my heart's not in it. How is this supposed to make me feel? The Army and prison - one and the same.

"So here I am," Apperson says, "but I don't know for how long. This ain't exactly my scene."

"Not mine either," I reply evenly, "and it just got worse."

"Yep, might have to check out."

I almost drop my tool. "You mean go AWOL?"

"Don't act so surprised. How hard would it be? This ain't exactly Leavenworth. Probably the only fence out here is around the general's flower garden."

"But they say that's the worst thing we can do," I reply. "You get hunted down like a convict and thrown in the stockade. I don't like the barracks. I don't even want to see anything with bars."

"Shit, they only catch you if you go home. You could be sunning yourself three doors down and the MPs would drive right past. They're dumber than we are."

"And you wouldn't go home?"

"Fuck, no. I'd head for Mexico. Nogales, maybe. Send a postcard with me in a sombrero. Hi, Mom. Bye, Mom."

I look Apperson up and down. There's no swagger in what he's saying. No put-on trying to make himself look big.

If the mood hits, this guy is gone.

Supper is the worst yet. Liquid mashed potatoes and a chunk of liver curled up until it looks like a third-baseman's mitt.

Skebo and I buy a boatload of Vienna Sausages and a bag of pretzels at the PX. We feast against the side of a long-abandoned Quonset hut and watch the sun set over the operations shack. That figures. Not only does the Army have us by the balls, it's got the solar system, too.

Skebo has something else on his mind.

"Quarter ounce of sensimillia, man. What a time for a number. What a time for 10 numbers."

He hurls a Vienna sausage tin in disgust.

"But I threw it in the hole that first night."

"Chickenshit?" I ask.

"Yeah."

We talk about the .44.

"Maybe my stash landed on top of it. I can see the sergeant of the hole reporting to his captain. 'Weapon won't fire, sir. Weed in the barrel.' "

I tell him about Apperson and the Army being the same as Sing Sing.

"Part of me has always wondered what it's like in the Big House," Skebo says sagely, running his fingers through what used to be hair.

"Do you think we'll make it?" I ask.

"Yeah," he replies. "But we'll need a last-ditch rally."

CHAPTER 3

The last thing I want this first day of basic is a sudden siren. I want it to go off on my terms, not theirs. I want to ease into the moment, not have it spring-loaded on me.

I call on a skill I developed in college. "Bonanza" sleeping. A one-hour episode at a time.

2 a.m. Still forever until 5:00. Rest secure. Rest relaxed. Rest unscreamed at. Another sleep cycle and it's 3:15. I plan my morning. At 4:45 I'll sneak to the bathroom, fatigues in hand. I'll take a leisurely piss and, with any luck, a shit. I'll get dressed ahead of the cycle. Plenty of time to pull up the socks, lace the boots, calm the nerves.

Game plan finalized, I re-enter dreamland. Stay there while Hoss eats, Adam broods and Ben stops an ambush. It's 3:45. Wake up to guys' moaning. Pick out the girls' names. Rhonda, Tanya, Donna, Anita, Kelly. Give myself pep talk. You can do this. You've got more common sense than you think. Just let someone else go first and do what he does. Go back to sleep. Think of Ben Cartwright, patriarch of a land mass only slightly smaller than the plains of the Serengeti. Think of Little Joe getting the girl, but not consummating the act because the friction from his chaps would start a range fire. Still plenty of time until lights come on. I rest satisfied-lover style with pillow propped up and hands folded behind my head. 4:15. I'll be pissing soon. 4:30. I'll be dressing soon. 4:40. Nobody else is stirring. They're sucking the last minutes of sleep out of the bottle. Somebody coughs. Must be air in the nipple.

How can they be snoring at a time like this? How can they be so confident they can handle the morning without a head start? They should be like me. Heart racing faster than a Jimi Hendrix power set. Enough anxiety to fuel an aircraft carrier.

I grab the fatigues, cap, socks and boots from under the bed and sneak into the toilet. Uncertainty clocks in. Should I dress first or brush my teeth? What if I stay in the bathroom too long and lose my advantage? Should I wear my watch? Should I do the foot spray? Will they think I'm a pussy if I use Chapstick?

I order myself to be decisive. Watch, yes. Shit, no. Foot spray, yes. Mouth guard, no.

4:56. Finish dressing. Lean against door. Prepare for quick dash to the operations shack. 4:58. 4:59.

Suddenly Haddox bounds up the stairs. No siren today. He's going to administer his own wake-up call.

"Let loose your cocks and grabs your socks," he shouts.

A guy's foot is dangling off the top bunk. Haddox yanks it. A troop left a towel on the floor beside his bed. Haddox snaps it an inch from the unfortunate's ear.

He seven-league-boots it down the long row of bunks. So much to say. So few syllables at his disposal.

"Get the fuck dressed. Move the fuck out of my way. What I just stepped in better not be piss, soldier, or you're one dead dick."

Haddox trashes an open footlocker and throws an unattended electric shaver against the window.

One flustered guy put his Army-issue boxers on backward with his ass looking out the hole. Haddox makes the thoroughly frightened guy stand at attention while he lectures on the right way and the wrong way to stow one's privates.

I look on, fully dressed, from a safe distance. This is the first chance I've had to size up the DI. A shade under six feet. Mid 20s. A chest that could stop small-arms fire. Chin a perfect marriage of unsightly growth and molten muscle mass. Flattened nose, probably from a mishandled

400-pound barbell.

And he's working over somebody else.

Thank you, Ben. Thank you, Hoss.

The bathroom is a madhouse. The precious minutes until formation are counting down and squirming guys are arguing over who gets dibs.

"I've got one half in and half out," one extremely anxious guy says, begging to shit first.

Another guy is jumping up and down. "Diarrhea, and it doesn't care about the floor."

Kippler steps in the middle of the squirming bodies. "OK, OK, who just has to pee?"

Five times more hands go up than there are urinals.

Kippler notices a trash can filled with soda bottles. "You men grab a bottle, go outside the door and do your business."

Nobody moves, never having taken orders from a 140-pound lieutenant of the piss.

"I said go and stick your binkies into the hole."

Several dozen puzzled looks.

Kippler realizes where he is. "Uh, your dicks. Stick your dicks into the hole."

The urinators take their leave.

But there's considerable congestion of the No. 1 variety, and even more angry debate.

In Trumanesque fashion, Kippler nationalizes the crappers.

"OK, if you're going to go in your pants in the next 30 seconds, stand over there. If you think you can hold it at least 90 seconds, fall out over here."

And so on as Kippler prioritizes the shit into two-minute guys, three-minute guys and guys who are only in the bathroom to get away from Haddox.

Kippler directs traffic like George C. Scott in the tank scene from "Patton." We fall in on time.

Because Haddox lacks the vocabulary, another cadre member explains what's going to happen.

Our group of 200 will be split into five platoons. Alpha, Bravo,

Charlie, Delta and Echo. If you're in Alpha and your buddy is in Delta, he goes on, you won't have much daily contact except in the mess hall. But if you're in Charlie, and he's in Charlie, you're practically going to be holding hands for the next eight weeks. At the company level, there's a first sergeant and a captain. Two drill sergeants per platoon - 10 in all - plus a senior drill sergeant.

"Maybe we won't get Haddox," Ya whispers.

I'm straining under the load of two duffel bags, the humidity is bordering on rain forest, and there's a pimple on my chin the size of a cherry bomb. I get them from worrying too much. In college, I could have three exams the next day and only get a blackhead.

I'll get Haddox, I think to myself. I deserve him. It's written in eczema.

Cattle cars are parked next to the operations shack. Because our handlers know we'll probably never master the Alpha and Bravo concept, there are scoreboard-sized A's, B's, C's, D's and E's taped to the windows.

The cadre member goes down the list of names. While he's doing that, Haddox makes his assignment official and reports to the Alpha meat wagon.

I only half-listen to the recitation. I already know where I'm going. This has to be as hard as it can be. The lackadaisical-ass way I've conducted my life cannot be tolerated. I must be taught a lesson. Haddox must be my teacher.

Boil, Hibernation and Cleaning Lady go to Echo.

Gaines and Lit Cigarette to Delta.

Four o'clock to Charlie. Three o'clock to Charlie. They deserve each other.

Apperson to Alpha. Ya to Alpha. Kippler to Alpha.

There's a pause in the reading of the names. Kippler is only barely strong enough to carry his glasses. He would need a crane to get his two duffel bags to the cattle car in one trip. He grabs the one and pretends he forgot the other.

We know better.

Martin to Alpha.

Skebo sees Haddox in front of the door. Remembering what happened after the haircut, he tries to be especially manly. He hoists the bags on his shoulders and takes off in a trot. The unthinkable happens on the fourth stride. Ejaculation of gear. Not just a casual dribbling. Every tent peg. Every tent stake. Every item that was carefully folded, every item that was almost folded, every item that was thrown in at the last second.

Haddox doesn't say a word. He just looks at Skebo like's he's eight weeks' worth of dessert bar.

I pay little attention while the troops fill up the cars. No reason to. Our stars are aligned. I'm the radio signal and Haddox is the receiver. I'm the little lost boy and he's the truant officer.

A small part of me hears my name and fate. A soft "Al," then the "pha" like the DI is coughing up mucus.

I hurl a duffel bag with the grace of the longshoreman's brother who's taking his place for an hour to earn wine money. Because Skebo hasn't had enough bad happen to him, the buckle smacks him across the face.

I apologize, but it doesn't register. He's worse than me. I just think I'm going to die. He's halfway through the embalming.

"I'll jump out under the axle, let the thing run over me and then it'll be all over," Skebo says. "You guys'll get a couple of days off during the investigation, and the Army will have the corpus delicti it's always wanted."

Meanwhile, Haddox leads us in song.

"I want to be an Airborne Ranger," he screams. "I want a life that's full of danger."

I hold firm to the truth-in-lyrics policy. I absolutely do not want to be an Airborne Ranger. Ergo, I cannot lend voice to the choir.

"You fucks WILL sing," Haddox bellows, "and you WILL mean it."

There's maybe 60 percent participation. Most of the regular Army guys are in full throat, but the National Guard and Army Reserve troops only muster a half-hearted lip sync. We don't even want to be in Missouri, much less in a special unit where they beat their chests and play for keeps.

Haddox does his best Julie Andrews. The hills might not be alive, but, by God, our cattle car sure is.

In between choruses, we pick out landmarks from the first night. Baker Theater. Walker Service Club. Nutter Field House. We see row after row of brick buildings. One-story. Two-story. Three-story. There's no rhyme or reason to the construction. If the foreman overslept, the workmen simply kept going until they added a second level. If the foreman called in sick, they put in a third floor. Let the foreman go into a coma, and you'd have an Empire State Building of brick and mortar.

We see basic-training troops marching, emptying garbage cans, being inspected, falling out for mess, looking like they need medical attention. We can tell how far along in the cycle they are by the gear they're carrying. Only a pistol belt means early in the first week. Poncho, bayonet, canteen, ammunition clip and gas mask and they can see the end.

I want to see a bunch of guys throwing Frisbee, or watching cartoons, or shooting hoops.

I long for just one sunbather. To hear just one car stereo blasting out a Creedence Clearwater song. To see just one person with no particular place to go.

But all around us is work. And purpose. And shouting.

It feels good to be out and about, even if it's so tight in the cattle car we're in violation of every packaging law known to man. Like that first night, I don't want to get where we're going. I want to keep circling the wagons until the Fort Leonard Wood Zoning Board outlaws brick, multi-resident housing and votes in Frisbees.

But Haddox guides us straight to the barracks.

"We're ruin't," Ya whispers.

Ours is the fifth and last cattle car to arrive. In an airless gesture of togetherness, the other four platoons are made to swelter inside until we park.

When the doors finally fly open, too many drill sergeants in Smokey the Bear hats are on us like aphids to a vine.

Screaming aphides.

"Put your shit in this pile and come with me."

"Not that pile, you dick."

"What's the chain of command? Don't shake your head at me, boy. Gimme 25 pushups. No, gimme 30. Not only are you stupid, you're shiftless."

"Whose fucking tent peg is this, or am I gonna have to ram it up somebody's ass?"

"What are your general orders? Don't look at me like I'm a spaceman. What are they, goddamnit?"

"Never mind how crowded it is. Tighten up the ranks. Make your buddy smile."

"That's the worst parade rest I've ever seen. Get it right. This ain't the safety patrol."

"I thought I told you to put your shit down and come with me. What's the matter with you, boy? If I had that much shit, I'd want to put it down. You wanna carry my shit, too?"

It's a panic mentality. Go somewhere, even if it's wrong. Don't let them catch you standing still. Some guys are running to the barracks. Some guys are running from the barracks. Some guys are running around the barracks, waiting for their turn to get yelled out. All of us are getting eaten up.

Somebody tells me to go to a room on the second floor. I carry and kick my gear to the nearest cot, slide it under, wipe off an amount of sweat that would fill a pontoon boat and stand more or less at ease.

Defending my bunk against all comers, sir!

Then somebody tells me to go somewhere else.

I carry and kick down the hall. Another room. Another set of floor tiles to call a hearth. I look at the footlocker. About as homey as a Port-A-Potty, but it's my dresser for the next eight weeks. And my bureau. And my nightstand. And, should the enemy advance that far, my bayonet blocker.

I hear footsteps. My roommates, no doubt. Well, I was here first. The bed in the front corner is mine. They can wake up looking at my ugly red ass.

The footsteps aren't friendlies. They're DIs.

Move the fuck, I'm told. Where to is not important. Just move the fuck.

I slump to the floor. It's all too much. The shouting. The confusion. The nobody-wants-me.

Let them trample me. Let them take me to the hospital. At least then I'll have an address.

"What's the matter, son?"

Crying, I look up. It's a Smokey hat. I start to snap to.

"Never mind that. What's wrong?"

"I can't take it any more. I haven't even moved in yet, and already I can't take it."

I'm expecting him to kick me in the balls or, if that's against regulations, in the face. Or maybe in both places like one of those Chinese kickboxers. Eyes closed, I'm thinking where I'll fall and how much it'll hurt when I feel a hand on my shoulder.

A soft hand.

"Trust me, son. It's not that bad."

He's short. Maybe 5-9. Dumpy. Freckle-faced. Thick black hair on his forearms that look freshly combed. Mustache that's all the law allows. Nametag that says "Waldsburger."

I try to stop crying. This man has the power of God over me and I don't want to be a leaky valve.

"First of all, you need to relax," the DI says softly. "And understand that 99 percent of this is bullshit. If I call you a dickhead, it's just a word. If I say you ain't worth diddly, it's not you as a person, it's you as a troop. There's a big difference."

I can't believe I'm hearing this from somebody who wears insignia for a living. These guys are supposed to be heartless, emotionless, mutilators, even. This man is talking to me like I just made a bad grade on his production management test, and he really wants me to do better next time.

"We've all got our jobs out here," Waldsburger says. "I'm supposed to stick it to you. You're supposed to stick it out. It's that simple."

This is unbelievable. He's "supposed to" ream us out. Doesn't he want to? Isn't reducing us to ashes a jolly at the end of his rainbow?

"Uh, are you Alpha's drill sergeant?" I ask hopefully but timidly, staring at my shoes.

"Yes. I wasn't with you at the reception center. They gave me a week off from the previous cycle. Went to the beach."

I want to ask why he's not bossing us around. I want to ask why he put his hand on my shoulder.

But I don't dare. He's who he is, and I'm lower than sewer pipe. If I try to get too familiar, he'll only pull rank and tell me to move the fuck.

So I just stand there, bobbing my lips. A serf to the throne.

"Did you come out here by yourself?" he wants to know.

I nod.

"Found a buddy yet?"

"Yes, sir. Skebo, er, Martin, sir."

"Would it help if he was in your room?"

"Very much help. Yes, mister sir." The words aren't coming out like I'd like, but I hope he'll edit for content.

Waldsburger writes something on a piece of paper and sticks it in his pocket.

"I've got to go. Remember, it's just eight weeks. You can stand on your head that long."

I can't for more than three seconds, but I appreciate his confidence.

There's nothing to do but stand in the hall and await further abuse. I count 10 of us without a place to stay. With our gear at our feet, we effectively block passage to all but championship hurdlers. We're uniformed refugees, the worst kind.

Suddenly, I hear a bass bellow from where a few seconds ago had been a tepid tenor.

"Get where you're going, you shits. I'm not your mama. Look at me. Do I got tits out to there?"

It's Waldsburger.

He looks at me until I summon the courage to make eye contact.

Then he winks.

Loud whistle. Our presence is requested on the patch of dead grass that separates the long rows of barracks. We sprint downstairs, but hit the brakes before the door. Which row do we get in? Who lines up beside who? Nobody's told us. Better to be late than wrong, so we cower.

"Over here, dipshits."

It's Haddox. He's standing next to the horizontal bars that flank our building.

"I AM in charge of your PT," he barks. "You WILL do good in PT. One of the events on the PT test is the bars. Today we WILL learn the bars."

This must be the 30th time I've heard him talk like this. Changing only a word or two from one sentence to the next so we cretins can follow along.

I want to yell back, "I am in charge of my brain. There is thought inside my brain. My brain could be three days dead and still be smarter than your brain. Your brain is only attached to your body by Scotch Tape. By comparison, mine is held in place by 10 layers of Polident. So quit talking to us like you're Carl Jung and we're protoplasm."

But I keep quiet. Haddox is built like an office complex. Out here, that means he's Jung.

"Here is how you do the bars."

The DI spits on his palms, jumps up and grabs the bar with both hands, all the while keeping his legs gymnast-straight.

There are 14 bars. I'm thinking he'll go down and come maybe halfway back. That's plenty to demonstrate the proper technique. He doesn't have to take the PT test. Why should he risk pulling his shoulders out of their sockets?

Haddox goes down 14, comes back 14 and then does 14 more. He isn't even breathing hard. Indeed, his shoulders have been given a go for three more trips.

"Fourteen plus 14 plus 14 is 42," he says, turning to face us. "That's what it takes to score the maximum points on this event."

I'm thinking, OK, OK, he's made his point. He can come down now.

But Haddox continues the lecture while hanging from the bars.

"The key is strength and balance," he says.

Never mind that. When's he gonna drop? Guy did all those bars and now he's talking. Guy's been up way more than a minute. He could be Tarzan. Give him enough vines and he could swing to the other side of the base and be back before lunch.

Haddox goes on and on about proper form and keeping a good grip. He actually thinks any reasonably conditioned office complex should be able to dangle until the bars rust.

Finally, he lets go. I'm watching to see what he grabs first. To see what hurts. To see where he's vulnerable.

But all he does is scratch his armpits. He didn't drop because of socket-searing pain. Just an itch. Get his pits up to speed and this guy's a human meat hook.

I imagine Haddox in combat. Hanging from a branch. Defenseless. Enemy sharpshooter squeezes the trigger. Haddox raises his heels, bends in half, catches the round between his toes and returns to the full, upright position. Judge from Bulgaria scores a 9.4. Italy gives him a 9.3. Tunisia awards a 9.5. America wins. War's over.

It's our turn. Nobody does more than 26 bars. I fall down at 18, Skebo at 10. Haddox calls us all pussies. It's easy to see why. He and Jane are on their fourth movie and here we are slipping on the first vine.

Waldsburger stands in front of the door. Clearly, he has something to say, but it's not in him to scream to get our attention. He waits patiently until Haddox gets disgusted with us and leaves.

"Who doesn't have a room yet?" he wants to know.

We squatters raise our hands.

"Who doesn't want a room?"

My jaw drops. Waldsburger has told an unauthorized joke. He can't do that. This is serious business. Doing the horizontal bars. Being a dick. Moving the fuck. There are no punchlines here.

Waldsburger, the housing authority, reaches in his pocket and pulls out a scrap of paper. He calls out my name. He calls out Skebo's name. Match game.

We grab our loads and head upstairs. There's almost a bounce to our step. We have a home. We have neighbors - guys who, if we don't make it, will say, "Yeah, they were really good persons. Sure wish I had known them better."

Skebo and I walk in our four-bunk bay. A large black man is in the bed furthest from the door with a tent stake in his hand. Suddenly, he lashes out at an imaginary enemy, slicing and dicing, all the while humming the theme from "Shaft." His foe dispatched, he returns to the ready position. It's like he's shadow-boxing, except with the closest thing he can find to a knife.

Home doesn't look so good. Skebo and I check the room number, hoping to God we made a mistake. Our shoes squeak. The black man looks up, sees us and immediately flashes his weapon.

I figure I've got five, maybe six seconds to live. Two for him to jump across the room, two for the actual cutting up and then a proper allowance for him to remove the stake so the bleeding can begin.

Skebo is frozen in place. A six-foot helping of lime sherbet with a splash of whipped cream at the top.

How stupid we've been. Haddox isn't going to kill us. Our roommate is.

I muster a greeting.

"Uh, hi." I back up until I'm out in the hall. He can have the room. I'll just live out here.

"Aw, shit," the black man says, throwing the stake on the floor. "Two more."

He says it in the manner of an Alamo defender who looks onto the horizon and sees the entire population of the Yucatan prepared to charge.

I bite. Two more what?

"White motherfuckers."

Skebo, he of the commune and good will to all, pursues the matter. "Er, what's your name?"

"Why do you care, you piece of blue-eyed shit?"

"Uh, well, since we're going to be in the same room and all."

"Fuck you, fat boy."

That's more than enough to snap my interviewer's pencil, but Skebo persists.

"Er, you know, what with all of us being thrown together and all, might as well get to know each other."

This guy has almost the same molecular structure as Haddox. But taller. And wider. Who's the more homicidal? Don't know. That game's in extra innings.

The information comes out slowly, reluctantly, and only after Skebo gives him a bag of Fritos.

William McKinley Carouthers. Regular Army. No Daddy. High school dropout. Cooks at a chicken restaurant. Says he hates whites. Says he wishes we were dead.

"All of us?" Skebo wants to know. "That's an awful lot of Caucasians."

He's being facetious. Why is he being facetious with someone who can cause his funeral? Leave the guy alone. Let him detest us. Let him hurt us. Hey, we couldn't get out of this on a mental. Maybe we can get out on a gurney.

"We're in the hundreds of millions," Skebo goes on. "You'd need a natural disaster."

Why can't Skebo let it go? Carouthers isn't going to live in his commune.

But I forget. Skebo is a sociology major. The big black man has become his research project.

"Do you think it's OK to hate whites?"

He's trying to tap Carouthers' subconscious. But what if the guy doesn't have one? What if that id is a 2-by-4?

"Hell, yes. Caucasians are devils." Carouthers is fingering the tent stake. If he throws it, I'm leaving. I don't care what they say.

"I cut me one once," Carouthers says, smiling. "We was in gym class. He's putting on his pants. I'm putting on my pants. And in a hurry. I want to get out of the locker room."

"Because the white man is a devil," Skebo says, finishing the thought.

"Yeah. I'm lacing my sneaks and I see the Caucasian looking at me and talking to his white buddy. He better not be calling me no nigger."

I look at Carouthers. If I called him a nigger, I'd go in the witness protection program for the rest of my life.

"The white guy raises his hand to me like he's in class. Wants to know if he can ask a question. I say, go ahead, motherfucker."

Skebo, the behaviorologist, is getting off on this. Carouthers could disembowel us both and all my friend cares about is annotated footnotes.

"Tell me, what did the white guy want to know?"

God, Skebo, there isn't any ivy on these walls. Give it up. Knowing Carouthers for the three minutes I've known him, if you publish, you perish.

"Man wanted to touch my head. Said he's never felt the top of a

Negro's head before."

"So, did you let him?" Skebo asks.

"Shit, no. Ain't no Caucasian gonna let his fingers do the walking over me. That's when I got the knife out."

I'm thinking, geez, a little anthropological curiosity gets a guy killed. Why didn't the Whitey study business like I did? He'd be bored out of his mind, but at least he'd be alive.

"Motherfucker started in to get his feel. Got him across the wrist, man. Blood starts zigging and zagging. Thought for a second I cut that thing clean off."

Skebo, the chronicler of our times, wants to know if Carouthers had a court date.

"Black judge, man. Six months suspended sentence. I was back in the Chicken House the next night."

Say what you will, the troop is good at what he does. Some guys sell insurance. Some build cabinets. Some design skyscrapers. He cuts the hands off white people.

And I get to live with this person for the next two months.

A Thanksgiving turkey.

And he gets to carve.

Loud whistle.

Skebo runs into the hall and bumps into Haddox. Afraid he'll have to do pushups for practicing sociology without a license, he comes to attention. Nobody told him to, but better to be stiff than sorry.

"You couldn't hit your dick with a stick," Haddox concludes.

Never mind that we haven't finished moving in. We are to report to battalion headquarters. The colonel has something to say.

Another panic attack. We don't know who to fall out beside. Worse than that, we're mostly strangers. How can we possibly march when our heels haven't been properly introduced?

Waldsburger to the rescue.

"Look, guys, just get in four rows, OK? Doesn't matter where. Just remember that you're Alpha Company, second battalion, second brigade. If someone asks, it's A-2-2. Got it? Even if that's the only Army thing you know, it should be enough for right now."

But what about marching? Isn't that important?

"Today, no," Waldsburger says. "Just walk. Move your hands up and down a lot. That'll make 'em think you know what you're doing. And take big steps. Confident steps. Little steps are like little peckers. Remember that."

We unranked-and-filed aren't so sure. People will be watching, won't they?

The other four platoons are ready to take off. Alphabetically speaking, Alpha should be in the vanguard.

Waldsburger hollers to the Bravo DI that he's got two puking troops.

"We'd better bring up the rear," he advises. "Take me that long to get 'em out of the can."

Bravo's Smokey the Bear nods and passes it on. Alpha will be last and two of its trainees won't be of sound fragrance.

At first, I try to keep in step with the guy ahead of me. I look at his left bootlace and try to put my left bootlace in the same place.

But it doesn't work. He walks fast. Then all of a sudden he walks slow. I'm striding. Then I'm shuffling.

It's like this all up and down the line.

"You guys look like a centipede with 50 broken ankles," Waldsburger says.

But he's smiling.

The strategy works. We get to the gymnasium a football field behind Echo. Nobody notices that we're just a bunch of guys in black boots out for a walk.

"Shit, we was in better step than this when we walked across the stage to get our GEDs," Ya says as we file in.

There's a podium with a half-dozen officers plus a scraggly troop who looks like he's got even less rank than me. The colonel claps his hands and a St. Bernard bigger than a PT boat trots to his side. It's not encouraging. The dog does forward march better than we do.

"The next time you see this little fellow will be graduation day," the head man says, patting his pal. "You'll be 10 times the soldiers you are today."

No way. If I'm 10 times the soldier I am today, I'll actually be one and that'll never happen. Might be 10 times a better actor. Maybe 10 times better at dealing with the certifiable. But that's all.

They show a Vince Lombardi film about doing whatever it takes to win. After we watch five defensive guys tackle the quarterback really hard, the commoner is brought forward.

"This AWOL standing to my left decided he couldn't take it," the colonel says, his voice picking up speed. "He thought he could just leave. Thought he wouldn't be caught.

"But he was picked up by the MPs. He went to the stockade. He thought he was winning, but he got beat 100 to nothing. Sergeant, read the report."

A soldier with a shiny helmet buffs himself, shoots the AWOL a sneer and acts like the manilla folder contains his own personal writ of mandamus.

I'm thinking, hey, another hall monitor makes good.

"Seay, Michael R., on or about 0300 hours on 8, August, 1971, left the military reservation without permission of his commanding officer.

"At 1630 hours on 10, August, 1971, said troop was apprehended outside an ice cream establishment, in Troy, Ohio, known as Tastee-Freez by the civilian population. It was without incident except for minor damage to a milkshake."

The colonel retakes the podium.

"Today's lesson, men, is don't go AWOL. Remember, you can fuck something, anything, and be in less trouble."

"Just my luck," Skebo whispers. I'd escape to the end of the Earth, but that's where the MPs buy their shiny helmets."

The dog barks.

"We'll see you in eight weeks. Dismissed."

We file out of the gym in front of Waldsburger. When we get to the sidewalk, he confirms what we've already heard, that the first few days of basic training will be nothing but classes, PT and learning to march better than we did today.

"And ragging on us," Skebo says under his breath.

"Oh, yes," Waldsburger adds, "and plenty of individual instruction."

We are dispatched to personal-hygiene class where we watch a film on trenchfoot and frostbite. Shot just after the advent of talkies, it features several dozen forlorn-looking GIs who won't be going to the 1933 prom.

Then some inverted crawl action and a spirited move-out phase in which we charge straight ahead and bounce to the ground upon command. None of us fall down hard enough. Pretend you're sleeping on a hammock, Waldsburger suggests, and a couple of assholes cut the rope on both sides at the same time.

Then a 20-minute trot and we're in front of the barracks.

Where Waldsburger teaches us our first marching cadence:

"The prettiest girl I've ever seen ...

"... was smoking pot in the boys' latrine."

Catchy lyrics. Good to dance to. Could be a hit.

"Left foot here, right foot there," Waldsburger barks. "C'mon, guys, Custer's men did it better than this and they knew they were gonna die."

He soon gives up and sends us inside. First inspection is tomorrow morning. Low quarters and extra pair of boots shined. Brass polished. Uniforms hung up in the closet. Footlocker arranged as per boxers, socks and undershirts.

Carouthers puts on "Shaft." In the spirit of preserving life, Skebo and I sing along.

8 p.m. Footsteps. Heavy footsteps. The footsteps of a none too happy soldier.

A shadow in the door, a loud "Fuck the Army" and then...

Apperson.

His gear is wrapped around his person in more layers than a 6-year-old from Duluth on New Year's. It seems Haddox caught him giving the colonel the finger and lined him against the bleachers for a royal reaming. Halfway through it, Apperson extended the same greeting to Haddox, who went berserk and had to be held back by five cadre members. He broke through long enough to rip Apperson's duffel bags open and call him a dick-sucking cocksucker.

Another DI told Apperson he'd better gather his shit quick, that Haddox has really lost it when he calls you a double queer.

Screaming that the troop won't live to see the sun set, Haddox was removed from the field. Apperson was advised to put on as much of his fallen gear as possible, sprint in the opposite direction and hope to Christ that Haddox gets a buzz-on at the NCO Club and forgets what happened.

After telling us all that, Apperson drops his load in the middle of the room and shakes in the manner of a just-bathed dog. Shirts, pants, socks and poncho fall to the floor.

Carouthers does a quick skin-color check.

"Shit, one more."

Skebo and I sit back, waiting for the confrontation between Apperson, the pissed, and Carouthers, the cutter.

Disappointment sets in almost immediately.

Apperson doesn't tap his fingers in rhythm to "Shaft," but doesn't ask that it be turned down.

Carouthers leaves the tape on, but quits singing.

Apperson calls Haddox a talking turd, the worst kind.

Carouthers says there are so many white people that each time he walks in the room it's like touring the cracker factory.

Standoff.

I'm nervous about tomorrow.

Not the training. I'm thoroughly accustomed to sitting through classes. And I'm in good enough shape to handle any PT they throw at us. It's the inspections that are going to kick my ass. The arranging of gear just so. The only things in my life I've ever been neat about are my rejection letters from newspapers. Got them in a folder in alphabetical order on my desk back home. Every other piece of personal property is thrown in a pile.

I get called away. Some idiot told the DIs I'm interested in higher office out here, and my name got put down both for platoon guide and squad leader. I miss valuable folding and shining time waiting in line to tell Waldsburger I'm definitely not leadership material, and whoever said I was created a fictional character.

Somehow he already knows this. I'm not halfway through gurgling the words out, and already he's looking down the list to see who's next.

I return to the bay at 8:45, only 15 minutes before lights out. My footlocker and closet sorta just sit there, but Skebo's area looks like it was targeted by a commando unit from Good Housekeeping Magazine.

Hey, what gives?

"Kippler," Skebo replies.

What about him?

"A bunch of us were in the bathroom talking about how we aren't ready for the inspection. Then somebody said we ought to walk down the hall and get a load of Kippler's footlocker, that it looks like some kind of religious shrine.

"I've never seen anything like it," Skebo goes on. "Not a blemish. Not a crease out of place. I tell you, Kippler should be somebody's wife.

"Kippler took a look at my shit and starts laughing," Skebo says. "Told me I couldn't pass inspection if Stevie Wonder was conducting it. That's when he told me about the 50 bucks."

"Fifty dollars?" I ask.

"I fork over the money; he arranges my shit for the next eight weeks. I believe he used the words 'on retainer.'"

"But what if you don't pass?"

"Are you kidding?" Skebo replies. "How can an altar flunk?"

"Say a miracle happens."

"Then I'm out the money. Kippler says he doesn't fold on spec."

"How can you afford that kind of cash?"

A sheepish look comes over Skebo.

"Mom and Dad thought I might run into a few problems out here."

I remember the first time I saw him at the reception center. Hair down to his ass. Flip-flops. Belly of Buddha. Roller of numbers. Yeah, he might have a little trouble out here.

"So they gave me, what do you business-types call it, a discretionary reservoir I can dip into."

"Your own little slush fund, in other words." Got to tweak the guy a little. I'll get gigged out the ass tomorrow and he's going to come out looking like Mr. Feather Duster.

"My parents love their little Skebo, what can I say?"

It's crazy, but I find strength in my friend's lack of it. I'm going to screw up tomorrow. I know that. But at least the screwing-up will be on my own. There's nobody I can call on. But there's nobody I want to call on.

At least that's how I feel now. Ask me again in the morning.

CHAPTER 4

4:30 a.m. I wake up and put an extra coat of polish on my shoes. But it doesn't take. Lord knows I'm rubbing hard enough. Some footwear, I'm convinced, are determined not to excel. If polished, they will not shine. If buffed, they will not glow.

I need a gimmick. Something like you see on those Chevrolet commercials on TV when the car goes around in a slow circle so you can see all its features. Maybe put my shoes on some kind of little platform, hook up a motor and let them rotate. Maybe add some flashing lights and a pretty girl who lifts the strap of her evening gown and purrs, "Now, ladies and gentlemen, for your viewing pleasure, our top-of-the-line model for 1971...(drum roll) ...the highest example of the cobbler's art...(more drums)... black Army shoes."

Just a thought.

I get my usual head start on shitting and showering. 4:40. 4:45. I'm stumbling around trying to put my pants on.

Suddenly it's not dark any more. Haddox has seized the night. And 15 minutes early.

Standing at the door, he screams, "Which one of you dicks gonna say, 'At ease?' "

It seems this is what you call out when when an NCO is about to enter your living space.

Not, "Hey, there are a bunch of naked guys here, Sarge. Can you give us a minute?" Or, "It's not visiting hours yet. Kindly take a seat, and we'll let you know when we're ready."

I'm frozen. So is Skebo.

"At ease!" Carouthers sounds off.

"At least there's one goddamn soldier in here. As you were."

Then he goes down the hall to pull the same early-alarm-clock routine on another bedroom community.

I turn my attention to making my bunk. Top sheet pulled tight and something called a hospital corner on the sides. Waldsburger showed us yesterday. You hold the flap like so and then you pull it over until the crease makes a 45-degree angle.

It looked easy when he did it. Tuck, tuck. Fold, fold. Then squish under the bed.

But I have trouble. The sheet is full of wrinkles. I try to beat them out. No good. I manage a flap, but it's lopsided. I try again, but can only muster a 5-degree angle. Will Haddox notice? Did he take geometry?

Apperson bitches about where he is. Carouthers complains that his laundry bag isn't where he left it last night and one of the white motherfuckers must've stolen it and, oops, never mind, it's in his closet.

I try to relax. I've done all I can to pass this inspection. Now it's up to my underwear, socks and pistol belt.

Haddox is coming back. I can tell by the rapid, confident-in-what-he's-doing strides. Boot-campers plod along in don't-know-for-sures.

He's still 50 feet away, but I holler "At ease!" at the top of my lungs. If I show him the proper respect, maybe he'll judge my low quarters kindly.

The DI walks around the room tugging on blankets and pillowcases. He stops in front of my shoes, checks them for star-light, star-bright and, finding none, kicks them into Skebo's cabinet.

But he saves his serious anger for my bunk.

"Is this made to the best of your ability, troop?" he hollers, his face two inches from my face.

"Yes, uh, sir. Very much well made well, sir."

My shoulders are in reverse as far as they'll go. I'm puckered up so much my lips look like a wad of chewing gum.

Haddox leaves me like this while he noses around my bunk. Suddenly, he grabs the top sheet, jerks the thing completely off and throws it on the floor. I've never seen such a display of power. This guy could undress a statue.

I'm praying he'll walk away. I don't do linen so good when I'm by myself. I'll never get through a command performance.

But Haddox stands there with hands on hips. The fate of 40 footlockers can wait until my mattress gets properly attired.

I grow six extra hands. They slap at each other in a vain attempt to create a crease. A fold is out of the question.

I look at him helplessly in the manner of a beached octopus.

"Goddamn, you're pitiful."

He kicks the bunk twice and then moves in for the kill.

But he's interrupted. The DI is needed in the toilet. There's a piece of shit in the shower.

"The men are refusing to clean it," the messenger reports. "Something about E coli."

Haddox stares clean through me.

"I'll be back and this bed better be made."

The six hands beget six more hands. Then the skeletal frame they're attached to starts shaking out of control.

I fall back on the bed, which only worsens its condition. I don't care. The condemned man might as well be comfortable.

I put the pillow against my face. A solution presents itself. I'll smother myself. It'll drive Haddox crazy knowing that he was so close to killing me, but didn't get the chance.

Then I feel a fist. The pillow offers little in the way of protection. The Army needs to make these things better.

Eyes watering, I try to stand. But something is in my way.

Carouthers.

"Shit, the man was right. You are pitiful."

But he tucks as he talks. And folds.

"Uh, what are you doing?" I ask.

"Fixing your bed," Carouthers replies. "You're too busy whining."

I decide to make his hitting me in the face a complete non-issue. He's at the crucial hospital-corner stage of the procedure and I don't want to break his concentration.

He pulls the sheet tight and does the squish bit. In 90 seconds, he has taken what was an out-of-shape, wrinkled bunk and turned it into a sleep zone worthy of the front of a Wheaties box.

"Uh, thanks. You really bailed me out."

Carouthers ignores me. A response would require an interpersonal exchange and our relationship hasn't progressed to that point.

But he helped me, something he didn't have to do.

And he didn't call me a motherfucker.

Something to build on.

We hear that Haddox successfully arbitrated the bathroom work stoppage by threatening to have the E coli served for lunch.

He returns in a trot, hollering that he'd better damn well see a tight-ass bunk.

Which he does.

A 40-year maid at the Holiday Inn couldn't make a better bed.

Haddox tries to yank the sheet out. It will not be moved.

He tosses a quarter on the bunk. The coin rockets to the ceiling.

The dumbfounded DI walks away. He knows he's been had, but doesn't know how. Hmm, only gone for five minutes. Is that enough time to air-mail a perfectly made bunk from one of the service academies?

I leave him to ponder the shipping costs. We've got breakfast to swallow and then a sit-down with company commander Litton. He spoke to us briefly when we got out of the cattle cars. Jawline riveted in place. A chest full of medals. Temples indented as if they'd been stamped at the foundry.

But what I noticed most was his adam's-apple hair. A giant tuft that can't be contained by mere collar. I stood in awe. He has more hair there than I have around my pecker. Never mind his command record, this alone qualifies him as a leader of men.

First, a class on military traditions and customs. Where we learn:

"The chain of command is the President of the United States, Then the Secretary of Defense. Then the Secretary of the Army. Then the Chief of Staff of the Army. Then the Army commander. Then the corps commander. Then the division commander. Then the post commander, brigade commander, battalion commander, company commander, platoon leader, squad leader and then me."

I'm thinking, if it gets down that far, might as well give Ho Chi Minh the keys to the Oval Office.

Then a class on map-reading. Where we learn:

"For accurate compass readings, stay 55 meters away from high-tension power lines, 18 meters from any motor vehicle, 10 meters from telephone wires, two meters from machineguns and a half meter from steel helmets."

I'm thinking, for really accurate readings, follow the paths created by troops from previous training cycles. Then, a PT session of jumping jacks, wind sprints, bending-over exercises and seeing how many sit-ups we can do in a minute.

Nothing to it. I'm not even breathing hard. I wish they'd say, look, guy, we won't make you fold anything or shoot anything, but we're going to run your hind parts off and make you do calisthenics until you develop hinges. I'd coast through this place.

Litton addresses us in a great place to play Frisbee if a miracle happened and that was made the order of the day. Don't wise-ass to the DIs. Don't leave your footlockers open. Don't fuck over your buddy. Yeah, yeah, we've heard it before.

Then he talks about Vietnam. The trip-wires. The punji sticks. The explosive devices intended not to kill, but to blow off an arm or a leg. Men get immune to death, he says quietly, not to seeing one pants leg swaying in the breeze.

"I've been there," he tells us. "Twice."

I don't doubt it. He didn't get all those stripes on his sleeves because he had some free time with a sewing machine.

"How many of you guys are regular Army?" Litton wants to know.

About 100 hands go up.

"About 50-50, right? Half regular Army and half National Guard and enlisted reserves."

I listen hard for a negative tone, something to indicate he thinks we're pussies for taking the easy way out, and he's going to make it as miserable for us as he possibly can.

"How many of you RAs knew you could probably get in the Guard or reserves if you worked at it hard enough?"

The show of hands is less than two dozen.

"You just took what the Army gave you, right? The Army didn't tell you there was a choice. The recruiter said sign here and that's what you did."

Measured agreement among most of the RAs.

"You NGs and ERs, how many are college boys?"

The overwhelming majority.

"You RAs, how many of your daddies could afford to send you away to school?"

No hands.

"How many of you finished high school?"

Less than half.

"You know you're probably going to Vietnam, right?"

More murmuring in the affirmative.

"Kill as many of them goddamn VC as you can, right?"

The RAs don't know what to say. We don't either.

"Poor man's Army," Litton grunts.

If Fort Leonard Wood is a newspaper, that was its first editorial.

The captain puts the cap on his poison pen. Enough point of view. Now it's back to hard news.

"I'm gonna push you these next eight weeks. The DIs are gonna push. The cadre at the rifle ranges are gonna push. Some of you will ship out for Southeast Asia. Some of you will ship out for a steno pool in Pottstown. We don't have time to go back and forth to see which is which. So we train like you're all going for a walk in the jungle. Everybody got that?"

He presses the point until he gets a loud "Yes, sir!"

Litton wants to know if we have any questions.

I'm dying to ask about his adam's-apple hair. Does it itch? Do the ladies like it? Is it a good place to hide ammunition?

But I keep quiet.

I just wilt under Haddox. With Litton, I wilt the fuck.

He calls us to attention and announces he will conduct the barracks inspections for at least the first week. If you think your DI is hard to live with now, he warns, just wait until your platoon comes in last.

Another session on personal hygiene. We look at slide after slide of rotting teeth that ages ago said "So long" to the gum line. Guys start nodding off after the 20th picture of pus. We've been up since before 5, our stomach linings have finally negotiated a peace settlement with breakfast and fourth-stage gingivitis looks better with eyes shut.

One of the DIs from Charlie Platoon is in charge. Sensing a rapid loss of audience, he adds fresh slides to the mix. Suddenly, there's 100-percent interest in teeth that have chewed their last.

Unclothed women. And in much better focus than the pus.

Every fourth or fifth flick of his switch calls to the screen a rouged, pouty vision of heaven.

But only for an instant.

Then it's back to looking at incisors that tried to bite their way through a minefield and suffered heavy casualties.

"You want me to start this class all over again?" the DI threatens.

We assure him that's not necessary.

"Then you gotta prove to me you're paying attention."

He has 200 willing students. Just tell us how we can help.

"Every time you see a naked chick, you holler 'pussy' as loud as you can."

No problem.

Slide of inch-deep cavity. Slide of tooth being yanked out. Slide of blood cascading down what's left of a bicuspid. Slide of 46-inch tits.

"Pussy!"

Third-year dental college students aren't any more alert than we are. And our knowledge base is increasing. Show me a few more extractions and I swear I could perform the procedure.

Finally, he turns off the projector and ushers us out of the building. The other platoons in Alpha Company immediately move out, but Waldsburger is in no hurry.

"Got an hour until supper, men," he says, leisurely. "What do you think we should do?"

We're astonished. The reins are loose around our shoulders. They're supposed to be strangling us.

"Go home?" one troop suggests cautiously.

"No can do. Sorry," Waldsburger says pleasantly.

"All go get a beer?" another troop chimes in.

The DI grins. "Maybe later in the cycle."

We react with surprising maturity to Waldsburger's easygoing nature. For once, we're being treated like human beings. Nobody wants to screw it up.

"What say we head back to the barracks?" the DI says. "You could probably use a little rest. Let's line up. Remember the squads we put you in after breakfast?"

We remember. In seconds, we're doing the dress-right-dress bit. And on our own, without somebody screaming in our ears.

We want to prove that Waldsburger's way of doing things is the best.

Nordquist, our newly appointed platoon guide, does not wait for the command; he gives it. "Right, right, your military right," he barks, more or less confidently. Waldsburger is just along to get his constitutional. We march ourselves.

It's the best two-stepping we've done since we got here. If you grade on a curve, Alpha Platoon is in step.

"Dismissed," Waldsburger says. "Fall out for break time."

We've never heard that command before, but we quickly embrace it. We're upstairs before you can say "sleep deprivation."

In the hall, I see a guy working on the bulletin board. Mud flaps for ears. Flattest head in the platoon. Looks like somebody took a sander to it. Shirt starched so much he crackles when he walks. Big enough that you don't mess with him.

It's the troop everybody has been calling "General."

Breaks into military-history lecture during mess. Puts a GI Joe on his footlocker at night. Knows where William Westmoreland went to high school. Tacks pictures of the Army's haircut policy on the bulletin board on his time off.

If basic training was a play, he'd be Haddox's understudy. Follows him around. Asks who his favorite sports teams are. Asks how you get to Khe Sanh from Saigon.

A tired-looking trainee sees General putting pictures of backs of heads on the wall.

"What are you doing that shit for?" he asks.

"So we can see what we need to look like," General explains. "I saw these in the CQ and thought I'd put 'em to good use. You got a problem?"

The guy walks away. Maybe next time he'll start something, but not when his eyeballs are rolling around like they've been in a centrifuge chamber.

This is amazing. General could be taking it easy, but he's doing the Army's work.

And what he's displaying isn't even news. Everybody out here knows hair is considered a disease. The more you have, the greater the potential to infect others.

Forget "Bonanza"-resting. I want to see this.

General arranges his pictures just so. First, the acceptable. Hair the length of stubble, and no follicle within an inch of the ears. Then the unacceptable. Hair that's had a shelf life of more than five days. Hair that might consider coming off during a vigorous combing. Hair whose ancestors were parted.

Despite fully illustrating the heroes and villains of good grooming, half the bulletin board remains blank. Can't have that, so General goes downstairs and comes back with signage that may not be new, but will never grow old.

WHAT YOU SEE STAYS HERE

They've got that right. No telling what the enemy could do with the piece of shit in the shower.

LOOSE LIPS SINK SHIPS

If anything I do or say at Fort Leonard Wood causes one of our naval vessels to go down, you can beat me about the head with a pier.

General retreats a step and, in the manner of a great artist, cocks his head from side to side and puts his fingers under his chin. Composition?

Perfect. Spacing? A slight downward adjustment of the mustache policy and, ta-da, the Renoir of bulletin boards.

Just then his buddy Haddox whizzes past. His face looks like it's been given a boil order.

"Fall out right fucking now," he screams.

We're on the sidewalk in seconds. I take my place in the third row beside Ya. Thirty-eight other men take their rightful places. But Haddox is too angry to praise us for hitting our marks.

He pulls out a piece of paper.

"Guess which platoon finished last in this morning's inspection? I don't mean just last. I mean fucking last. Captain didn't like your footlockers. Didn't like your boots. Didn't like your bathroom. Didn't like nothing."

Haddox walks between the ranks. I swear I feel the heat when he brushes past Ya.

"Do you dicks know why I know this?"

We assume the information was handed down from the mountain on a large stone tablet and presented to an old guy with a long, flowing beard, who promptly turned it in to the CQ.

"Because the captain gave it to me," he says, waving the sheet of paper. "And how do you think it made me feel when the captain informed me of this? Bad. Real fucking bad. And I don't see why I should be the only one who feels bad. So, guess what? You're gonna feel bad, too."

If the red gets any higher on Haddox's face, we're going to have liftoff.

"ALPHA PLATOON," he screams, "ASSUME THE LOW-CRAWL POSITION!"

Imagine losing a quarter and having to look for it on all fours without getting higher than 18 inches off the ground. It's propulsion by knees and elbows. Speed? Compared to this, a turtle has a motor up its ass.

"You're gonna take a little trip around the block, dicks. Could take an hour. Could take two. While you're down there, you think about today's inspection. You think about tomorrow's inspection. You WILL do better."

The only time I've done anything like this was in Babe Ruth League when a foul ball rolled under the fence and I squeezed under to get it. The difference is that was only three feet. Now I might have to stay in lost-ball mode for half a mile.

The journey begins. What must we look like to passersby? I wonder. Green-suited aliens who must breathe from the cracks of sidewalks to sustain life.

First to bleed are forearms, followed quickly by knees and ankles.

"Move faster, goddammit," Haddox barks.

I'm getting a serious pain in my balls. I try to crawl in such a way that my pecker absorbs most of the punishment, but my nuts keep bouncing back in play.

"Slide them bellies," Haddox shouts. "You can't be hurt yet. We're just getting started."

Someone rushes up from behind. Someone important-sounding.

"As you were, men," he orders.

Which we interpret as assuming the full, upright position.

It's senior drill instructor Robison. Black. Squat. Little or no neck. Until now, he's been content to stay back and leave the day-to-day screaming to his subordinates.

He hustles Haddox inside the barracks where he thinks we won't hear.

But we do.

"What do you think you're doing with these men?" Robison explodes.

"Nothing that says I can't," Haddox replies.

"You're fucked, mister. I'm saying you can't."

The two men are practically lip to lip. Haddox is saying he low-crawled his troops all the time last cycle including once, he brags, in the middle of the street without bothering to stop traffic. Robison is saying that was under some other SDI and he won't tolerate such bullshit. He's particularly pissed about the street thing. He tells Haddox somebody could have gotten killed.

This is great. There's shouting, but it isn't directed at us. We use the bills of our caps to squeegee the blood off our forearms and listen on.

"The men are soft already," Haddox says. "You're just making 'em worse."

"Then it'll be my ass," Robison counters. "No more low-crawl on the sidewalk. You got that, mister?"

Haddox is anything but contrite. "Yeah, I got that, mister," he says sarcastically.

"Glad we understand each other. Now tell the men they're done with low-crawl."

"You tell the dicks. It's your order."

Which prompts a fresh round of screaming.

Finally, an "All right, goddammit, I'll do it, but this shit ain't over."

Haddox bolts out of the building and calls us to attention. We pretend we didn't overhear the best three-minute exchange of obscenities of our entire lives.

"I decided that's enough low-crawl for today," Haddox announces. "You were doing it so bad it hurt to watch."

He looks at Robison, then back at us.

"But fuck saying that, wouldn't wanna hurt nobody's feelings."

We march to guard duty. Where we learn:

"All guards in a combat zone are exterior guards. The first type of exterior guard are listening posts, where two or three men hide in the bushes and listen. The second type of exterior guard are observation posts, where more than two or three men climb up in a tower and observe. The third type of exterior guards are patrols, where more than two or three men go out on patrol and may or may not hide in the bushes."

Then it's back to the CQ to get our military IDs. Kippler notices a mistake with his blood type. Which prompts this exchange with the Echo drill sergeant in charge of the paperwork:

Kippler: "This is wrong. I'm not O."

DI: "I don't care."

Kippler: "I'm AB negative. I want the card to say AB negative."

DI: "Card says what it says."

Kippler: "What if there's a transfusion? Somebody could die."

DI: "Could it be you?"

Kippler: "Yes."

DI: "Good."

Kippler, concerned: "So you won't change it?"

DI: "That's right."

Kippler: "Then can I put an asterisk by my blood type followed by a 'See me first before starting IV' at the bottom of the card?"

DI: "You deface that card, troop, and I'll break your nuts."

Kippler, not wanting to die on the Army's operating table with the wrong red stuff coursing through his veins. "Then can we just leave that part blank? Personally, I'd rather see a 'Guess what' on that space than a 'type O.' "

DI, searching through desk for the sharpest thing he can find, settling for a letter-opener. "Personally, I'd rather see this sticking out of your neck."

Kippler waits until the DI's back is turned, takes out a pen and corrects his body chemistry. He starts to return the card to the stack, but sees something else he wants to fix.

Out comes the pen for a series of small, but deft, strokes.

"Always wanted to be 5-foot-7."

It's 8 o'clock before we finally get upstairs. The inspection report is posted beside General's war slogans. I was gigged for shoes, brass and handkerchief. But my bunk passed.

And it will pass tomorrow and the day after and the day after. That's because I'm going to call on yet another of my bedroom skills: coffin-sleeping. I can stretch out and remain almost completely motionless the entire night. My heels don't cause the covers to ride up. I don't toss and turn. I don't even scrunch the pillow. When I wake up, the bed looks like a strip of cellophane spent the night on it, not a 180-pound man. I'll sleep on top of the sheets and keep Carouthers' tuck-and-fold handiwork in place for the rest of the cycle. A top o' the morning bunk first time, every time.

Sept. 28, 1971

Dear Carl,
Just a few lines to let you know I'm at this shit depot. One thing that helps me get up in the morning is the hope that one day a scared basic-trainee-to-be will seek my sage advice, and I'll be able to come through half as well as you did that night back at the dorm.
You painted a perfect picture, buddy. How the DIs try to

stress you out. How the fate of the free world hinges on how well we fold our socks. How if you never want to be found, all you have to do is move to Central Missouri.

I'll put this Haddox asshole against any DI you or anybody else ever had. You see the other cadre members talking with each other. Sitting together at the PX. Getting in and out of each others' cars. They take a break from this crap. Probably go home to their wives and laugh their asses off.

Not Haddox. Never removes the mask. Never orders himself to fall out. Like our man Ya says, he's ate up with it.

If Haddox kills me, please enter this letter into evidence to prove he had prior intent.

Our other DI is the exact opposite. Just a few minutes ago, Skebo was shining his boots to "L.A. Woman." Waldsburger walks by. We're saying, oh God, turn it down. Violation 10 E, Section 4, Code 5, or some such shit. Guy sticks his head in the door, says a polite hello and walks down the hall humming, "Never saw a woman so-o-o alone." It's like he's really one of us, but he can't let on until the eight weeks are over.

Skebo lives in a commune called the Farm. He was staying in a beat-up school bus when he heard about a place where a whole bunch of other hippies who used to live in beat-up school buses took off to. Skebo put air in the tires, gassed up and took off before his french fries got cold.

Housing is free in the dozens of log cabins. Meals are free at the common kitchen. Utopian society, Skebo says. Neighbors love neighbors and nobody worries about cash flow. Children have names like Astar, Kingson, Sky and Queen. Nary a Bob and a Ruth Ann. Meditation is encouraged. Psychedelics aren't, he says, but all-night boogies are a happening thing after the elders go to sleep.

Skebo talks about the common treasury, and the no private ownership of property, and midwives delivering babies right and left. He's trying to teach me village ways, but it's slow going. I know comparative economics. He knows Adzuki beans.

Let's review some of what's happened so far:

Kippler's pissed because his Wall Street Journal keeps getting sent to the post library.

Rodriguez, my squad leader, sometimes plays guitar in clubs around El Paso. Says his idea to have me clean the heat duct with a pipe cleaner came to him in a song.

Peavey is well on his way to becoming the platoon fuckup. The DIs don't like him because he has the attention span of a foil ball. We don't like him because he's a lying little snot. The troops are cleaning the bathroom and he comes staggering in like he's high on something. Holds an empty bottle of pills like he tried to OD. Starts babbling and almost falls down in the shower.

Then Ya comes up, pries open Peavey's mouth and whacks him in the back of the head. Small chunks of green, red and yellow come out.

"Sweet Tarts," Ya says. "Boy tried to fool y'all."

It seems Ya saw the stash of candy, saw the pill bottle, saw Peavey practice bobbing and weaving, and added up two plus two.

Peavey begged us not to turn him in, and I guess we won't. But he's at the bottom of the algae pond and I don't see any surface bubbles any time soon.

And then there's Hercules, or at least that's what we call him. Ran the mile in under 5 minutes wearing combat boots. In pushup contest with Bravo DI, rattled off 85 without stopping. Keeps to himself. Only says the minimum to get by. When it's his turn to do something, he does it better than anybody in the company, and then goes to the back of the line like it was nothing. He's like God in fatigues. I'm trying to work up the courage to ask him to say a few words over my low quarters.

Well, that's about it. Downshift the dump truck once for me.

Sept. 29, 1971

Dear Osgood,

Still padding your wallet on "Jock Time," or do you have too much dignity now that you're a senior?

You were the best, man. The government ought to study your nipples and develop a new compound for making bullets.

No doubt you're sitting back, sucking on a cold one and celebrating your 299 draft lottery number. Maybe you're wondering what those of us are doing who weren't so lucky with the little white balls.

Making it, that's what. Not making it up. And definitely not making out.

Khrushchev died and all hell broke loose at the Attica prison in New York. Did I hear about it with any dispatch? Hell, no. Out here, only generals have TV sets and they probably get lousy reception. And newspapers. You're more likely to see a Dead Sea Scroll.

One of the things we have to do to pass basic is get a decent score on the PT test. The events are the mile run, the bars, the crab crawl, bent-leg sit-ups and a serpentine course the DIs call dodge-and-run. No problem. Then we take a test on all the classes - map-reading, first aid, military traditions, manual of arms and such. No problem. Then we have to shoot down a minimum number of targets with the M-16. Big problem. I barely know which end the bullet comes out.

*They're giving us a chance to go to a St. Louis Cardinals'
football game, but I think I'll skip it. We'd have to wear the
uniform and march in and out of the stadium by platoon. I'd like
nothing better than leaving this place for a day, but not if I have to
play soldier in the public sector.*

*I get fire guard about every fifth night, usually the 1 to 2 a.m.
shift. We're supposed to walk up and down the hall holding the
stupid paddle, but most of us just sit on the top step and write
letters. If you're really brave, you sneak downstairs and get a
Coke and a pack of peanuts out of the vending machines. A DI is
supposed to be in the CQ to prevent such lawlessness, but most of
the time they're conked out. Or reading fuck books.*

*I'm not platoon guide or a squad leader, so that means I have
guard duty. And KP. We run-of-the-mill types can look forward to
pulling it about once every three weeks. I had my first session two
days ago. It was everything the other guys in the platoon said it
would be. The stinkiest day of my life.*

*The fire guard woke us up at 3:45 a.m. so we could be at the
mess hall by 4. To a man we arrived tired and in slow motion.
The cooks had already been slicing and stirring for an hour. They
have even worse attitudes than we do. Bitching, cussing and
jumping our asses for having the audacity to be only amateur
food preparers.*

*I wanted to say, look, shitheads, you're permanent party.
You signed up to get up in the middle of the night and spoon out
lard on the bacon trays. You should have thought about 4 a.m.
in the middle of nowhere when you raised your right hand at the
induction center, and said I do solemnly swear to set out the butter
patties.*

*But I keep quiet. I will do nothing and I will say nothing that
could increase my time at this place by 15 seconds. Pop off to one
of these sauteed assholes and no telling what he'd do. Or who
he'd tell. Best to just stay out of the way.*

*Dining room orderlies pour coffee for the DIs, fetch pancake
syrup for the DIs and pick up napkins that the DIs dropped.*

*This is bad duty. You would need a promotion to be an
indentured servant.*

*Back-room guys stand in front of gurgling, steaming garbage
disposals, and scrape off plates that have been refitted with
cigarettes, matches and nasal matter to reflect diners' disgust with
the meal.*

*This is worse duty. You feel like a decal on the back of the
trash truck.*

*I did the dining-room gig for breakfast and switched off for
lunch and dinner. I'd rather have food stuck to my skin than be a
lackey.*

In between meals was the worst. You can't leave the mess hall.

Then you'd go on report and the enlistment judge would prescribe extra time. You're not expected to do a great deal of work other than wheel new caldrons into place so they can be filled with more shit nobody is going to eat. You just have to be there.

The other KPs hid behind the pallets of brown beans. I went to stall No. 2, locked the door and assumed the position. I'm thinking, hey, they can't accuse me of goofing off if my pants are down.

In all my life, I had never gone to the bathroom for more than five minutes. If it hasn't come out by then, it's not going to.

But this is different. Out there is getting yelled at for not knowing which end of the potato peeler is up. In here is peace. A half hour I stay in the can. I hum Beatles lyrics. Dylan lyrics. Jim Morrison lyrics. Paul Simon lyrics. Then I start writing the words on the walls. Even though I wasn't very comfortable - try sitting with your pants at your feet and leaning over to reach the composition area - I lost myself in lyrics that took me back to college. I'm writing and singing and thinking about Newton and his Dear Abby letters, and pissing in Brick's sink, and the night Slim and Gino got high and put a marshmallow on a Santana album and watched it go 'round and 'round for two hours.

Inspired out the ass, I drew pictures of miniature hippies carrying guitars and driving beat-up vans and sitting under a maple tree waiting for something groovy to happen. I drew Frank Zappa. I drew Melvin Laird. I drew Richard Daley. I don't know what got into me. Every time I heard one of the cooks holler something about where did the dickhead KPs run off to, another mural popped up in my mind.

Osgood, I swear I was in there almost three hours. So long I actually did shit twice. It was like the Neil Young song. There was a band playing in my head and it took me away from here.

I smudged out where the previous fecalator wrote "The Army Blows" and replaced it with the words to "Eleanor Rigby." "For A Good Time, Meet Greta Outside Building 321" became the chorus to "Love The One You're With."

You should have seen the walls of that stall when I got finished, Osgood - a Picasso of rock 'n' roll. I was particularly impressed by the way I wrapped my "Day In The Life" display around the toilet-paper dispenser.

What started out as a way to kill some time became a shrine. Why don't you make some discrete inquiries at the Smithsonian? Maybe they'd be interested in a free-standing example of how the counter-culture lives within the nation's war machine.

Just a thought.

Before supper, I was merely in serious need of a shower.

After supper, I smelled like a six-month garbage strike.

The sinks backed up and our hands became covered with this gooey red shit that felt like half-scum, half-beets. Because it was at least 130 degrees back there, the sweat broke free from those stupid white hats they made us wear.

And what did we use to wipe with? Why, our red hands, of course.

So now our faces felt like we were bobbing for a dirty fork in the Army's dishwater.

Did the cooks let us clean up, Osgood?

And leave the Pentagon's plates unguarded? Are you crazy?

I had never been so filthy in my life. I swear things were crawling around on me. I could feel them organizing block parties. And inviting the kids over. And collecting for Easter Seals.

And did we get to go back to the barracks as per the usual time, or 45 minutes after our last customer phlegmed in his mashed potatoes?

Hell, no. This had to be the night before the mess hall's IG inspection. Cooks, cooks' bosses and KPs were comrades in cleanser. For two extra hours, I scrubbed bread ovens, silverware dispensers, the bottoms of chairs and the plastic covering on the clock that always says 3:46. Others buffed, sprayed, Boraxed and otherwise labored mightily on the principle that if the white-glove guy found so much as a speck of dirt on a caldron, they'd be making their next batch of tater tots at Khe Sanh.

And so it went until 8:30 when meltdown hit. It doesn't matter if you're on loan or the major of the macaroni. There comes a time when you can no longer function as kitchen help. Your reservoir is drained. Your geyser is tapped. Collapsing isn't allowed, so you do the next best thing, which is stop dead in your tracks and lean over like a hat rack that's lost its base of operations. Your lips tremble like you really want to work another six hours, but your body has ruled against it. All command centers have been shut down except for the cardiovascular system which has been allowed just enough energy to maintain low-level respiration. Only if you follow this strict military procedure can you officially be declared exhausted.

Finally, some dick with a spatula in his hand dismissed us. I was expecting a, "Thanks for working so hard under less than hygienic circumstances. It's not every night that we have to burn everything the KPs were wearing." Or maybe a, "We appreciate everything that you did. If this KP results in your being quarantined, you qualify for the Distinguished Service Spoon."

Nothing. Just a, "Christ, you guys smell like crap. Get outta here."

Naturally, the bathroom was off-limits when we got back. Litton was conducting a walk-through the next morning and everything had been precleaned. No shitting, no pissing, no showering.

The first two matters were of little consequence. We left our loads in the parallel bar pit in front of the barracks and covered it up like a bunch of cats.

But climbing into bed feeling like a bag of peat moss was another matter. I tried going to sleep for one hour. I tried for two hours. Couldn't do it, Osgood. The things that were crawling on me had gone beyond friends and family. Now they were hosting a lawn and garden show.

I was bone tired, but knew I wasn't going to close my eyes until I had been doused. But how? It was almost midnight. All the barracks in all the quads were dark and their CQs wouldn't take kindly to an unauthorized dirtball.

I remembered a hose outside the first-aid classroom. We took a drink in between tying off tourniquets, but spit it out because the water tasted like a corroded door knob. But it would do to wash off flesh scum. The problem was that the building is more than a mile away. Did I want to walk that far just to get clean? Did I want to risk getting spotted by MPs who could throw me in the slammer for being absent without bed?

Yes, yes and yes. I grabbed soap, shampoo, a towel and a change of fatigues and was gone.

As weary as I was, I got a rush from doing something against the Code of Military Justice. I had been afraid my entire time on this installation. Now, because cooties were standing-room-only on my person, I was striking a blow for the right of a buck private not to smell like a sacrificial raccoon. I was making a statement to the Pentagon: I'm going to lather up and I don't care whether you like it or not.

In front of God, crickets and a pile of rotten roofing tiles, I got naked and hosed myself down.

I don't mind telling you, Osgood. I almost climaxed. It felt that good to be clean. I luxuriated in the moment, turning the thing on full-blast and watching the caked-on grease cascade down my body.

I didn't know when I'd get the chance again, so I gave myself the most intense cleansing of my life. I almost got carried away. Another minute and I would have flushed out an eyeball.

For the first time at FLW, I felt good about myself. The Army had thrown everything it had at me - filth, asshole cooks, a day without end - and I battled at least to a standstill, if not outright victory. I was still standing. I was clean. And I was close to passing my audition as a fugitive.

An hour after feeling like I had been hung out to dry at a landfill, I was more antiseptic than the Joint Chiefs' hand dryer.

I didn't sleep like a baby, Osgood. It was beyond that. It was like my skin had moisture put on back order, and it all came in at once.

I was so tired the next morning I didn't get up until Carouthers threatened to kill me with his tent stake.

But he didn't.

Like I said, I'm making it.

If you get the chance, send me a picture of your nipples. Sign it "With Love." I'll show it to the cadre. Maybe get out of here yet.

CHAPTER 5

Skebo wakes me up 15 minutes earlier than my usual "Bonanza" 4:45. I open my eyes to see his big butt standing over Apperson's bed like it's a crime scene.

"God damn," he's saying. "God damn."

I spring up. There's a wad of toilet paper on Apperson's pillow with shit on it.

And a note:

Later, boys. Haddox, pretend my dick is a chili dog.

His military gear is thrown all over the floor. Suitcase gone. Laundry bag gone. Troop gone.

I start to shake. So does Skebo. We've never been this close to major wrongdoing before.

"He couldn't have gotten far," Skebo says. "I got up to piss at 3:30 and he was still here."

My friend might have the bloodhound in him, but I don't.

"Are you saying we should track him down? I say let him go. He's where he wants to be."

Skebo agrees but has trouble reconciling the shitpaper on the pillow.

"Political statement," I explain. "Primitive but effective."

"Yeah, but there's a whole half turd on there," Skebo says, backing away like it's a bomb.

"Symbolic," I explain. "White paper stands for purity. Shit represents the ultimate violation of that virtue."

Skebo looks at me like I'm on drugs.

Hey, it's not even daylight. That's the best psychoanalysis I can come up with.

We agree that going to the CQ would be bad. They'd bombard us with questions. Did Apperson talk like he was going AWOL? Did we see a stack of road maps on his bunk?

We decide the best strategy is to pretend nothing happened. There's only one snag. In order for the entire bay to achieve ignorance, Carouthers has to be in on the plot. That means somebody has to play Mr. Alarm Clock. Somebody white.

"Carouthers can't stand us when he's awake and we're 50 feet away from him," I say. "No telling what he might do if we touch him while he's asleep."

I look at the big black man whose legs are hanging over the end of the bed. I don't want him to face an inquisition come 5 o'clock, but I don't want to be the cracker who taps him on the shoulder.

Skebo is no less eager to administer the wake-up call. So we hatch a plan.

The hall closet is filled with cleaning supplies. We'll fetch a broom and gently poke Carouthers from what we hope is a safe distance.

I target his ankle and tap with the pressure of a baby kitten taking its first steps.

Nothing.

"You'll have to do it harder than that," Skebo says.

I put the handle between his toes, pretend they're guitar strings and lightly strum.

Naturally, Carouthers' involuntary reflex system picks that exact moment to go haywire. His left foot goes into full-blown spasm and powers down on the handle.

"Ow, shit."

And what's the first thing he sees when he wakes up? A white person standing over him with a stick in his hands.

Carouthers grabs the tent stake and comes at me.

"No, no, it's not what you think," Skebo shouts, jumping between us. It's the single most bravest act I've ever seen.

Carouthers pauses, perhaps in respect for one white motherfucker's willingness to give his life for another.

"Apperson," Skebo breathes. "He's gone."

Caucasian conspiracy is written all over Carouthers' face until he sees the shitpaper and the note to Haddox.

We explain that the thing to do is to retreat to the bathroom and let the DI make the discovery for himself. It's like Haddox getting a letter. He'd want to open it himself.

Carouthers goes along. 4:58. 4:59. Haddox thunders down the hall, throwing light switches and hollering for everybody to get the fuck up.

We watch him enter our room. How long will it take for him to find an ass that's not only been wiped, it's left the building?

"Jesus Christ. Jesus shitpile Christ."

We take that to mean Haddox has been forced to revisit his worst subject in school - subtraction. There's one less of us than there was the night before.

"Fuck the MPs. I'm going after this prick myself."

He looks at Apperson's bed and then at us.

"Don't touch a thing."

Never has an order been met with more agreement.

The DI sprints downstairs. The rest of the troops can get up on their own. The message is clear: You clean your ass with Haddox, you've got a manhunt on your hands.

We sneak to the edge of the steps, our gateway to the CQ. The place quickly fills with DIs from our company and from those in adjoining barracks. Ten minutes pass and officers begin to arrive. When they aren't huddling, they're whispering.

Soon we're given our new orders for the morning. Our quarters are off limits until the investigators finish sifting through Apperson's leavings.

Kippler sees evidentiary matter right in front of us.

"They do carbon-dating," he whispers. "Why not shit-dating?"

No inspection. Classes delayed. We are to arrange ourselves by room assignments for bay-to-bay questioning.

The bad morning for Carouthers just got worse. First, he was awakened by a white person with suspicious intent. Now he must endure forced togetherness.

Skebo is getting off on the opportunity to study the large black man. Like an overeager maitre d', he gets our little group preferred seating next to the horizontal bars.

I'm squirming. It was OK talking about race with Gaines, who is as engaging as he is unintimidating. Carouthers is brooding, menacing. If I had the gift of gab - and I'm not saying I do - this man would make me want to give it back.

Skebo has prepared some opening remarks, but he's more than a little nervous.

"Uh, er, to get this discussion off on the right foot, it seems, uh, that we need to come to a mutual, er, understanding."

"What the fuck you talking about?" Carouthers wants to know.

"In the room," Skebo goes on, still staring at his shoes, "there's, er, something that bothers, uh, us."

I shake my head. Don't include me in this. I'm happy that Carouthers has seen fit to let us live. I'm not the least bit bothered.

My friend plods on.

"There's this, uh, word that you use when you refer to us that's, uh, not a very nice word. We'd, ah, sorta like for you to call us a different word, er, if you don't mind."

"What goddamn word?"

"Uh, er, when you look at us and say 'motherfucker.' We, uh, have never had conjugal visits with our moms, and we don't expect to in the future."

This is Bravest Thing No. 2: Pointing out a vocabulary shortcoming to someone who ignores the manufacturer's suggested use of the tent stake.

Skebo's lips are running in place. I take that as an indication he'd appreciate some help, and quick.

I wring my hands. Merely swallowing courage pills won't work at this point. I must mainline.

"Uh, I must admit it does somewhat bother me when you say I'm a motherfucker," I stammer.

Carouthers exhales, which I interpret as a hostile reaction.

So I quickly backtrack.

"We're not saying that you stop calling us motherfuckers altogether. Not at all. Just maybe adopt a gradual stepdown program. For example, instead of calling us motherfuckers four times in a row, you throw in a cocksucker on fifth reference. Then the next day, let it be two motherfuckers, a turdball and a pissant before you get back to motherfucker."

That's it. I've done for Skebo's lips all I'm going to do.

"You're 'fraid of me, ain't 'cha? 'Fraid of the tall, dark Negro."

I don't have any problem nodding to that. Neither does Skebo.

For the first time, Carouthers acts like he's tired of that role. That he wants a new character to play.

"Aw, shit, man. I ain't so bad."

Skebo takes that as a signal the roundtable is at least temporarily in session and asks the first question.

"Uh, when did you, er, go to an integrated school for the first time?"

"Fall of 1964," Carouthers says. "Up to then, I rode a bus 40 miles one way every morning to the black school. Four white schools were by the side of the road, but we just kept on going.

"You don't know how that makes you feel. You ain't good enough to go to the white school with the new brick building and the nice paved parking lot. You gotta go to the colored school where the roof leaks and the janitor is the math teacher."

I think about how he could beat the crap out of me in less than five seconds, and ask if he played sports when he went to the white school.

"They started a wrestling team the first year I was there. No other brother tried out, but I said, shit, the white folks are trying something new, I'll try something new. They didn't have enough money for a mat, so the coach went out and bought piles of used carpet. I remember the day I learned a reversal. I went home and said, 'Mama, I know how to get away when a guy's on top of me.' She started laughing and shit. I'm thinking how to score two points and she's thinking queer love. But she never said nothing and paid the 10 bucks so I could have a team sweater.

"The day came for our first meet. We were going to the biggest high school in that part of the state. They had a portable mat that they put on the basketball floor. We kept hearing that seven, eight hundred people come out for the matches."

Carouthers is warming up to this talking concept. I can tell by how far he's pushed the tent stake under his bed.

"I'm excited, man. At lunch I wrote down all the moves I knew on a napkin. I'm studying that napkin all the way through fourth and fifth period. I'm gonna do this, I'm gonna do that, then, bam, the ref's gonna raise up my hand.

"It's 2:30 and the coach pulls me out of math class. He's got this look on his face. Something was up. It snowed the night before, so I thought maybe the match got called off.

"The man wouldn't look me in the face. He talks sideways-like and tells me I ain't gonna be wrestling. I thought the guy I was going against couldn't make his weight, or maybe got sick.

"Then he tells me he called the other team's coach and told him I'm black. This gave the man a chance to talk to his wrestler in my class and find out if the kid had a problem with that. He had a problem all right. Big problem. Said he'd quit if he had to put his hands on a nigger. Other boys on the team found out about it and they said they'd turn our bus over if I wrestled."

So what happened? Skebo wants to know.

I chime in. "Let me guess. The principals got into it and yours caved. He said there was no sense in everybody getting all riled up because of one wrestler. We'll just leave our little problem at home and go on with the match. Right?"

"They asked if I wanted to go as the team manager, but I said fuck that," Carouthers goes on. "Went home that night and cut my uniform into little pieces. Coach never came up to me. Teachers never came up to me. Boys on the team never came up to me. Everybody went on like everything was just fine. End of that week came and I just left. Walked out of school right in homeroom. Teacher watched me go and then went on taking the lunch count. Didn't make a shit to her or anybody else."

I think about the wrestling incident, and what I hope will be my career after leaving this place.

"Maybe you should have gone to the newspaper," I say. "Told your story. Raised a stink."

Carouthers looks at me as if to say, hey, glad you asked that.

"When my daddy passed, Mama took the death notice in. The woman behind the desk said she couldn't put it in the real paper. We'd have to wait 'til Sunday when they ran News from the Colored Community. She put the piece of paper back in her purse. Mama knew her place. The white people called her Mrs. Miller's Bessie on accounta that's who she cleaned house for. She walked in the door. I'm playing with my Dinky Toys on the floor. I can tell something happened, but I'm too little to know what. She started to put Daddy's picture back in the frame real careful-like. Then all of a sudden she throws it down. Glass flies all over the place. 'Ain't that some kind of shit?' she said. Only time I ever saw her get mad."

My turn to testify.

I remember aloud the summer we visited my grandparents when I was about 12. My brother and I did the hug-and-kiss routine for a polite period of time before asking to go to the municipal pool.

My grandfather said there wasn't going to be any swimming this year because the niggers decided they wanted to go to the same pool. The grownups in the living room were in unanimous agreement that the uppity niggers were at fault, and the town council had made the correct decision.

The next day we drove by the city park. There was the pool. Blue as blue can be.

And not a soul in the water.

One of the grownups in the car said black people are filthy and the chlorine can only do so much. There'd be disease all over that water, somebody said in explaining why we should be content to just sit on the porch.

I gather these thoughts, and begin to understand why the person sleeping across from me in the bay would holler the lyrics to "Shaft" and keep a tent stake at the ready.

Skebo isn't saying much. You're the master of ceremonies, I tell him. You can't let your guests monopolize the proceedings.

"I was a member of the Key Club in high school," he says softly. "One of my best friends was this black kid named James. He beat me on every French test. I hated that."

Skebo hesitates as if the tale is too painful too tell. He looks over as if to ask permission to remain silent. Carouthers shakes his head. The troop will talk.

"My stock in the club wasn't too high. One reason was because I studied too much. Another was that they saw me driving around with James in the front seat, and the word got out that I was a nigger-lover.

"For some reason, James wanted to join the Key Club. He had this weird notion that they'd forget he was black and take him right in. James kept asking me to get him an application. I could see bad things coming and I didn't want any part. I'd either tell him I forgot or lie and say the club secretary was out of forms. He finally ended up getting one from the faculty sponsor.

"The day for deciding the 1966-67 pledge class came. Each member got a copy of the roster. One of the football players had printed 'Nigger' in big letters beside James' name.

"Somebody noticed that James used me as a recommendation. The room got quiet. Was this true?

"I denied James and I were friends. Denied we walked down the hall together on the way to French class. Said we just happened to have the same-length stride, that's all. Said the only reason he was in my car was because it was storming real bad that day, and you wouldn't want to see even a nigger get killed by lightning.

"That seemed to satisfy them. The next step was listening to the speeches. An applicant's name would be called out and one or more club members would say a few words in his behalf. James' turn came. No one said anything. I wanted to tell them James was a great guy, and they'd really like him once they got to know him. But I didn't have the guts. There was this long silence and then the next name was read.

"This went on for about 45 minutes and then they passed out the ballots. I couldn't acknowledge James in public, so the least I could do was give him the satisfaction of getting at least one vote, right? But I didn't even do that. I was afraid somebody in the club would recognize my handwriting. He'd see the check mark beside James' name, know it was mine and I'd be called 'nigger-lover' the rest of my life.

"James called that night to find out if he got in. I said, God, it was close. We bounced all the applicants around for more than three hours. I spoke up for you at every turn, though, old buddy, but, damn, you came up two votes short.

"And you know the worst part? James bought it. Thanked me for going the extra mile for him, and then joked that he was going to beat me again on the French test tomorrow.

"I put the phone down and started sobbing. Right in front of Mom and Dad. I told them I wasn't going to school the next day. They could make up some song-and-dance for the principal if they wanted to, but I didn't care. Wasn't going to study the lessons either. Get some Fs for a change. I screwed over my friend. The least I could do was screw over myself."

Carouthers can't believe what he's hearing. It's as if Skebo and I are at confessional and he gets to listen inside the little room.

"We were never the same friends after that," Skebo goes on. "James would phone to talk, but I'd tell him my dad needed to keep the line open because he was expecting an important call from his boss. I couldn't face up to him after what I did. It was like there was this deed to our friendship, and I sold it out from under him.

"I've kept up with him, though. Two years at San Jose State and then he started studying film at UCLA. When he's not making 15-minute shorts, he's flipping burgers at the Jack-in-the-Box. Probably be the next David Lean."

"How do you know all this?" Carouthers asks.

"Talked to his mom and dad," Skebo says. "Made them promise not to let on. I've got his address in my footlocker. I'm trying to work up the strength to tell him the white guy who sat behind him in French class is a shitty excuse for a human being."

I recall my high school and the black homecoming queen who wasn't. Five girls were nominated, and you voted by stuffing money in campaign jars that were put under their pictures beside the trophy case. Carolyn was well-liked by all the kids and the quarters and half-dollars just rolled in. I think we were trying to send a message that times were changing, and a predominantly white high school could have a black homecoming queen if it wanted to.

The teachers were appalled that Carolyn could win one of the school's highest honors. The last day of the contest, they sneaked out in the hall during classes when they thought no one was looking and stuffed Penny's jar with dollar bills. At the end of sixth period, it was announced that the Caucasian chick had amassed a veritable fortune and was the winner hands down. The quarterback kissed Penny at halftime as per usual and all was right with the world.

Awkward silence on the podium until Carouthers pounds the gavel.

"You two are some all right cottontails, you know that," he says.

He has to translate.

"Whites. You know, the tails. You're a couple of OK whites."

From motherfucker to cottontails in one roundtable. I need to take my step-down program on the road.

The investigators - if that's the right word for three Junior Achievement MPs who shave less than 3 percent of their faces - call us to the CQ.

"Did you know Apperson was leaving?"

Three heads shake as one.

Do you have any idea where he went?

Skebo, solemnly: "The Black Hills of Dakota."

Me, taken aback by the baldfaced lie, but able to think on my feet: "Yes, he often talked of going there. Said he has an option on some property."

Carouthers: "The Dark Hills, that's right, man. Wanted to live next to some Negroes."

Alpha Platoon is allowed upstairs in time to see one of our interrogators take the piece of shitpaper off the pillow and flush it down the toilet.

"Now they've got no case," Kippler whispers. "They disturbed the chain of evidence."

We report to personal hygiene class.

Where we learn:

"Use clean clothing. Have a clean body. Have clean mess gear. Wash hands after using latrine. Why are these measures important? To prevent the spread of disease. Always clean and dry feet, especially between toes. Do not get debris or mud into canteen when you fill it. Add one iodine tablet for clean water, two for cloudy water. Why are these measures important? To prevent the spread of disease."

Then a class on troop movements.

Where we learn:

"On command of forward, shift weight to right foot. Fingers are curled. The right hand is nine inches in front of the pants seam. The left hand is six inches to the rear of the seam. Arms swing close to side. A step is 30 inches. There are 120 paces a minute. All marching steps from halt are started from left, except right-step march. The command of double-time march is given from halt or quick-time. Make a fist with forearms parallel to ground. Take 180 steps a minute at individual distance of 36 inches per step. On right-step march, raise right foot 10 inches from heel. No arm-swinging. Halted command given when heels are together."

"Why are these measures important?" Kippler mimics. "To prevent the spread of stroll."

Then an exercise PT followed by a running PT forced on us because of dickhead Peavey, who lost his glasses while we were marching. When he leaned over to pick them up, Hercules and Ya double-timed right over top of him. Despite the fact Peavey put up the resistance of a kite tail, the rollover effect was devastating and troops went down like flies.

Four different DIs got in his face, but Waldsburger got off the best line.

"Peavey, this ain't no comedy show on TV. You'd better change your channel."

Followed by a class on military customs and traditions.

Where we learn:

"The salute is always with the right hand. The salute is six feet before passing officers or when making eye-to-eye contact. The index finger will touch helmet liner or the eyebrow if not wearing a hat. If on a detail, the man in charge will salute. If double-timing, slow to quick-time and salute, then resume running. If sitting in a group, call attention and all salute."

"Just get an artificial arm and attach it to your forehead," Skebo suggests. "Save wear and tear."

Then our first look at the M16s.

We're marched to a nondescript brick building across the street from the mess hall. They open the door and we see row after row of high-powered rifles locked down high and low by thick metal bars. We're introduced to a thick-necked individual with teeth the color of a football who pronounces himself the armorer. He acts like we're getting ready to walk into a cathedral.

"Inside this supply area, men, is the most advanced infantry weapon known to man. The M16. 5.56 caliber. Magazine-fed, gas-powered, shoulder-fired. Semi-automatic or automatic. Weight: 6.55 pounds. Weight with cartridge magazine and sling lift with 20-round clip: 7.6 pounds. Cyclical rate of fire, 700 to 800 rounds per minute. Maximum effective range: 460 meters."

I expect him to genuflect at any moment.

The man is so overcome by all the muzzle velocity at his disposal that he cannot find the words that give justice to the killing potential.

So Kippler whispers a suggested text.

"Blessed Father, the enemy knows not what they do. Let us blow their brains out."

Waldsburger herds us into a classroom where there's an M16 on the table. After that buildup, I'm expecting the thing to resemble a torpedo, but it's more like a billy club with a trigger mechanism. The barrel is light. The stock is light. You could beat the enemy over the head with it and not even raise a welt.

"Let's have a show of hands," the DI calls out. "How many of you guys are familiar with weapons? You've hunted or gone target-shooting or something like that."

About two-thirds of us. Ya not only raises his hand, he waves it. The troop's been waiting for just this moment. He can't run and he can't march, but he damn sure can pour lead.

"OK, now how many of you have had at least a little experience with rifles?"

I start to say "Yea, verily," but opt instead for hands-down honesty. I've never fired a real gun in my life - something they'll find out in three seconds on my first day at the range.

If this was Haddox asking, I'd wiggle a finger or two because I wouldn't want him to think I'm any more of a pussy than I already am.

But it's Waldsburger, and he's worthy of the truth.

Only one other man in the room makes a similar admission of unmanhood.

Kippler.

Waldsburger just shrugs.

"You two might want to pair up. One might pick up something and rub it off on the other. The rest of you can sit anywhere you want."

He picks up the M16 and clears his throat as if to begin the lecture. Then he thinks of a better use for his time.

"How many of you are afraid of your first day at the range?"

A smattering of hands.

"C'mon, I was scared out of my mind."

A few more hands go up.

"I thought one of the shitasses out there would get pissed and shoot me."

A lot more hands.

"That's more like it. The rifle can wait. Let me tell you what to expect."

I can't believe it. Waldsburger is about to break the drill instructor's code. He's going to give us prior knowledge.

"The big thing is not to get the range cadre mad at you. They do the same thing day after day and have absolutely no patience. Worst I ever got hollered at in basic was at the quick-fire range. I lost my firing pin for a few minutes and they 'bout had a shit fit."

Laughter all around, something I'm not hearing in the other classrooms. I'm not surprised. Waldsburger is rarer than a gemstone in a grease rack.

"It's about three miles to the shortest range and five to the furthest," Waldsburger goes on. "Sometimes you'll march both ways. Sometimes you'll ride cattle cars. Changes every day.

"And speaking of every day, that's pretty much what rifle training is. You've still got a lot of classes and guard mounts and shit like that, but you'll see Armorer Fickey just about every morning from here on out."

The DI looks at Kippler and me.

"They can teach a fox terrier to shoot. Don't worry about it."

Any structure the presentation might have had is completely gone. Waldsburger fields questions on everything from the color of tracer rounds to did Haddox really take off after Apperson.

"Orange" and a diplomatic, "The Army felt its interests would be best served if drill sergeant Haddox remained on post."

Kippler and I look at the M16 the way an aborigine would a blow-dryer.

"I'll tell you why I can't shoot if you will," I offer.

"OK," Kippler replies.

"Well, go on," I say.

Not a sound. He plays a quiet game of hold-'em. His need to testify is a king-high. Mine is four jacks.

I last maybe three seconds before throwing down my cards and spilling my guts.

"I was 11 years old when I found the BB gun in Dad's closet. Seems this stray dog was getting too close to Mom's roses. Dad was going to light up its ass a few times to keep it away.

"I picked up the gun and walked out the back door. There was this robin in the birdbath. Tiny thing. Must've thought it was in a 25-meter pool.

"I wasn't thinking about killing it. I just wanted to see what the bird would look like after I drew a bead on it. Some hidden force was moving my finger on the trigger. I swear it wasn't me."

"Wait a minute, wait a minute," Kippler interrupts. He has this exasperated look on his face. "I know exactly what you're going to say. The gun couldn't shoot itself, so it must have been you. The BB penetrated the robin's breastplate, killing it instantly. The thing fell like a stone. You were so traumatized you vowed never to pick up another firearm as long as you live."

He is smugness personified. "That about right?"

"Yeah, except I tried to break the gun over my knee, couldn't and the bruise didn't go away for a week. How did you know?"

"Because it's the biggest childhood cliche there is, that's why," Kippler explains. "You ask a million people why they don't want to shoot, and at least half of them will say exactly what you did. Maybe the bird fell off a telephone line instead of a birdbath. Maybe it was a .22 instead of a BB gun. Maybe the shot missed by a mile, but the bird keeled over from fright. Same thing. Just variations on a theme."

"Why would I lie? I shot a bird."

Kippler shakes his head. "Your psyche is saying you shot a bird, but in reality you're just falling in lockstep with the sample group."

"The 500,000, right?"

"Exactly. They didn't all go out one day after elementary school with a gun and a taste for bird. The story made the rounds of the halls and cafeterias and they bought into it. Maybe 100 kids in this country were triggermen. Everything beyond that is just legend."

"You're full of shit," I say defensively. "I can still see the feathers on the ground."

"Oh, yeah? What color were they?"

"I don't remember. That was more than 10 years ago."

"What time did the alleged homicide happen?"

"I don't know. Daylight. Yeah, it was daylight."

"What did you do with the bird after you killed it?" Kippler's questions are coming in too fast. I can't even deflect them, much less provide answers.

"Disposal of the body. That's pretty important, wouldn't you say?" the lawyer-in-waiting bores in.

Looks like I could remember that. We played baseball earlier in the day, that much does come to mind. Roger was at the house. And Robert. And David. If I shot the bird, they would have seen it. For the life of me, I can't call up that exact image. Dad did have a BB gun. And I distinctly recall our cat putting a dead bird in his mouth and how mad we got at him. But was there a burst of fire? And was there a beaked victim?

God, what if Kippler's right? What if I just invented killing the robin so I'd have an excuse for my lack of accuracy if I ever have to pick up a gun? What if I heard the story at the sliding board and bought in to it?

I look at Kippler. He's smiling like Perry Mason always did in the last three minutes of the show when he rehashed the case with Della and Paul Drake.

Damn his 1450 SAT score.

"Uh, let's talk about something else."

"Didn't kill it, did you?" he crows.

The guy can't leave well enough alone. He's got to insert the cutlery a little deeper.

"OK, asshole," I sputter. "Why can't you shoot?"

"I'm about 11, same age as you and your make-believe birdbath. There was this guy in our town named Dave who fixed TV sets. Everybody knew him. Howya doing, Dave? Got any used picture tubes I can have for my science project, Dave? Can you hook us up to the cable on the sly so we won't have to pay the five dollars? That kind of thing.

"The man loved beagles. When he wasn't fixing televisions, he'd be out in the woods hunting rabbits. We had this purebred named Queenie. Best rabbit dog in the world, Dave said. Mom and Dad were always in court and didn't have time to play with her. Dave called a lot. He'd say he was going hunting first thing in the morning, and was it all right if Queenie stayed overnight so they could get an early start? It was like a doggie sleepover.

"It was one less thing for my parents to think about, so they said OK. It got to where Queenie was spending almost as much time at Dave's house as she did with us. Dave already had a half-dozen other beagles, but he was always looking for more. We heard he even cooked steaks for them.

"Dave lived about a half mile from us in an old house that was full of parts. TV parts. Car parts. Stuff other people didn't want any more. They'd call Dave to say they couldn't pick up Channel 5 and could he come over. To show their appreciation when the job was done, they'd load up Dave's van with whatnots.

"The man had no family and no close friends. Just television sets, piles of greasy junk and his dogs. He'd be real nice and polite while he was working on your television, but nobody ever got close to him.

"Queenie didn't come home for three straight nights. She never was gone that long before, so Mom and Dad sent me over to Dave's house to pick her up."

For the first time since I've known Kippler, there is not the first trace of smart-ass on or about his person.

He continues his testimony.

"When I got there, I found Queenie in the pen with his other beagles. Plenty of water, plenty of dog chow and enough steak bones to chew on for a week. Dave's van was out front, but it was quiet inside like nobody was home. But there had to be somebody home. Dave was always where his van was.

"The back door was open so I walked in. I always wondered where he put all the parts. Now I knew. Wherever there was an un-spoken-for inch in his house. Under the sink. In the hall. Even in the bathroom."

Kippler is twitching. The story is getting harder to tell.

"Dave must be doing something in his back yard or maybe he's doesn't know he's got company. So I hollered out his name and stomped my feet so he'd know I was there. I didn't want to scare him.

"I went in the den and Dave was on the floor. Why would he sleep there? He's got a bed. Parts all over it, probably, but enough free space to squeeze in under the covers."

Kippler is biting his lip.

"Then I saw the dark red place by his head. And a shotgun that was bigger than I was. I screamed louder than I've ever screamed in my life. Then I passed out.

"When I opened my eyes, Dad was holding me as tight as he could. Nobody was on the floor and there was no gun, but I could see the traces of dark red on the carpet. Dad told me Dave was dead and they had taken him away. Mom explained that sometimes people can be real sick inside and nobody ever knows. They took me outside where the ambulance was. A policeman was holding the gun and writing something on a sheet of paper.

"That night I tried to go to sleep, but I kept throwing up. Mom had this thing about dogs in the house and she always made Queenie stay in the basement. Dad said something and the next thing I knew he carried Queenie into my room and put her on the bed. It was like Dad knew I was too old to sleep with them, but not too old to have company. Queenie left her load in the corner sometime during the night. As fastidious as Mom was, she didn't say anything. It was like she knew that in the overall scheme of things, two pieces of dog shit didn't amount to much.

"Ever since then when I've seen a gun, that's what comes into my mind. I think about firing it and I think of the side of Dave's head."

I don't know how to deal with this. My life's field of fire has been little more than maybe a dead bird and maybe not. Kipper walked in on a suicide.

Suddenly the guy seems more of a human being and less of a wad of brain waves placed end to end.

I put my hand out.

"What's that for?" he asks.

"Just shake it, OK?"

I saw the schedule in the CQ. This is where it's supposed to end for the day. M16 initial briefing. Then admin time, which is another way of saying jacking off in the company area.

Which is good. I've got boots to shine, brass to polish and a handkerchief to get with the program.

We're trying to turn Carouthers on to "Riders on the Storm" when we hear a whistle.

"Alpha Platoon, fall out."

It's Litton. We double-time down the stairs. If it's the captain at this hour, it must be serious.

We can tell he's pissed. His adam's-apple hair looks like the roots growing out of a manhole cover.

"Your platoon leads the company in AWOLs," he screams. "Did you know that?"

If this was a "Jeopardy" question, even Ya would have won a hundred dollars.

Litton is a man of few words. He prefers to let our actions to the talking.

"Start running in place."

It's almost 7:30. We've been whipsawed from place to place all day and now we're doing the trot to nowhere.

Fifteen minutes pass and we're still high-stepping. When it suits him,

Litton drops us for pushups. We do as many as we can until our arms collapse, and then we get back to running in place.

This is bullshit. Apperson didn't want to be here. Shouldn't have been here. Should have been at least in jail if not the penitentiary. But the Army cut him a deal. Put on these fatigues and we'll forget all about those silly felony convictions. The guy comes out here for a few days, starts missing his switchblade, runs afoul of Haddox and - surprise, surprise - jumps ship. He would have fled from any unit he was in. Alpha, Bravo, Gamma, Sigma Phi, whatever.

But this Litton, this West Point graduate, can't understand that. It's not our fault Apperson is gone. It's the Army's fault he was even here.

Twenty minutes and our legs are still churning. I know I've sometimes been guilty of complaining for complaining's sake. But the longer I'm out here playing Mr. Piston with my knees, I realize I have a mature, fully rational reason to despise this place and everything it stands for. From Litton on down, they're barbaric bastards plugged in like a power plant to the most anal-retentive approach to determining right and wrong.

Let's see what we have here: On the one hand is the Army recruiter. He talked with Apperson. Examined his file. Heard the story about the tourist who wet his wallet. Knew Apperson had as much business being in the Army as Rex Reed does in the NFL. But he signed him up anyway.

And then there's Alpha Platoon. We knew Apperson was a piece of shit long before he went public with his potty training. Nobody in Alpha Platoon would be a tourist in any state where Apperson ever maintained a residence. Nobody in Alpha Platoon would have signed Apperson up for more than the guy who passes out books and magazines inside the joint.

So, your OD Honor, who's at fault here?

A cough, plenty of time to deliberate.

"Alpha Platoon, guilty as charged. The men are hereby sentenced to run in place by the legs until exhausted."

Robison comes out of the CQ with his finger on his watch. Litton tucks in his adam's-apple hair and blows his whistle. We have two minutes of R & R to get the feeling back in our legs while the other four platoons fall out.

Skebo is puking up supper. So is Nordquist. There are at least six other guys who could start firing chartreuse at any instant.

"Those men had an AWOL," Litton roars to the entire company, pointing to our sorry asses. "See how sick they look. This is what's going to happen to a platoon every fucking time it has an AWOL."

If I had more balls, if I had 45 seconds until my enlistment is up, I would say, "Listen. Apperson was the lowest common denominator of our band of merry men. To punish us for his decision to take flight makes as much sense as blaming Marco Polo for the invention of the stop light."

But naturally I keep quiet.

We're almost dead on our feet, we've got blisters the size of tote sacks and our knees may never stop cracking.

So where does Alpha Platoon go?

To the chop shop.

There's no hair to cut off, but that doesn't bother Litton, who orders the barbers to use their instruments to scrub brush our upper regions.

If the guy is hoping to break us down, it isn't working. It's one thing to push us to be quasi-soldiers, but all Litton is doing is showing his ass.

He might have pulled all the right triggers at West Point, but right now his butt cheeks are spread wide open.

The barbers aren't into it any more than we are. I watch the one take a couple of quick laps around Skebo's bulging cranium, realize he has absolutely no idea where he's going or where he's been, and holler a quick "Next."

It's almost 9 o'clock when we get back to the barracks.

"This is really fucked," Ya says, kicking his pistol belt down the hall.

"Whoever wants my job can have it," Nordquist says.

"Litton is definitely culpable," Kippler says.

No time to shower. We go to bed as pissed as we are dirty.

All but Skebo, who is surprisingly thoughtful for a guy with vomit on his chin.

"Best performance I've seen since we've been here. Litton should get an Academy Award."

"Performance, shit," Carouthers says. "If that's what it was, how come the back of my legs are burning?"

I concur. Litton was put on this Earth to wear warpaint, not greasepaint.

"Couldn't you see what he was doing back there?" Skebo asks.

"Yeah," Carouthers replies. "Running our dicks off."

"Go on," I say, remembering that Skebo has been right before.

Litton's not stupid. He knows Apperson wasn't going to get on the career track out here. He saw the AWOL as an opportunity to foster esprit de corps."

"How the fuck was he doing that?" Carouthers says.

"By making us all mad, that's how. Would you agree that right now there's an entire platoon who would like to see Litton get run over by a tank?"

I see where Skebo is coming from. You can be as one happy, or be as one pissed. Our captain opted for No. 2.

Carouthers goes to sleep. He's too tired to listen to any more Human Behavior 401.

"And Litton played it for all he was worth," Skebo continues. "He wasn't more than 10 percent irritated at us, but he came over like we had firebombed his first-born. He wanted us to hate his guts in 40-part harmony."

"You could be right," I offer.

"Hey, I know I'm right, and that's the difference between Litton and Haddox. Just like that first big speech he gave us about Vietnam. Litton sees getting in our shit as part of a bigger purpose. Haddox only has the amount of troop-trainer in his system that allowed him to pass drill sergeant school. He gets in our shit because he's a bully. He doesn't care if we learn what we're supposed to. He just wants us to hurt."

Skebo is losing his audience. Carouthers is snoring and itchy things are crawling across the top of my dirty head. I'll be lucky to sleep a "Bonanza" commercial.

"Think he made it?" Skebo wants to know.

"Who?"

"Apperson."

"Oh, yeah, him. I had almost forgotten. Don't care much one way or the other."

"I think he'll get caught," Skebo says, "and I think he'll bring it on himself."

"How?" I ask.

"The fugitive will be in the bus station, something will set him off and he'll shitpaper the bathroom."

"But how will he get caught?"

"An alert crapper in the next stall will call the Interstate Commerce Commission. They'll bust him. Those guys don't play around."

"And what will be the upshot in court?" I ask, yawning.

"Kippler will get Apperson off on a technicality. He'll have him plead intestinal insanity."

"An ass memo. Can you believe that?" I say.

"You kidding? That's the Army's notepad."

CHAPTER 6

"We need a ball-checker. Who wants to be ball-checker?"

The head poobah at the rifle range has set his M16 on automatic. The presumption is that the weapon will kick like a stegosaurus. Our professor wants to prove it doesn't.

And how to best get that point across in a Neanderthal setting?

Why, by putting the thing against his crotch and firing.

"Gotta have a pecker-checker before and after. Who's it gonna be?"

The troops holler "Pea-vey, Pea-vey" like a football cheer. The company fuck-up is practically thrown to center stage.

"What's your name, son?" the cadre guy asks.

The rumpled troop mumbles a response, but the syllables become trapped in all that acne and suffocate.

"Here's the deal, son. You examine my private parts before I shoot off a 20-round clip and then after. If there's any damage, you get to go home and I get to go to the hospital. Is that fair?"

The rest of us are in hysterics. Peavey winces, closes his eyes and starts to feel around.

"Can't do it like a blind man, son. Gotta see what you're getting. Go for it, son. Do I got one pineapple or two?"

Peavey puts his hands on the man's balls for the length of time it takes a hummingbird to hit passing gear.

"OK, son, now tell the men where the butt of the weapon is located as we speak."

"Your nuts," Peavey whispers to the assembled multitude.

"I'm proud of 'em, son. You be proud of 'em."

"YOUR NUTS," Peavey screams.

With ruffles and flourishes, the cadre guy proceeds to gun down an imaginary enemy with the M16 firmly braced against his reproductive region.

Twenty cartridges fly every which way, but the shooter's ability to have interest in a vagina appears undiminished.

"OK, son, inspect the goods."

In front of 200 troops. In front of all the DIs. In front of the entire range cadre. In front of more green than at Camp Chlorophyll, Peavey gets another hands-on experience.

"Umm, feels good, son. What are you doing Saturday night?"

"Aw, shit," Peavey says, shriveling up.

But not everybody is convinced. We're going to need a phase two.

"How many of you men still think the M16 has too much bang for your buck?"

Several dozen hands go up, including mine. It could have been a trick. They can do a lot these days with mirrors.

"So what you're saying," our prof goes on, "is that my balls have been hardened to the M16 after teaching 10,000 dumb asses to shoot"

He smiles. Clearly, his favorite part of the lecture is coming up.

"So we need to use somebody else's nuts. Somebody whose nuts aren't so experienced."

I can see where this is going.

"Peavey, come over here a minute."

The cadre guy loads another clip.

"Spread your legs, son. Got to put the weapon in proper position."

Which is directly against Peavey's pouch pack.

"You ready, son?"

Peavey is clearly embarrassed, but not to the point of no return. There seems to be at least a small part of him that relishes the attention, even if it's negative. If he'd get mad, the cadre guy might pick on somebody else. But Peavey just stands there with a shit-eating grin.

"OK, son. You just hold tight and I'll do the rest. Troops, let's have a countdown before our man here loses his nuts to a burst of automatic fire."

"Three! Two! One!"

The cadre guy pulls the trigger. Peavey's lower body gives a little, but there's no shriek of pain. In the storm of bullets, his genitalia hold firm.

The troop is amazed. He thought his dick would be going end over end.

"So what conclusions can we draw from this little demonstration?" the cadre guy wants to know.

"The M16 doesn't hurt," Peavey stammers.

"Put it in language the men can understand, son."

"Your nuts won't come off."

Alpha Company goes to a large classroom where 200 disassembled M16s are on top of 200 schematics. With the care of Santa's elves, the innards of each weapon have been perfectly placed inside the blue lines.

There's the charging handle.

And the bolt catch.

And the bolt carrier group.

And the buffer assembly.

And the catch button that releases the magazine.

And the firing pin.

I don't care what the Davey Crocketts in the unit are thinking. To me, it looks like somebody made a withdrawal from the mystery bin at the hardware store and dumped the contents on my table.

And remembering where everything fits?

A parakeet would have an easier time memorizing "Old Ironsides."

We listen to a lecture on characteristics and capabilities of the M16. Then one on operations and functions. Then we pour over the diagrams and tinker with the parts. It's like Erector Sets except this is war. The range cadre file between us like proctors at the SAT test. Screw up the first time and it's, "Come on, troop, think." After that, it's hands on hips and, "Goddammit, dickhead, if you insert the firing pin there, you'd better hope the enemy has signed a peace treaty."

Waldsburger was right. Their ditty bags contain little or no patience.

The pecker-checkee orders the film screen rolled in and the projector turned on.

"I used to have to explain this shit," he says, flexing his pineapples, "but now I got me a movie."

Lights, camera, horrible music, a grainy troop holding the M16 as he would his girlfriend and wavy letters in 350-point type that scream out, "RIFLE TRAINING AND YOU."

Several dozen men are lying on the ground with their firing machines resting on sandbags.

"This is battlesighting, or zeroing, the weapon," Walter Winchell's first cousin intones. "This is the first stage of your training. You fire from the prone-supported position at a 25-meter target. You will make windage adjustments to the rear sight and elevation adjustments from the front sight. You successfully zero your weapon when you can place a three-shot group within a half dollar."

Naturally, the film breaks. While Pineapple Man's helper is trying not to asphyxiate from the resulting duststorm, an anxious Kippler raises his hand. Which leads to the following exchange:

Kippler: "What if I can't put three bullets in such a little space?"

P.M.: "Then you bolo."

Kippler: "Is that good?"

P.M.: "It means you stay at the zero range while everybody else in your unit is one step closer to getting out of this place."

Kippler: "What if I put two bullets in there?"

P.M.: "That's not good enough."

Kippler: "What if I would have put the third bullet in there, but the sun got in my eyes?"

P.M.: "Too bad."

Kippler: "The sun's pretty important."

P.M.: "So is hitting the target."

Kippler: "What if the shade gets in my eyes? What if there's a weeping willow?"

P.M.: "There ain't a fucking tree within 800 yards of the range."

Kippler: "What about a dogwood? It grows in this kind of soil and they say it springs up almost overnight."

P.M.: "Wanna be ball-checker for the rest of your life?"

Kippler: "No."

P.M.: "Then shut up."

Spliced to within an inch of its life, the film is once again ready for its matinee showing.

"After you zero your weapon, basic rifle marksmanship training continues at one of the field-fire ranges," the narrator goes on. "You will fire at 100-foot targets from the prone-unsupported and the prone-supported positions."

Cut to hail of bullets from a cast of E-1s.

"You will fire at 200-foot targets from the prone-unsupported and the prone-supported positions."

Cut to range officer in control tower giving the "Clear to fire" command. He is at least twice as wooden as the rear-numbered stakes.

"You will fire at 300-foot targets from the prone-unsupported and the prone-supported positions."

These things look at least a mile away. I couldn't knock them down with a mine sweeper.

Lights on.

Pineapple Man explains the silhouette targets.

"They pop up electronically. If a round penetrates any part of the half-soldier, the shooter at that station is credited with a kill. You'll get all the practice you can stand, and then we take you to record-fire where you get 100 shots from different positions and distances. To complete BRM, you need a minimum of 54 hits."

Continuing with the director's cut.

"As you become more proficient with the M16," the narrator drones on, "the training will become more and more difficult."

The camera pulls back.

A 200-foot silhouette pops up for about two seconds and then goes back into its den. The shooter barely has time to draw a bead when, to the extreme left, a 100-foot target rises from a dirt mound. Then, somewhere off in the next county, there's a glimpse of enemy green at the 300-foot mark. Like its buddies closer in, it comes up only long enough to reject Missouri as a natural habitat.

We're thinking, oh, shit, they expect us to hit a target that could appear almost anywhere and at any of three distances and only stays up for the time it takes to fart.

I am only moderately depressed until I hear Ya say not even squirrels move that fast.

Then it hits me. I won't die out here. There would be too many messy investigations. I'll just never be able to leave because I won't qualify with the M16.

Here I am at 50 years old at record-fire, more than a hint of gray in my hair and range cadre young enough to be my sons calling me a near-sighted bolo.

Here I am at 60 with a geriatric Pineapple Man kicking me in the ass for not knowing how to adjust the windage knob.

Here I am at 85 when I'm not strong enough to fire a three-shot group, much less give it proper placement. A medic gives me a breathing treatment, they tape the M16 to my fingers and I try again.

Back to the film.

Where we learn:

That all firing takes place while wearing the steel helmet that feels like you've got a Quonset hut on top of your head.

That basic trainees say "No brass, no ammo" more often than their prayers.

That we're going to hear, "Ready on the right? Ready on the left? Ready on the firing line. Firers, watch your lane," an awful lot of times in the next few weeks.

That the range cadre see absolutely no humor in the term "butt plate."

We file out of the building and see Haddox stretching his legs and grinning. The cattle car that brought us out here nine hours ago is nowhere in sight. We'll be taking the cardiovascular route back.

Haddox is PT instructor for the company. That means he's the leader of the pack for the three-mile return trip to the barracks.

It's his call. He could decide on a slow march. All this M16 nomenclature is hard to swallow, and he doesn't want the road to pound it out of us before we can digest it. The fall colors are coming in and he could decide that a quiet nature walk is just the thing to cap off a crisp September evening.

Or he could take the position that we're all pussies and if he doesn't whip us into shape, who will? Fuck the fall colors. Fuck crisp. We're going to get back to the barracks a close second to the wind.

It's not even close.

"You WILL keep up," he screams. "You WILL NOT fall back. You WILL NOT get on the loser's bus."

I absolutely do not want to be on board. It's probably a nonstop straight to the stockade.

Haddox takes off backwards, the better to monitor our pace.

"Pick it up," he shouts as his knees damn near hit his chin.

Alpha Company is charging for all we're worth, but we're loaded down by our rifles and the steel pots and the stupid galoshes they make us attach to the backs of our pistol belts.

Faster and faster Haddox goes. He's in reverse, but we'd need starters' blocks to catch him.

But what's that ahead? It might be. It could be. Yes, it's a Dumpster.

And right in the DI's path.

"Who's gonna pull even with me? C'mon, dicks, who's it gonna be?"

Fifty yards and counting.

"You're weak and shiftless, and now you're slow. What else is wrong with you?"

Twenty-five yards.

They could give me the Pentagon, NATO and the Strategic Air Command and I still wouldn't tell him.

Ten yards.

"Move them legs. Move them arms. You ain't stickmen."

The joyous moment comes in slow motion. Haddox raising his knees to the edge of the Earth's atmosphere and calling us sub-humans. The back of Haddox's head hitting the Dumpster and ricocheting like a tee shot off a telephone pole. Haddox going down as if the ground has been pulled out from under him. A train wreck without the choo-choo.

But even with a fast count, the referee wouldn't get past two.

Bleeding profusely, Haddox rights himself and turns around to discipline the Dumpster for not yielding right of way to a non-commissioned officer. He kicks the thing in an area corresponding to its groin and continues with the march.

This is unbelievable. The DI has an open wound near where his brains are. He didn't have a surplus to begin with. The slightest ooze could be fatal.

So what does he do?

Wrap his poncho tourniquet-style around his head and lead the singing of "I Want to Be an Airborne Ranger."

The oversized bandage is crimson within seconds, but Haddox goes down the road - forward, this time - crooning about the river of Mekong as if nothing happened.

We slow down, expecting him to collapse and, if we're really lucky, die. Haddox is not a maple tree. Getting tapped deep enough to draw gray matter can't be part of his wellness plan.

But the DI has the gait of a thoroughbred as he speeds down the road. The back of his head must be made of knotty pine.

"Goddammit, let's go," he screams.

The man has forgotten all about teaching us to band together, to function as a group. As little interest as I have in the proper movement of a company of soldiers, I know that the idea is for us to arrive at the same time.

Haddox is turning the 5 o'clock hour into a test of machismo.

He could have a permanent dent in his fender. He could need an emergency footer transplant. He could have the red-blood-cell count of a spent shell.

But by God he'll still beat us back to the brick building.

Throw away the training manual. This is personal.

I stay close enough the first two miles to watch the blood work its way under his collar and down the back of his shirt. My fast-twitch muscles fight the good fight, but fade as the DI's belt begins to turn a gooey red. I fall farther and farther back.

But who's this coming up on the outside?

Hercules, and gaining like a Derby hopeful in a field of claimers. The guy isn't even breathing hard. With less than a furlong to go and Haddox bleeding to death, this is who you want your money on.

The troop pulls even, then slightly ahead. Not only is there a motor up his ass, it's finely tuned.

Around the clubhouse turn and it's Hercules by a length. Looks like Haddox will have to settle for second - not bad for someone who'll need a transfusion.

But hold on to your tickets, race fans. Haddox grabs Hercules by the strap of his M16. Never having been interfered with in a stakes race before, the troop doesn't know how to respond. Haddox seizes on this moment of indecision and throws him down.

Hercules comes to rest in a ditch. It's Haddox in a walk.

Which is good for the DI because that's all he has left. Blood has finished with his pants and is draining into his boots.

Nordquist and I finish side-by-side. Haddox has just enough blood pressure left to recognize the platoon leader.

"Carry on," he tells him, staggering into the CQ.

It takes a full five minutes before all of Alpha Company gets to the sidewalk. We're a mess. Pistol belts akimbo. Straps flapping. Some troops had their galoshes come off and are carrying them. One guy threw a shoe. Another is breaking out in hives. Kippler is telling anyone who'll listen that he realizes the steel helmet is supposed to be slightly oversized, but his is bigger than some atolls in the Pacific.

Waldsburger isn't around. It seems somebody threw up on somebody and hostilities commenced.

Echo Platoon's junior DI leads us back to the armorer to turn in our rifles and announces we're free for the rest of the evening.

Two hours. Just short of forever.

The mail brings a package from Dad that includes three letters from newspaper editors who read my articles from college.

"Unfortunately, this material does not work for our newspaper and, I daresay, not for any other publication." - Miami Herald.

"You, sir, fail to understand that writing does not come out of thin

air." - Boston Herald.

"The article about the brassiere that shines in the dark to show male students the way was poorly thought out and extremely offensive. I didn't look at the other samples." - Kansas City Star.

I look on the bright side. One editor made it all the way through the bra article. Maybe he just didn't like the part about the flashing lights in the cups. Next time I'll take out the batteries.

It's clear that bras make for interesting reading. I make a note to write a funny article about a lonely man who buys the newspaper just to clip out the Maidenform ads. The walls of his apartment are a tribute to cleavage. Thanks, Kansas City.

I put the returned columns under my boxers. There's a typewriter over in supply. Maybe I can get in there long enough to crank out new cover letters for Philadelphia, Houston and Salt Lake City.

Skebo, the sociologist, hears about a guy from Charlie Platoon whose father knew Che Guevara and flies out of the room. Carouthers leaves right behind him to get new batteries for his cassette player. Some things might operate on reduced power, but not Shaft.

Ya comes in and asks for some gum. He likes to have a topper for his Beech-Nut.

An idea hits.

"I want to write stories for newspapers when I leave this place," I tell him.

"So?"

"It would help if you would give me some feedback on some of the things I've written. Who knows, you might even like them."

He reaches in his back pocket and pulls out a fuck book.

"Is it anything like one of these?"

"Close," I reply. "Real close."

His face drops.

"But I hate to read."

"The words will fairly fly by. Trust me."

"Aw, shit. OK."

This is great. I have an audience for my work.

"It's real simple," I explain. "You read one of my stories and tell me what you think."

Ya looks at his watch.

"You've got five minutes. If I ain't finished by then, too bad."

Not exactly the attitude going in that I'd like from my one-person sample group, but I'm not complaining.

"Which article would you like to read?" I ask, pulling out a sheath of papers. "Nixon's expansion of the war. Coed dorms. A teacher who got fired because his hair was too long. Suicide-not-so-prevention centers."

Ya determines the suicide story is the shortest by five lines.

"This one."

He starts in on it in the manner of a convict breaking rock.

"Don't mind me," I say, getting my pen in the ready position. "I'm just going to make a few notations. You proceed with the text."

"What kind of notations?" he asks suspiciously.

"I call it my guffaw meter," I explain. "I watch your reactions when you get to the funny parts. If you smile, it's one point. A chuckle is two points and a guffaw is three points. Ten points is considered a good score."

"What's a guffaw?"

"When you laugh out loud."

"I don't do that unless Haddox gets his dick caught in a drill press."

"Look, all I ask is that you don't fight the feeling. If you're overcome by hilarity, let it run its course."

Clearly, this is Ya's first time with a humor-measuring mechanism.

"It's hard enough to get from one word to the next. I can't do it if you're gonna look at me."

"You can. I know you can. All I ask is that if I make you laugh, laugh with every inch of your being. Anything else and you skew the test results."

Ya looks like he's about to be executed. If I coax so much as a grin out of him, I ought to be head writer for the Bob Hope Show.

"Are you relaxed?" I want to know. "Can I get you anything? Some Fritos, maybe?"

"Let's get it over with."

He reads. I watch.

Suicides have been on the increase in this country in the past few years. In some of the larger cities, notably San Francisco, Suicide Prevention Centers have been provided by the city at no cost. Volunteers man the telephones and follow a standard procedure.

They are primarily taught not to panic but to be gentle and persistent in getting the necessary information. A call like this one perhaps would not be very unusual to one of these busy people.

R-R-R-I-N-G. "SPC Desk 2. Are we in time? I know that's a silly question but it gets us off to a cheery start. Now what's your problem?"

"I'm tired of living. I'm lonely, I have no friends and I know nobody cares about me."

"Of course they do. Don't be silly. What's the name and social security number? Joe J. - we don't take first names. Just last name and number, please. The other phone's ringing."

"Jones, 228-65-7635."

"Thank you, Jones. Now tell me why you feel this sudden urge to kill yourself?"

"Many things. I haven't had a promotion in 20 years. I caught my wife in bed with the paperboy. The Klan gave me control of three counties, and my daughter married a Negro."

"Where are you now?"

"In a pay booth on top of the Mutual Building downtown. It had your number on the door so I thought, what the hell, you know?"

"You did the right thing, Jones. What kind of a funeral would you like? We're sort of a middleman for the Undertakers Syndicate. We get 25 percent."

"Methodist will be all right. I never went. Hey, how much does that cost?"

"How much would you like to spend?"

"As little as possible. I just want to die."

"That rules out a lot of things. You probably want an old sea captain to officiate instead of a priest. Burials at sea usually save $400. But since you have no friends, you'll have to rent four pallbearers."

"Can't you just get two strong men?"

"All right, Jones, but you're cutting it tight. We had one poor fellow who didn't have enough money for the gravediggers, so we just let his body decompose on a park bench. By the way, what's the height and weight? Medium build, I hope. One time somebody took our $200 plan and cheated the hell out of us. He was seven feet tall and weighed 400 pounds. We had to hire a bulldozer and a crane to handle him. We would have lost money but his wife drove the bulldozer, so we cleared $10. I'll tell you what you can do to save money. Take some nude photos of your wife and we can make a program out of them and push them at the graveside ceremony. Add some poetry or something. Maybe that last letter. Include a little handkerchief and I guarantee you no trouble whatsoever at selling 100. You should also consider where you will jump and how you will land. The programs won't sell if people have to look at a busted-up head and body. One guy jumped off a 75-story building and his bill included $300 more than usual. It cost that much for the sanitation department to put him back together.

"I would suggest pills. That way the undertaker can make you look real contented and peaceful. Nobody will buy your programs if they think you died with a chip on your shoulder. Also, you can save three hours of an undertaker's time.

"We've also been requested to try to sell you a dark suit. They're usually $100, but if you buy sight unseen it's half price. The reason I offer this is that you fall in the Poor-Friendless category and most of these guys are in pretty bad shape. One wino wanted the cheapest possible so we buried him in his Jockey shorts. I'm glad he didn't sell programs. His own mother wouldn't have bought one of his ugly body lying in state.

"Jones, it's been nice talking to you but our time's up. As you can probably tell, we're all clinical psychologists trained in this sort of thing and we don't come cheap. As we say, your time is our time...for a little while."

Ya is expressionless. He might as well be reading the Constitution.

No score.

I can't believe it.

"What's the matter with you? Sea captain, renting pallbearers, can't you just get two strong men - that's funny."

"I told you I don't laugh."

"Hire a crane, get his wife to operate the bulldozer, cleared $10. How can you not guffaw at that? You're holding back. I told you not to do that."

Ya shrugs his shoulders and hands back the pages.

"Next time, write about pussy," he suggests.

I'm devastated. It's one thing getting a negative review in the mail. It's quite another to hear it from someone in your same squad.

"Aw, don't take it personal," Ya says. "I probably ain't the best person for your survey no how. I didn't even know who the vice-president was until last year."

That does make me feel better. If you don't know Agnew, you're not going to know comic juxtaposition.

"I'm going to the NCO Club," Ya says. "Wanna come?"

I decide to put my writing career on hold and go to this new and exciting place. Rodriguez and Nordquist went the night before. They filled our sleep with first-hand reports about the Honey Buns, and the no-cadence, and the beef jerky, and the no duty rosters, and the waitresses in tight skirts with the important parts sticking out so much they were giving off shade.

But something caught their eyes even more than tits.

A cat.

They said watching the thing lick itself was the first time they felt like they were somewhere near civilization. This shithole actually contains a water dish, a scratching post and a litter box. There's Army going on all around, but somebody still makes time for Scruffy.

Ya and I find our own treasures on the walk over. There's a Weekly Reader, a tag off a McGregor sweater and a stray hamburger wrapper. Ya and I take turns smelling it. The mustard glob is still moist. Couldn't be more than an hour old. Ya swears he got a whiff of a french fry, but I think that's just wishful thinking.

No cat, though.

Must be on maneuvers.

The ancient building is painted white, proof of its decadence. It's like the land the Pentagon forgot. Guys with rank are walking up the steps beside guys who got here four weeks ago. The screen door has a hole in it and nobody is assigned to fix it. The butt can on the porch is overflowing and nobody is emptying it.

The bread man is struggling under the weight of three boxes. He's wearing wing tips, the first I've seen since the airport. He leaves this place after the last delivery. He could bring news of the outside world. I think about slipping a note under his windshield wiper. Are any more senators flashing the peace sign? Is Newsweek still being printed? Has Nixon heard of the Kinks yet?

Inside the NCO Club, there's more beer than I've ever seen in my life. By comparison, the Greek's back at school is a water cooler.

It's the measure of a man how many cans are at his table. Waitresses pick up napkins, plates and silverware, but leave the empties.

At several tables, the cans are stacked three-high. Some guys are drinking in groups, but a surprising number are by themselves. Some rest their heads above crossed arms like first-graders at nap time. Others put their hands behind their heads, lean back and look up as if awaiting further instructions.

Some stare angrily at their empty cans, ready to sweep them aside if they make a false move.

One such man puts his chin on the table so he can be at eye level with the enemy. Just try to break through the perimeter, cocksuckers, he's saying with his eyes.

A dozen basic trainees have gravitated his way. Word trickles out that this guy is just back from Vietnam and still wound up jelly tight. Comes here every night. Drinks two six-packs and then puts his head on the table. He looks like he's passed out, but every sensor in his body is lit up. Ears on full alert, eyes darting, neck veins throbbing.

Some nights, we're told, he just sits there and twitches. Nobody gets anywhere near him for fear he'll go off. Other nights, he raises his head and talks as pleasantly as Dennis James.

The RAs get the closest. They want to know what they've got coming.

The bravest of the group pipes up.

"Uh, you've been in 'Nam. What's it like?"

The vet orders another beer with an arch of his eyebrow.

"I'm 19 years old, man. Flew into Cam Ranh Bay on commercial. It's like we were on vacation. Stewardesses laughing it up and giving out free drinks. One guy put his hand up one of their dresses. Like, what are they gonna do to him?

"Cherry-boys, that's what the new ones are called. They put me in a forward observation unit in the bush near Chu Lai. Elephant grass so high you had to hack your way through. Leeches all over the place. One hundred thirteen degrees in that jungle. You move, you sweat. Our mission was to draw enemy fire and then call in artillery to take it out. We had another name for what we were doing. You know what it was?"

Nobody says anything. We don't feel worthy.

He jumps up out of his chair.

"I said, what do you think they called us, motherfuckers?" he screams.

Scared silence.

"Bait. They expected us to stay out 72 hours at a time. We'd snort this stuff that was like speed. It looked like powdered mustard and made you throw up your socks, but you kept awake. The VC would pass by on the trail, and we were so close we could smell the fish on their breath.

"I get flashbacks all the time. My buddy was hit and I almost shot the medic because he treated someone else first. Another buddy's got both legs blown off and he's gasping for air. I take hold of his arm to steady him and it comes off in my hand. Guy looks at me one last time and dies."

He says he's tried to commit suicide twice since coming back to the States.

"Put the .45 in my mouth. You gotta do it quick. Can't swallow. You feel when you swallow. And hear. That makes you want to put the gun down. Just hold your breath, set your jaw and pull the trigger. But I swallowed. Both times."

He says he almost killed a full-bird colonel a week ago.

"I was driving a Jeep and the little motherfucker comes up behind me at the stoplight. I didn't pull away fast enough to suit him so he blew his horn. I've always had a bad temper, and Vietnam just made it worse. I jump out of the Jeep, grab my service revolver and put it against his ear. Swear I could smell him shitting his pants. He didn't want no part of me. Turned around and went the other way."

He tells a growing crowd he doesn't know how to write his name.

"Didn't bother the Army none. I was just what they wanted. They put a blank test paper in front of me, let me sign it the best I could and then they had some other guy take the written test in my name. Passed with flying colors. I was just what they wanted for Vietnam. High-strung and ignorant. All they had to do was give me a gun and point me in the right direction."

He says the big, heavy raindrops of a summer shower sound like incoming groundfire. The burning of wet leaves smells like Vietnam and sends him ducking for cover.

"The VC gutted one of our guys so bad you couldn't tell what was flesh and what was ground. It made me crazy-mad. I rang up and said there was a sniper in this village and he needed to be taken out. I knew there were women and children, but fuck 'em. Artillery came in and wiped 'em out. Everybody told me what a good job I done."

Some asshole asks if he remembers when he killed his first VC.

"Gook's lying there with his guts in a pile and I see this little bag he's got around his neck. I open it up and here's this picture of little girls. His, I guess. I showed them to one of the other men and he started crying. I didn't give a shit. The motherfucker shouldn't have been there. I threw the picture in the hole they buried him in."

His head goes back down on the table, the signal he's clocked out of our world and gone back in his.

One night he won't be served his 12th beer, or somebody will ask how he killed his 95th VC, or he'll imagine there's a sniper behind the jukebox. It'll take a platoon of MPs in riot gear just to make him put down the pool table. There'll be more casualties than at two firefights and a siege. This man is the monstrous creation of the Joint Chiefs' secret laboratory. Done their bidding. Deflected bullets. Stomped trip wires. His war is over. Now what are they going to do with him?

"I saw a guy just like that back home when I was in the Rescue Squad," Ya says as we walk back to the barracks. "He couldn't kill himself so he kept trying to get us to do the job for him. Put a knife to a clerk's throat at the Montgomery Ward. Got jail time for it. Then a week after he got out, he laid down naked on the railroad tracks. Train came and he snapped out of it. Rolled over and almost broke his dick on a crosstie. They finally said he was tetched and sent him off."

The troop swallows the last of his beef jerky.

"You know what the man back there wants somebody to do, don't you?"

I shake my head.

"Shoot him. Blow him out of this world and into the next. Bound to be a better place."

I'm forgetting who I'm with. Usually I hang out with Skebo and Kippler. Like me, they're ERs. Four months active duty and back home. Defender of our nation's honor one weekend a month and two weeks in the summer.

Like the mindless gook-slayer, Ya is RA.

"I thought I was gonna be a hero like the pictures in the magazines," he says. "I thought it would be like pulling somebody out of a burning car, but better. Go off to a foreign land. Whip everybody who gives the U.S.A. the finger. Prove we've got the best soldiers in the world. Then I see that nutball back there and I say, shit, it ain't worth turning into that. Nothing is."

I think of the unfairness of it all. Army Reserve and National Guard folks know all the right people downtown. A wink and a nod and we'll never be down range of anything more dangerous than an empty beer truck.

But men like Ya, who took industrial arts instead of trigonometry, are going to Cam Ranh Bay. No pissing around at the reserve meeting for them. They'll be in the rice paddies with mud up to their ass, and praying their next step won't get them put in a body bag.

"Do you wish you were in the reserves like me?" I ask.

He shakes his head.

"Wouldn't work. I ain't smart. You're smart."

Smart shouldn't have anything to do with it. Ya is a man and, relatively speaking, so am I. Both our asses ought to be up for grabs. I shouldn't get to stay out of Vietnam because my dad is more tuned-in than his dad.

But I'm not going to petition anybody's court to change the rules. I want to write. Find a woman who'll have me. Raise a bunch of baseball players. I can't do that if I'm dead. Or insane.

Sorry, Ya, but better you than me, pal. It's not my fault you picked up a copy of Look Magazine one day and wanted to be like the gung-ho grunt with vines in his helmet who jumps off the Huey giving a Rebel yell.

"It don't bother me none, if that's what you're thinking," Ya says.

"What doesn't bother me?"

"That I'm going and you're not."

"It should bother you."

He smiles.

"I couldn't do the college shit. I'd flunk panty raid."

I start to say that's not part of the core curriculum, but I hold off.

"And you can't do Army."

Ya's got that right. I'll flunk bolt-carrier group and everything that comes after it. Compared to that, he'll be tapped into the Fort Leonard Wood Honor Society.

"So maybe the right thing is happening for both of us," he says.

Sure, it's the right thing. Everybody who couldn't finagle his way into college gets to shoot at targets that shoot back.

I can conjugate verbs. I get to go home.

Ya would rather go squirrel-hunting. He gets the window seat to Southeast Asia.

I want this to be wrong. I want everybody to be vulnerable. Verb guys and squirrel guys.

But I want an asterisk by my name. An official exception. A special case. An extraneous circumstance.

Smart? OK, yeah, I'm smart.

I can live with that.

Oct. 8, 1971

Dear Mom,

Things are starting to take shape out here. By that I mean we've progressed to the point there aren't any major surprises.

Leave a button open on your shirt and it's 50 sit-ups in front of the entire company. First time, every time. Same thing for hands in pants. And looking off to one side when marching. And not knowing the difference between a captain and a lieutenant.

It's called getting dropped and it happens all the time. We were marching to lunch from first-aid class and guys were going down like bowling pins. Don't know the chain of command? Gimme 50. Don't know that the initial course of action upon stoppage of fire is tap the magazine, pull the charging handle to the rear and look for a spent cartridge? Gimme 50. Our platoon didn't have enough men standing for a quorum. Remember when you liked to go bowling? One more question about failure to fire and we would have looked like the 7-10 split.

Oh, by the way, had half a tooth knocked out in bayonet training.

I did fine on running up to the target, letting out a primal scream and carving it a new insides. You just imagine you're holding the little Exacto knife they gave us in school to cut paper. Then you multiply it a few hundred times until you've got something that will rip through human flesh.

It was the next phase - close-quarters fighting - where I became a casualty.

Same straw-man target, only this time you're just a couple of feet away. You've got to take him out, but you've got to do it in a space equal to that of a phone booth.

I tried to go up side the scourge's head. Wipe that smile off its stuffing.

Mom, there's no courageous way of saying this. I hit myself in the mouth with the butt of the rifle.

Hard.

I felt this sudden rush of cold. It's like its heat shield got blown off and all of a sudden I've got lake-effect tooth.

I looked on the ground, and there was a chunk of dental matter that will never again engage an ear of corn.

Waldsburger came over and gave me the first degree. He's not capable of the third degree.

"Thbroke my thtooth," I explained.

Here's where you have to know Waldsburger.

He could have dropped me for 50 for losing a combat decision to an inanimate object. He could have dropped me for 100 for practicing dentistry without a license.

Instead, he sent Nordquist for cold compresses.

And reacted as I had been gut-shot.

"This man is hurt. Get help," he shouted.

Then the DI stood watch over me in case the enemy counter-attacked. I tried to make it look good by grabbing my jaw, but there just wasn't enough wound.

No matter. Within minutes, two medics came running and whisked me off to the dentist. The guy put some kind of cream on it to kill the pain, and told me I'd be better off if I got my mouth fixed when I get back home. Laughed and said he pulls 'em better than he caps 'em.

Don't worry about the tooth. I almost like it this way because it makes me look tough. The other night I was at the movie theater and two Spec/4s let me get ahead of them in line. They said it was because they had to go through their pockets to find enough change for popcorn, but they didn't fool me. It was the fractured bicuspid. I looked like bar fight and they wanted no part.

Maybe tomorrow I'll hit myself with a grenade launcher.

Just kidding, Mom.

Here's a partial list of the things I'm screwing up on:

- Shooting. I keep forgetting to use the front sight. The range cadre say I'm missing the targets by as much as Rhode Island.

- The buffing machine. I never used one before and it shows. I get the ride of my life every Sunday night when we wax the bay. Until the tooth, my most serious injury was letting it run me into Skebo's bed frame.

- Breaking the M-16 down and putting it back together fast enough to suit them. I can't keep straight which piece goes where, but I've figured out a way to skirt the system. It's like music-appreciation class in high school when Miss Boone made us learn the composers of classical music. She'd play the record and we had 15 seconds to write the answer. I beat everybody in the class, even the kids who took piano lessons. How did I do it? Not by my knowledge of bass and treble clef, I can tell you that. Every one of her tunes sounded the same. It was like trying to tell the difference between Blood, Sweat and Tears and the Ides of March. So I did it by the color of the record labels. Bach was pink, Chopin blue, Mozart black, Rimsky-Korsakov green and so on down the line. I had the answer before the vinyl hit the turntable and Miss Boone thought I was a prodigy.

So what do I do with the gun? Memorize which parts have to be in place just so the M-16 will close. The other stuff I put in my field jacket until I get the chance for more permanent installation. Sometimes that opportunity doesn't come and I have to turn it in light. The first time, I was scared to death the armorer would notice and have me recycled for trying to skim the Defense Department. But, no. I got it back the next morning missing the same stuff. I went in the bathroom after breakfast, locked the stall door, fished the items out of my field jacket and put them back where they belong. I'm seriously considering color-coding the troublesome parts. If you see Miss Boone, tell her thanks.

Skebo is known as Mr. Grocery Store Man. They let you have a drawer for personal stuff and his is filled with potato chips of every description, Fig Newtons and little boxes of Sugar Pops. Troops come around for handouts. Skebo is generous to a fault. He doesn't like Peavey. Nobody does. But a little while ago he let the kid take his last bag of spicy barbecue.

Mom, I've never met someone so unselfish. And I'm not the only one who thinks so. If there was a mayor of Alpha Platoon, it would be Skebo. Hands down.

There's no ulterior motive. No banner with his name on it

that he expects us to fly. It's just the way he is to help people. A couple guys in the unit can barely read. Five minutes before lights out and Skebo is helping them write home. One kid's mother didn't know how to apply for disability. Skebo spent a Sunday afternoon drafting the letter.

Skebo asks what I want to do when I get out of here and I tell him write funny stories for newspapers. He's OK about the writing part, but he wants me to explore the human condition. He sees General behaving like a caged animal, pokes me in the ribs and says, write about that. I think on it for a few minutes, nothing happens and I go back to suicide-prevention counselors who were on speed when they should have been on call.

The other guy in the room, Carouthers, is OK, too. Oh, I didn't think so at first. I was almost as afraid of him as I was the drill sergeants. He talked tough, acted tough, even snored tough.

But then the Army put the three of us in the same mixing bowl. In between marching and shooting, we learned about being black and he learned about being white. Wary turned to tolerant. Tolerant became understanding. Understanding got to, "I'm headed for the PX; You need anything?"

Other than a brief outburst when I turned the volume down on "Shaft," you'd think we were the Three Musketeers. Just don't touch his head. He hates that.

We've gone to Walker Service Club together. Played basketball together. Helped my footlocker pass inspection together. It's like every day Carouthers wakes up, sees that we're just a couple of career Caucasians and scrapes off another layer of veneer.

You'll like this, Mom.

Remember how I wouldn't eat unless each food was in its own individual area? Absolutely no brown bean juice running into the creamed corn. No broccoli parts infiltrating the mashed potatoes.

Remember how I'd construct a little fort with my silverware and make you pour all the tapioca pudding on that side of the plate and that side only?

Remember how you'd fix something really good like brownies, and I'd turn up my nose because it was served with a stray french fry?

Well, no more.

We eat lunch at the range most days, and that means the cooks have to set up a field kitchen. The food's not that great when it's prepared on home turf. Go on the road and your stomach's really going to churn.

Breakfast is around 5:30. There's time for maybe a dozen swallows and then we move out. Lunch is six or even seven hours later. Even with a stowed-away nibble item from Skebo's kitchen,

I'm starved by 10 o'clock. I swear I could eat triggers. Add some tracer rounds. Make a great stew.

And how is lunch finally served?

Why, on paper plates, of course.

And what is the consistency of these paper plates? You ask.

Why, the same as the lace doilies on Granny's living-room chairs.

So here's what we have:

Famished troops holding plates they can almost see through. Cooks doling out chow that makes up for what it will lack in taste by being scalding hot. Food Group C is piled on top of Food Group B which has already deflowered Food Group A. Lunch a la heap.

Nordquist and his major in chemistry calculate that we have maybe 20 seconds to eat before the meal burns through to the ground. Guys chow down face first like dogs. No compartments. No pride. If it gets in your cap, you can always scrape it into your mouth on your own time.

When I get home, I will not require silverware or even a plate. Just put my supper in a trough and I'll be fine.

That's about it from your Missouri correspondent.

Please write. I get as much mail as a World War 1 barracks orderly.

Oct. 10, 1971

Bluefield, W. Va., Daily Telegraph
Richard Wesley, editor

Dear Mr. Wesley,

You don't know me. I'm in basic training at Fort Leonard Wood, Mo. I graduated college this past June with a degree in economics. I am not interested in a career in business. Instead I want to write funny stories for newspapers. Enclosed please find several from my files to include articles on Nixon memorizing the lyrics to Emerson, Lake and Palmer's "Lucky Man" so the kids will think he's cool, and strippers who bare their breasts for the United Way.

I recently showed one article to a troop who shares the same room, and he couldn't find the words to express his feelings.

I have been sending these articles to editors of big-city newspapers. While their responses have been encouraging, some say I might need just a little seasoning before I reach that level.

I get out of this horrid place in January of 1972. I wonder if I could get that experience at your operation.

I feel I can write you like this because I am familiar with your newspaper. A kid I knew in school, Brian Osgood, is from Bluefield, and he got the paper every day in the mail. He passed the issues on to me and I read them with great interest. I especially enjoyed the articles about coal and coal mining. Maybe I could take an occasional break from the funny stories to write about that.

You'll find me a hard worker. In college, I almost never cut class and made Bs in subjects I couldn't stand. And I'm good at managing my money. The guys on the dorm got hungry for hamburgers every night at 9 o'clock, but they were too lazy to walk the two miles, so I hired out my services. I charged a flat 15 percent fee plus an additional quarter per order if it was below 20 degrees. If you wanted your change in a separate enclosure, that was extra. Same with straws and napkins. I could make $5 last all week. What I lack in newspaper training, I make up for by being able to live on or below the poverty line.

And you'll find me good at making do with the materials at hand.

Last Saturday, they made us parade in our Class A uniforms. Twenty minutes before we were supposed to fall in, the DIs said that our shoulder insignia had to be in place. Panic. If the parade went OK, we were off for the rest of the day. If we screwed up, we were confined to quarters. Not having insignia was screwing up.

Troops were running around like crazy looking for needles and thread. But not me. I calmly sneaked off to the woods in back of supply and found a tree that leaked stickum. I applied my private's patch to the bark and then slapped it on the uniform. There was some curling up around the edges, but the thing held up long enough to get through the parade. With that kind of composure, I'd be your MVP at deadline.

I've thought of several other reasons to hire me.

- At least twice a day, they make us holler that more than anything in the world, we want to be on the river of Mekong. We've shouted about it so often I feel like I could swim the thing blindfolded. It would be good to have someone on staff with such navigational knowledge of a body of water that's in the headlines so often.

- No doubt there are many college students in your circulation area who are protesting the Vietnam war. It would be good to have someone on staff who knows about that. Skebo, my buddy out here, would have been arrested on the Ellipse last spring except they ran out of D.C. cops who could lift somebody his size.

- Tunes. I know the modern ones. No offense, sir, but I'll bet a lot of your readers listen to Dave Dudley, Connie Francis and that "Big Bad John" guy. I could turn them on to Cream, John Sebastian and the Paul Butterfield Blues Band. It would be good to have someone on staff who could write music reviews on songs

that came out after Khrushchev slammed his shoe on the table.

If you enjoyed these funny stories, I'll be happy to send more. I'm almost finished with a new humorous article about what happened at the grenade range a few days ago.

We sat through this long class about delayed-action fuses and fragmentation, and how the grenade is much better than mail call at clearing trenches, and how the concussion alone is enough to put you in the emergency room. We threw practice grenades that looked like pine cones and then it was time for the real thing.

I don't know how much you know about basic training, Mr. Wesley, but the drill instructors scream at you almost every second. I have been called every profane word in the dictionary, especially the morning I put the bayonet on backwards and the DI from C platoon asked if I went to remedial school.

But all that changed when we were given the live grenades, and that's what I wrote the funny story about.

We're waiting in this long tunnel. Every time a troop lobs a grenade, we can feel the shrapnel raining down on us. Fear sets in. What if we drop the grenade? What if we throw it like a second-grade girl, it goes six feet and we get fragmented?

It's my turn. I walk into the concrete bunker, and here's this cadre guy who's even more scared than I am. Then I see why. He's got to sit in the chair beside me. If I screw up, there will be two eulogies on the village green.

He hands over the grenade like it's the crown jewels. He calls me by my first name. Asks about my family. Asks about my high school baseball team. Asks what I want to be when I grow up. No cussing. No hollering. I'm holding a lethal weapon and he wants me completely relaxed. I could have requested 10 Valium and he would have called for special delivery. Anything so I don't roll it under his feet, and a crater is formed below what used to be his lower body.

"Son, I want you to pretend you're playing right field, the grenade rolls against the fence and you have to get it to the catcher on the fly for the play at the plate," he said calmly. "Do you think you can do that?"

I almost felt sorry for the guy. There are troops in this platoon I wouldn't trust to throw a light switch.

The thought hit to do a behind-the-back number with the grenade, or maybe toss it high in the air and do a 360 before catching it and letting loose. The NCOs put the fear of God in us. Why not let them see what it feels like to have your adrenal glands working a triple shift?

But maturity won out. I hurled the grenade like Johnny Unitas hitting an open receiver. The shrapnel didn't start flying until I had time to ice down my arm.

I lingered, thinking that I had made a friend. Maybe he'll tell me about his high school team. Maybe he'll ask me to come over Sunday to meet the wife and kids.

But, no. You don't get on this guy's Christmas list that easy.

"Get the hell out of here, dickhead," he said, officially severing our relationship. "Send the next buttcheek in here."

He was abrupt, oblivious of my feelings and this close to hollering at me for leaving my shadow in his bunker.

Back to normal, in other words.

That's what my article is about, Mr. Wesley. While the grenade was in my hand, I was somebody. Without it, I was just taking up valuable breathing space that could be better used by a crustacean.

Unless I hear from you to the contrary, I'll forward the grenade story as soon as it's ready. I write my articles longhand and then wait until we get a work detail so I can volunteer to type for the supply sergeant. He thinks anybody who can find the backspace key is just a notch below Gutenberg. The guy gives me a handful of purchase orders to type. I'm thinking, hmm, 30 minutes for the job, maybe 40 if the "m" key gets stuck like it did last time. The supply sergeant is thinking, hmm, if the big-eared kid can't finish by supper, maybe they'll let me have him again tomorrow.

I'm done in a flash and spend the rest of the time doing funny stories and writing letters. If he looks in on me, I tell him the backspace key could use a little oil. He gives me the thumbs-up sign and I get back to wasting the Pentagon's time.

That's about all I have, Mr. Wesley. I hope I've convinced you to hire me. I've got more paragraphs in me than the Army has gunpowder. Please let me be the fire in your hole.

Oct. 12, 1971

Dear Kathy,

You don't have to do this, I want you to know that up front. Feel free to totally disregard this part of my letter. Rip it to shreds. Throw it in the fire.

Having said that, I'd sure appreciate it if you'd send me one of your garments. I think you know what my first choice would be, but I want you to be comfortable with your decision. If you'd rather send me a hat or a belt or even a purse, I'll understand.

I am not to blame for the tone of this missive. It's the fault of the personal-hygiene cadre guy who finished 20 minutes early, and showed us a stag film about two mothers of Girl Scouts who were desperate for their daughters to get the award for highest cookie sales.

They went door-to-door with their free samples until they hit the jackpot at the apartment of these two naked guys who obviously had the biggest butternut budget in the county.

They wallowed around a sufficient amount of time for me to determine there wasn't a case of trenchfoot in the entire bunch.

Something neat happened in the bathroom the other night.

A bonding kind of thing, although not one the Army would put on any of its recruiting brochures.

Carouthers had this weed mailed to him and was dying to fire it up. But a troop can't just decide on his own to toke a number. The DIs would put him away until he gets so old he'll forget where to put it.

So we had to work as a team to make sure one of our players could get high.

Carouthers went inside the stall. Ya stood watch by the stairs in case the CQ decided to make rounds. Skebo took the guard post outside the bathroom door. I was the inside man. If Skebo gave the signal, I was to create a diversion by pretending to have convulsions. By the time the CQ pulls my tongue out of my throat, Carouthers should have ample time to de-toke himself.

Other guys in the platoon knew how important this was to Carouthers, so they put their shits and showers on hold. Black guys, Hispanic guys, white guys - everybody.

We're coming together, Kathy. Except for a couple of RAs, we hate the Army. Hate the DIs other than Waldsburger who's a saint in OD clothing. But we're like guys at the Rescue Mission. Nobody's holding any more than anybody else. Nobody's got a nicer place to stay. Nobody's got a fur-lined footlocker. And all our asses are up for grabs.

Three weeks ago, Carouthers would have done the number by himself. We weren't about to put ourselves in harm's way just so he could see the primary colors in Cinemascope.

But we've done pushups together. Run back from the rifle range together. Listened to Haddox say we're all a bunch of shiftless cocksuckers. Been told there aren't enough balls in our platoon to fill a Petri dish.

And how do we react?

By doing what it takes so one of our own can get a few minutes of eyes-in-the-back-of-his-head time.

I would not be a good reporter if I didn't tell you about Four Corners, a whorehouse a few miles off post in Waynesville. The CO said we shouldn't go there. Last weekend was the first time we could leave the post. Guess what? A lot of us went there.

Let the record show I was not among them. I played basketball with Nordquist and Rodriguez, and was the only player wearing fatigue pants to score more than 10 points. Haddox said we would never need shorts out here and should send all that civilian shit home. I made the mistake of believing him. Ever tried to defend the post in trousers?

Ya is my source on Four Corners. He says it's like any other sleazy beer joint except there are more than a dozen trailers out back where the girls live.

Nothing happens until a troop starts spending money. Drinks or 8-ball. Preferably both. The signal is given and then women magically appear and start rubbing against you. Fifteen dollars for 15 minutes. No haggling. You could be Tab Hunter or have one eye in the center of your forehead. Doesn't matter. Strictly cash and carry.

Ya's babe had so much makeup on that he almost had an allergic reaction while they were doing it. And about that particular part of her anatomy: Ya says he felt like a single-pump gas station trying to service a fleet of Peterbilts.

There was absolutely no afterglow. He says she had her miniskirt back on before he could clear his throat. By the time he got to the bathroom, she was out the door.

Peavey was also among the paying customers. Ya says he tried to act like this was something that happens every day, but he had a boner that would support the Wallendas.

Not much more to say from here.

Keep it warm for me and I'll see you after I've learned to shoot.

Oct. 13, 1971

Dear Dad,

You would have been proud of me earlier this week. You've always wanted me to be a tough guy, and I know most of the time I've let you down. Flailing away at my fellow man usually isn't my thing.

But let me tell you about pugil-stick competition. They give you this three-foot Q-tip padded at either end that's supposed to simulate a rifle without bullets. You're fired your entire clip, but the bad guys just shrugged it off. They're coming at you, and all you've got to stop them with is what you're holding in your hand.

For about 15 minutes, the cadre guy demonstrated the basic high-low hits to the face and groin. They put helmets on us as well as these diaper-like outfits that are supposed to protect your privates. Then it was gladiator time. The DIs sat back like they were on thrones.

At breakfast, Skebo and I agreed that we would volunteer to do battle. We'd snarl and all that, but just play patty-cake with each other until the DIs got bored and called on fresh meat who hadn't signed non-aggression pacts.

They want us to be barbarians, but we can rise about it, Skebo sniffed.

For sure, I replied.

But that was before my other pair of boots got gigged again for lack of shine, and before I got dropped for missing formation because my galoshes fell off the pistol belt and I couldn't get them back on, and before commode No. 2 was found to have a pubic hair I failed to remove, which helped our platoon finish last once again in morning inspection. It didn't happen, thank God, but the rumor was that Haddox was going to hold the thing up with tweezers as yet another example of how pathetic we are.

The humiliation was just beginning. After lunch, Litton inspected our M16s for cleanliness of bore. He looked at mine and I thought he was going to blow chow. He said my weapon looked like a furnace, and if it exploded in my face, I was just getting what's coming to me. He ranted at some other troops, but I was his whipping boy for a good five minutes. He grabbed the gun and I swear he was going to hit me with it. Then he got disgusted and moved to the next troop who, naturally, had a bore that was clean enough for an antiseptic ward.

I got mad for the first time since I've been here. Really mad. Enough screwing up. I made my mind up that I was going to be good at something by the end of the day. And not in personal-hygiene class either. Something physical. I was going to beat the daylights out of something or somebody.

And guess what was the next thing on the agenda, Dad?

Pugil sticks.

This was my big chance. No smarts required. No common sense. All I had to do was wield this thing like a psychopath who hasn't taken his medicine in more than a year, and I could finally get an "A" in something.

Poor Skebo. He's standing there in his diaper, the world's fattest 2-year-old. He's holding the Q-tip like it's a scepter and he's going to anoint me. I'm holding mine like I'm getting ready to pound a railroad spike.

As per our plan, he tapped me on the side of the helmet. You ring a doorbell harder. I pretended his head was a watermelon and my family hadn't eaten in three days. Bam! He went down like a wide receiver who ran into the goal post. It took three guys to drag him to the sidelines.

Do I care that I may have given my friend a concussion? Of course not. I'm stomping the arena floor like a bull that gets extra oats for each matador it takes out.

The DIs stopped slipping grapes into their mouths and took notice. This was the new, improved troop. More brightener. More red under the collar.

I know exactly how somebody on amphetamines feels, Dad. I didn't care who I did it to, or who was watching, or how many stitches it required. I just wanted to do it.

They put me against this guy from E Platoon who enters all these body-building contests and has a chest like a bridge abutment. Nostrils flared to the max, I popped him under the jaw and then declared total war on his balls. You know how Sherman marched through Georgia? Well, that's what I did to his reproductive region. Time after time. From the front. From the side. From down under. I'm thinking, by God, the bastard doesn't lift weights there. Game, set and truss to me.

I'm close to berserk by this point. I would have gone in the ring against an atomic bomb.

The throne-sitters huddled and then snapped their fingers. My next foe was a troop from C Platoon who's going to the stockade as soon as they process his paperwork. Found guilty of assault on a cab driver before coming here, he lost it one day during formation and attempted to run the guidon through his platoon leader. The DIs intervened, but not before the lead troop had to go to the hospital.

The felon pawed at the ground and said, "Bring it on, (real bad word)."

I whacked myself in the side of the head with the Q-Tip and said, "Can you hit harder than this, (real bad word)?"

Then I banged myself again as I rushed toward him. Then again, even harder. I didn't even feel it. I just wanted to knock his chin into his adenoids.

This has never happened before, Dad. The person occupying my body screamed horrible obscenities, and swung the Q-Tip like a ball bat, and didn't care if he ever again has a place in the social circle.

My foe put his hands behind his neck, which I would later learn was a signal that he didn't want to fight any more. But I was way too far gone at this point to recognize reconciliation. I clubbed him about the head until his helmet was almost off. Two DIs gently, and then not so gently, pulled me away. By this time, I had a mind only in the legal definition. I would have attacked anything that moved. If the Secretary of the Army got in my line of sight, he'd better have a spring-loaded Q-Tip.

The cadre had everybody gather in a semi-circle for the main event. They had the perfect opponent for the mild-mannered troop who suddenly turned into Barry Sadler times seven.

Hercules.

Six foot-three. Two hundred twenty pounds. Bigger than Haddox. Bigger than Carouthers. Bigger than 45 shitpots welded together. Best runner in the company. Best at PT. Best at commanding the DIs' respect. Best at being the total opposite of Peavey.

He held the Q-Tip like it was a ruler. Two whacks with that thing and I'll look like an accident victim. Three, and I'm on a *respirator.*

I'm pretty sure I don't care.

God, amphetamines are good.

I gripped the stick with all my might. This was for not being able to make the bed. Not knowing where the firing pin goes. Not knowing how to fold my underwear. Not finding that pubic hair.

This was for all those weeks of failure. All those weeks of being No. 39 out of 40. I could get it all back right here.

The whistle blew. Head down and eyes closed, I stampeded toward probably the most imposing troop at the military installation. I'm jacked up and all that, but this is Hercules we're talking about. I kept waiting for the blow to my skull that would bring on the rosary beads.

Nothing.

I sneaked a peek as the screaming person occupying my body raised serious mating issues regarding Hercules' mother. He should be preparing to knock my head clean off and then, to defend her honor, not allow them to treat the stump.

But Hercules just stood there. I slugged him in the rib cage. His response was a lame thrust to the knee that wouldn't hurt Kippler. On and on it went. I hit him as hard as I could. He gave me his 2 percent retaliation. His hardest blow was no worse than bumping your shoulder on the closet door when you're trying to find your bathrobe.

"You win, man," he kept whispering.

I couldn't understand it, Dad. The only thing I should be able to beat him at is waking up at 4:45.

"C'mon, you win," he said when we got in a clinch. "Nail me one more time and I'll go down."

I obliged. He was like the bad guy in all those Western movies after the shootout in the last reel. Grabbed his side. Grabbed his throat. Then he circled like the first-grader trying to see how dizzy he could make himself. Then he fell to the ground. The only thing missing were death throes.

Stunned silence.

The impossible had happened. The troop of troops had been KO'd by a typist.

Like an 18-wheeler going up the off ramp, I was easing to a halt. The foam was just barely visible on my lips. It only took one DI to keep me from jumping up and down on Hercules' midsection.

My head soon cleared completely and I realized what I had done. Lied to and then possibly hospitalized my best friend. Violated the Basic Human Dignity Act of 1787. Behaved like a rabid dog.

Skebo asked to be treated as far away from me as possible. Making up will take a while. A long while.

Cadre members suddenly treated me like the reincarnation of Sgt. York.

"Good hit," one said, slapping my back.

"Attaboy, tiger," another joined in.

The senior DI from E company started to extend congratulations, but jokingly pulled back, covering his face as if I might turn on him next.

Haddox barked that we had 45 seconds to either smoke 'em or (bad word) 'em, and then it was time for guard-mount class.

The rush from the hypo was gone and replaced by embarrassment. I wished I could erase the previous 10 minutes of my life and substitute it with anything else. I mean anything. The time I farted during Algebra 2 and everybody laughed at me. The time I couldn't climb the rope in gym class and the PE teacher said I was a pussy. The time I tried to kiss Sylvia during Weekly Reader time and she slapped me.

I got in formation and tried to pretend I wasn't myself back there, that I had gotten hold of some bad saliva. They weren't buying it. The Army's attention span is brief, but not that brief. I was still the lead story. It wasn't time for their eyes to move down the page.

We got a break after an hour of M16 assembly class. Hercules went into the toilet. I followed him. He's pissing. I'm pissing. A good time to talk.

Me: "What were you trying to pull back there? Why didn't you take me out?"

Him: "You needed it. I don't."

Me: "Needed what?"

Him: "To be the best at something. To have people crowd around like you're the place to be."

I had to admit that succeeding sure beat the hell out of being called a dickhead.

Hercules: "Yeah, I know. So I let you have that feeling."

Me: "You could have knocked me into Wednesday."

Him: "Or Thursday."

Me, in disbelief: "But you chose not to."

Him: "Look, did the DIs get off your case for a few minutes?"

Me: "Well, yeah."

Hercules: "Then it was worth it."

Me: "So you took a dive."

Him: "Ah, yes, but with choreography." He stopped his stream long enough to grab his lower body in mock abdominal breakdown from my withering attack.

Me: "You still haven't told me why."

Hercules, realizing I was trying to penetrate his outer perimeter: "Like I said, I've had it already."

End of discussion. He zipped up his pants and went back to being the mystery man of A-2-2.

One more thing, Dad, and I'll let you go.

We were zeroing our weapons, the thing that has to happen before you can move on to record-fire. Using the prone-supported position from the 25-meter range, you have to put three rounds inside the space of a half-dollar. That's supposed to mean your sights are adjusted, and you're ready to kill people from farther out.

Well, your oldest son was unable to achieve such a tight shot group. Not on the third try. Not on the sixth try. I'd either forget to use the front sight, or get so nervous the barrel went up and down like a yo-yo.

Three rounds into a football, maybe, but nothing involving coinage.

Even Kippler got the job done. I was the only bolo in the platoon.

Each time you fire three rounds at the target, you have to connect them with a pencil so those shots don't get mixed up with previous rounds. All gunmen have No. 2-bearing spotters to make sure there's no cheating. Mine was a straight-arrow from D Platoon who's never done anything wrong in his entire life. He walked the 25 paces with me every time and made sure I marked off the correct group of three. Then I trudged back, my spirits lower than the sandbags.

Waldsburger watches all this from the tower. One of his boys is going down. Must come to the rescue.

He whispers something to my goonie, and the kid double-times to the other side of the range. Ya becomes my new grader. He's grinning broadly when he arrives at my firing line.

"Waldsburger says shoot 'em up."

Now I'm smiling. There's been a change in the procedure. Same target, same M-16, same pathetic shooter. But we aren't going to play the circle game any more. I will keep firing until three rounds - any three rounds - are close enough for government work. It only takes a few minutes for a shot I just fired to be inside the same half dollar as two shots I fired earlier in the afternoon.

"He did it!" Ya screamed after connecting the bullet holes with Waldsburger's pen.

I prepared to take my, uh-hum, rightful place with my colleagues in cordite when a loud voice called out.

"Wait a minute. He cheated."

It's General.

He was in the firing line beside me. He saw how inept I was and then Ya comes over and, boom, a miracle happened.

"Check his target. There's got to be something wrong," he says to Waldsburger.

Naturally, General zeroed on his first three rounds. He strutted like he had just won a shopping spree at the armory.

A half-dozen or so other guys in the platoon were equally proficient, but they didn't lord it over me. So they can shoot and I can't. Big deal. I know about Czar Nicholas in 1917 and they don't. It all evens out.

But not for General.

To him, zeroing one's rifle is a part of our nation's military heritage like Valley Forge or something. There can be no shortcuts. No conniving. No evoking the name of the royal Russian family.

Honoring the troop's request, Waldsburger looked at my target.

"Damn. Fuck that. God damn."

He gets out a nickel and puts it over my shot group.

"It fits. Son of a bitch, it fits."

He bows his head.

"I am truly honored," he says solemnly. "I'm seeing something few DIs have been privileged to see. If I took my shirt off, you could see the chills going up and down my spine. Congratulations, son."

I don't know any more about what's going on than the guy who drives the coffee truck.

"A nickel? You mean a nickel?" General says incredulously, realizing his thunder has been stolen by someone who only uses the front sight the percentage of time Nellie Fox hits a home run.

As carefully as he would handle the evidence if someone murdered Peavey, Waldsburger puts my target in an envelope and seals it.

"Anybody got a tamper-proof container?" he wants to know.

We've got just about everything else on our pistol belts, but not that.

"Very well," Waldsburger said. "This will have to do."

He grasps the thing with his fingertips so as not to jostle the precious contents.

"Only one place for something like this, men - the trainees' museum."

Now I know Waldsburger is bullshitting. There is no such place. We're here to be screamed at and processed, not honored. If we're remembered at all, it would be for our sloth. Don't need a curator for that.

I'm thinking, geez, surely General can see through this charade. But, no. He has the insight of a garbage can lid.

"Er, shit, uh, you can really shoot," he says to me. "To get in a museum. God."

I don't know how to react to this hero-worship. Should I give him the nickel?

General goes back to my firing line and picks up the spent rounds. It's his way, I can only assume, of getting close to greatness.

Waldsburger watches, then winks at me.

Write when you have time, Dad. If I'm not too busy Clint Eastwooding pop bottles out of the air I'll get back to you.

CHAPTER 7

We gather around the little building that's set off in the woods like a hunting camp.

It most certainly isn't.

Nobody has been anxious for this morning.

If you can shoot, you look forward to going to the range so you can play pinball with the targets.

If you're a budding domestic, you look forward to the morning inspections because it's like rolling the cleaning cart down the hall.

If you're an athlete, you look forward to PT because you can run or jump or crab-walk to the head of the class.

But this is the Army's gas chamber. You only look forward to it if you want to walk in a double murderer's shoes.

The other four platoons in Alpha Company have already had their turns in the forest. Word has spread. You stand against the wall, protective mask and steel pot between your knees. The cadre guy sets off the tear gas canister. You shout out name, rank and serial number before scrambling to put the mask on. It doesn't matter how quick you are, we've been told. The stuff gets in your throat, and you feel like your esophagus is being burned at the stake.

To make matters even worse, Haddox is already seething and we haven't even done anything wrong yet. Seems he got a letter from an old adversary who's managed to elude justice.

Apperson.

Ya was cleaning the radiator pipes in the CQ this morning and heard the whole thing. There were two items inside the envelope: A sheet of loose-leaf paper calling Haddox everything from a dick-licker to a sheep-fucker. And a cottonball coated with shit.

Ya said Haddox kept screaming that Apperson is a dead man. Then he went back and forth from stomping the letter into submission to calling for the Postmaster General to throw the full weight of his office into identifying the cocksucker who sold the AWOL a stamp.

At one point, the DI talked about strapping on a holster and doing what he should have done the morning the Apperson tripped out. Tracked him down like a dog.

It was weird, Ya told us. While Haddox was raving about the pissant who got away, the other DIs quietly moved to the other side of the room and talked about something else. Haddox couldn't even get a "Gee, that's too bad" out of them. It was as if they half-understood why Apperson would share his bowel movement with the man.

The cadre guy starts the individual protective measures class.

"There are four ports of entry for chemical weapons - the eyes, nose, mouth and skin," he says, holding the M17 gas mask that looks like a blowup of an ant's mug shot.

"You will mask without command when spray-attacked, gas-attacked or smoke-attacked," the seen-it-all cadre guy intones as he has intoned for every training cycle for time immemorial, or at least since the Gulf of Tonkin Resolution.

"What if we're Haddox-attacked?" Peavey whispers.

"Forget the mask," Nordquist replies. "You'd need a tetanus shot."

The cadre guy tells us most trainees experience no lasting effects from the gassing.

"Usually you're just disoriented for a few minutes. You'll holler like hell, but pretty soon you can go on about your day."

Wily grin.

"However, a few troops don't take it so good. If you think you are having an adverse reaction, you are to raise your hand. If you're having a seizure and are unable to raise your hand, you are to have your buddy jump up and down. Eventually, someone will come to your assistance."

I'm thinking, yeah, right, when the war is over, or when the esophagus doctor makes rounds, whichever comes first.

Haddox looks right at home in his protective mask. Hardened. Battle-tested. Ready to prove he can suck up more noxious fumes than the exhaust system at Boeing.

We take our places against the woodwork. The lights go out, and we hear a loud hiss like a cobra that's been trying to shed its skin for two weeks, but it won't come off, and the reptile is severely pissed.

To the very end, we hold out hope that the other platoons were wrong. Yes, we will have time to get the mask on. Yes, the gas is slow-acting. Yes, there is a vent somewhere in here that will blow out the really bad stuff before it gets on us.

No, no and no.

Despite putting on the mask faster than Peavey can screw up, I feel an inferno on my neck. Then somebody tries to shove a hot plate in my mouth.

The door opens and we pour out like green A1 Sauce. And cough. Guys are rolling around in bushes coughing. Rubbing up against trees coughing. Hitting themselves in the chest coughing.

It's like group activity time at camp. Not for crafts, but to hack up pieces of bronchial tube.

Mucous flies everywhere. Collar, sleeves, shoes. I don't have the strength to fight the enemy, but I can phlegm him a new asshole.

Kippler, the wisest of us, is grabbing at his eyes and screaming that a horrible mistake has been made.

"Hydrochloric acid. The butchers used hydrochloric acid. We're going to dissolve."

I can't disagree. My pores are Code Blue. My nose feels like it's caught inside a refinery fire. Thanks to scalded vitreous matter, the most my eyes can do is glimpse.

Troops are following Kippler's lead and going out of their minds. But never mind that. I can't remember the last time I breathed. Chest heaving, I try ringing down there, but there's no answer. So this is how it's going to be. Sweet dreams, troops. An acid bath followed by the deployment of a powerful new vacuum cleaner attachment that reams out your cardiovascular system.

With the Grim Reaper awash in my eyelids, I can barely make out Haddox standing calmly a few feet from the gas chamber door.

Is he gouging at gaseous demons that have infested his body? Is he even scratching himself?

Hell, no. The bastard is lighting up a cigarette and hollering, "Shit, that was nothing." By God, tear gas couldn't challenge his alveoli. Bring on Brown & Williamson.

The biggest prick out here blowing smoke rings. That will be my last vision on this mortal sphere.

It's been a great 21 years. So I didn't get to have children. The Army has a reason for everything. They just would have become delinquents.

Fade to nothing. Cue harps. Cue sea of white. Cue perfect flesh tones. So this is heaven. Got a nice place here. Think I'll look into one of their long-term housing units.

Suddenly, there's light and a degree of function in my upper body. My nose is wet. And my face. It's lower to the ground than it should be. Much lower. And something smells really bad. Hey, what's going on? There's no jungle rot in heaven.

The same eyes that I thought had gone in the tank are up and blinking. The pharynx that had tendered its resignation is suddenly open for business.

I decide it would be a mistake to come back from the grave too fast. Deep-sea divers don't just zoom up from the depths of the ocean and flop right in the boat. It's the same for someone whose epiglottis has been hot-wired.

So to find out exactly how alive I am, I engage in a preliminary Q-and-A with myself.

Where am I?

Within hailing distance of the gas chamber.

Who am I?

The same person you've always been, only paler.

What am I?

Prone.

My mouth feels funny. What gives?

It should feel funny. You puked your guts out.

When did it happen?

About four seconds ago.

A polite distance away, right?

Nope. Right in your tracks. You could run a line straight down from your chin to the chunks.

You're lying.

Am not. You swandived into your puke.

And this wetness I'm experiencing?

Puke does that to a nose.

I spring up faster than one of A. J. Foyt's pistons. There's no towel handy so I use the next best thing: My pistol belt. I look around, half expecting to be yelled at for illegal removal of peristaltic matter.

But nobody is paying attention. It seems Haddox and Kippler are having a point-counterpoint.

The DI is accusing Kippler of causing a near-riot by loudly testifying that the cadre decided to do away with us by substituting hydrochloric acid for tear gas.

Haddox: "The rest of the men heard you jabbering and started running around like their dicks had been cut off. One shithead even tried to take off his buddy's mask. Thought he could breathe better if he had two of 'em. What the fuck were you thinking?"

Kippler: "Initially, it felt like my eye sockets were being eaten away. If that could happen to bone, I knew my endoplasm had no chance."

Haddox: "Fuck your endoplasm."

Kippler, calmly: "It's true, drill sergeant. If massive quantities of unadulterated hydrochloric acid are released onto your person, you're going to feel worse than the pig on the spit at the Eagles Lodge."

Haddox: "But was it hydrophonic acid, or whatever the fuck you said it was?"

Kippler: "No."

Haddox, revved up like he's finally going to win an oral argument against the near-Rhodes Scholar of a troop: "So you started hollering."

A hush falls over the platoon. The DI has him this time. No way the kid bullshits his way out of this one. Never mind that he's got a triple major in lying out the ass. He screamed that we were going to dissolve. We believed him and panicked according. Next case.

Kippler: "I suppose an explanation is in order."

Haddox: "You got that right, fuckface."

Kippler: "Never before having been treated like a black man picked up after a riot, I had no way to anticipate the effect of the substance in the canister. For those first few seconds, it did indeed seem as if asphyxiation was imminent."

Haddox: "Cut the crap."

Kippler, undeterred: "Then I could feel the stuff wear off and I realized the cadre probably had no intention of killing us, at least not at the present time."

Haddox, eagerly: "Go on. Then what?"

Kippler: "That's when I started thinking like, well, you."

Haddox absolutely cannot process this piece of information. He is not Kippler and Kippler is definitely not him. The DI struggles to find the response that adequately reflects how pissed he is that the bastard would even suggest such a thing. But his upstairs biology can't even defend its position, much less launch an offensive. He just sputters and stomps and calls the little troop a cockfucksucker.

Kippler: "I know, as you do, that many of us aren't very good soldiers. We're weak and shiftless and always take the easy way out. If the men believe they've been given less than a lethal dose, they won't take the gas chamber seriously. We'd have to go through it again, and I for one didn't want that to happen. So I exaggerated my condition. I considered several words, but went with 'dissolve' because it conjured up images of the worst possible death. Forty guys, 40 piles of ooze. The platoon envisioned being moped up and got their minds right."

This is the crucial moment in his performance. If Kippler's eyes dart, if his chin quivers, if his temple flexes - anything - Haddox kicks him out of acting school and into the stockade.

In previous go-'rounds with Haddox, Kippler was merely Barrymore. This time, he's the entire Motion Picture Academy.

Kippler, locking into his target: "I knew exactly how, in a perfect world, you would handle the situation, drill sergeant Haddox. You'd make the men think they were going to perish unless they masked exactly as they were told. But the Army has some stupid pansy-ass rule against DIs making death threats. So I did the next best thing. I became your representative. I made the men believe our lives were in danger so we would reap the maximum benefit of the protective measures training class. How did I do?'

Haddox, confused out the ass: "Uh, uh, shit."

He is shaking his head violently as if that will jump-start his mental circuitry into going faster than its usual two miles per hour.

Kippler: "Please. I value your opinion."

The man is in full brain overload. Kippler uses such big words. And he uses so many of them. His words come out so smoothly. And they seem to make sense. Maybe the little fart is telling the truth.

Haddox, looking for an out: "Uh, police the area. I'll get back to you."

Big deal. Kippler picks up Haddox's cigarette butt, throws dirt over the puke and the hunting camp is ready for the next batch of inhalers.

Once again, Kippler is hailed by troops who couldn't argue down an Amish carpenter, much less a brick-shithouse representative of the nation's military might. He's like the basketball player who banks in a leaning one-hander with two seconds left to win the conference championship. All that's missing are the cheerleaders running into his arms.

But what's this?

There are only 39 celebrants. General has left our group and is having an animated conversation with Haddox. Occasionally he points back at us as if he's explaining something. The DI is rigid, the signal that all receptors in his cerebrum have been activated to the maximum allowed by its meager housing.

General finishes his presentation. Then he backs away, proud of himself, so we can see Haddox's reaction.

Which is savage anger. It begins with his steel-plated eyes, continues with the little bubble on his upper lip, and works its way down to boots that are slowly grinding up all the weak, shiftless blades of grass. His ears are pressed against his head. I turn away. I can't even meet the man's gaze when he's sleeping. I want no part of this.

Kippler is too busy congratulating himself for winning another round of Debate The DI to realize what's going on. Alpha Platoon turns to Skebo for expert analysis.

"He fucking ratted us out," my friend says in language I thought sociologists only used when they spilled pipe tobacco on their tweed jackets.

"Who?" Ya wants to know.

"General, the dick."

Skebo is unusually forceful. General must have committed a grievous behaviorial-science transgression.

"He told Haddox about Kippler's little act. He told Haddox that the men know Kippler got the better of him and they're laughing about it. Haddox realizes that he's been had and he's boiling over inside."

We murmur that Skebo might be right.

"You damn well better believe I'm right. Remember that night he would have low-crawled us to Kingdom Come if Robison hadn't intervened? There's not always going to be someone there. He's going to be alone with us one of these days and something could really happen. This isn't like earlier in the cycle when we just fantasized that they might find us dead in a ditch. I'm telling you, this man is psychopathic enough to put us there."

Great. Basic training has been rolling right along. Shooting, cleaning up after shooting, falling in, falling out, falling down. And now we must lie in wait for a DI who would like nothing better than to see 39 of us succumb to trench warfare.

But enough about real, not imagined, fear. We're trucked back to the barracks to get ready for the overnight camp. SDI Robison sits us down for some prepared remarks.

"The next step of your training is the bivouac. You will march a distance of 12.6 miles in full gear. You and your buddy will pitch a tent using your respective shelter halves. Your excretory functions will take place in a cat-hole latrine dug one foot below the surface. You will do this. There will be no goddamn pissing on some goddamn bush. During the march, you will be tear-gassed and shot at. It is just make-believe. Do not charge in the woods after them like those two dicks from the last cycle. If you charge in the woods, I will kick your goddamn ass. Meals will be C rations. You are not to be in possession of food. Possession of unauthorized food can result in disciplinary action as well as confiscation of said food.

"The following personal items are approved for bivouac: Toothpaste, toothbrush, soap, washcloth, foot powder, lice powder, insect repellent, socks and shoe polish.

"The following personal items are not approved for bivouac: Tape players, dice, playing cards, marijuana, fuck books, what's that shit some of you had in college, oh, yeah, incense, butcher knives, beads and bitches."

We laugh.

He doesn't.

"Two cycles ago, some guy sneaked a chick into the tent. He was halfway through banging her when he got called out for guard mount.

"You will have your M16s at all times. You will place your M16 in the tent in such a way that it does not sustain water damage. If your M16 sustains water damage, I will kick your goddamn ass.

"You will dry-shave in your steel helmets. The whiteness of lather can give away your position to the enemy. If you give away your position to the enemy, I will kick your goddamn ass.

"You will prepare a foxhole observation point 10 meters from your tent. If I walk by your tent and do not see a foxhole observation point, you owe me five laps around the quads and then I will kick your goddamn ass."

"Any questions?" Robison thunders.

We're all concerned that a long march with 40-pound packs will leave us with curvature of the spine, but we decide not to bring that up.

Skebo agrees to be my tent-buddy, but only after I apologize 10 more times for pulverizing him with the pugil stick and promising that if I ever go berserk on him again, his lawyers will hold a lien on my balls.

We're given 15 minutes to prepare our gear. I need every second. Fill up the canteen. Clip on the ammo pouch. Tie off the galoshes. Tie off the poncho. Squeeze in the shelter half. Sneak bag of M&Ms in pants pocket to eat on the way. If Haddox catches me, I'll say it's the latest in lice protection.

I feel like I'm carrying a half-dozen cannonballs. If I ever get started, it's going to take me a football field to stop.

Skebo looks like a stuffed bear that lost his insides at pre-school, and the 4-year-olds desperately tried to put him back together before nap time.

Ya takes a final drag on his cigarette.

"Shit, I didn't even like walking home from the bus stop."

He needn't have worried.

We needn't have worried.

Something incredible has happened since that first day when we panted running up the stairs.

We're in shape.

All the hauling ass back from the rifle range. All the afternoons we ran the track until we could get around four times without being lapped by Hercules. All the wind sprints up and down Caisson Drive.

The jumping jacks until I thought I was going to split in two. The squat-thrust sessions that lasted longer than "Hey, Jude." The fireman's carries that began with almost dropping Kippler after 10 yards until now when most of us can get Skebo from Point A to Point B.

I didn't know it was happening. None of us did. But while we were surviving one day, and then another, and then another, we were becoming damn near buff.

They give us a break after five miles. We spend the whole time acting like a bunch of doctors making rounds.

"Are you all right?" we ask each other. "How's the neck? Are the knees holding up?"

Everybody gives a good report. Even Skebo. He's like the rest of us. It hurt for the first few hundred yards, but then it becomes a battle of endoplasms and ours won going away.

Of course, cheating helps.

Skebo is fine with the distance. Well, relatively fine. It's the load that gets him down. So, come dark, we divvy up the weight. I take his entrenching tool. Kippler takes his M16. Ya takes his pistol belt and all the add-ons. Carouthers puts on his pack. Skebo hid in the woods until Echo Platoon passed by, and then follows far enough back that he won't be seen.

DIs and troops blend in on the four-hour march. Cadence runs out. Rank runs out. There's only walking. And talking. Earlier in the cycle, there was a gorge-sized chasm between cadre and troops. They had stripes on their shoulders and tenure out the ass. We knew nothing. We could do nothing. We had experienced nothing.

But now, this far into it, we've earned the respect of most of the company's DIs. We've become accustomed to the long days. We haven't crumbled under the physical requirements.

They react to this not by praise, but by gradually including us in their world. By talking about things within our earshot that they never would have before.

The DIs take turns marching with us. We find ourselves abreast with the two drill instructors from Charlie Platoon - Hicks and Cannon.

Hicks is on one side of the road that leads to our night-night and Cannon the other. They can't see each other - we shuffling pack animals are in the way - so they have to holler over our heads.

Hicks asks Cannon if he knows there's been a change in M16 training.

Cannon says no.

Hicks tells him a two-hour block of the move-out phase has been at least temporarily discontinued.

Cannon asks if he means when the troops crawl toward the tower while live machinegun rounds are automatically fired overhead.

Hicks says yes. There was an accident a month ago at one of the other basic-training installations. As always, the men were told under no circumstances to stand up. Guess what happened?

Some kid lost it and jumped to his feet, Cannon guesses.

Damn near blew his head off, Hicks says.

Piece of shit got what he deserves, Cannon concludes.

It is against that backdrop of concern for our fellow man that Robison's Jeep driver arrives, going from 50 miles per hour to zero in the time it takes a cootie to shake a tail feather. If throwing gravel for a quarter-mile hasn't given away our position to the enemy, then I'm Westmoreland's protege.

Bounding out of the still-smoking conveyance, Robison sees that we're still standing and the stretcher-bearers are asleep in the truck. Their boards are cold. We made the trip on our own. Summed up in language the SDI can best understand, our Achilles tendons are with the program.

He asks the least of us the proper distance between platoons on a tactical march.

"Fifty meters," Peavey guesses.

A miracle has happened. He's right.

"Well, I'll be dipped in shit," Robison drawls, as button-popping proud as an SDI is allowed to be. "You boys are short, you know that. Real short."

We need a translation. For six weeks, short has been like dicks. Bad. Coming up short in PT. Coming up short on payday because we earn less than what falls out of McNamara's pockets. Now, all of a sudden, short is good.

"Goddammit, short means you can count the days you have left in boot camp," Robison explains. "You used to be long and it was forever until you got out of here. Now you're short."

I thought we were too tired to get excited about anything other than falling asleep.

But I'm wrong.

"Short." A troop's voice rings out of the darkness.

Silence for a few seconds while the crickets search for any hidden meaning.

Then a veritable cacophony from the rank and file.

"Short!" The shout comes from the darkened depths of Echo Platoon.

"Short!" Bravo answers.

"Short! Short! Short!" Delta screams. Their harmonies are lousy and the men are hopelessly out of key, but you've got to cut them some slack. This is a live performance.

Robison isn't a drill instructor any more. He's like a cheerleader, going from squad to squad and raising his hands like this is a pep rally.

"Louder," he exhorts.

Charlie lends its voice.

"I said louder, goddamnit."

Everybody screams, even me, the typist/observer from Alpha Platoon.

"Three more miles," coach Robinson calls out. "Got that many in you?"

We should be shaking our heads. Our pack straps have eaten their way down to the bone. Some of us would need a breathing treatment to give out name, rank and serial number.

But we're getting off on Robison so much that we forge ahead. Word spreads that no basic-training company at Fort Leonard Wood has ever made it to the bivouac without at least one guy dropping out. It's always something: Full-cardiac arrest, blisters the size of toasters, rigor mortis.

So this is why Robison is so worked up. He has a chance to make military history. Anybody can jump out of a plane at the South of France, or dodge one of Rommel's tanks in the African desert. By God, he can get 200 ignorant assholes to their campground without calling in Special Forces.

The SDI climbs on the back of the Jeep as it slowly goes up the road. There's an hour's march left. The men are tired. They need to be motivated. How best to do that?

Why, talking about pussy, of course.

"You troops wanna know what happened to me last night at Four Corners?" Robison asks.

The mere mention of that oasis of pleasure is worth a brigade of massage therapists.

"I'm standing against a pool table with a pecker just this side of a fire tower. I get up to take a piss and all of a sudden this chick comes up and shimmies against my balls. I whisper in her ear that I'll fuck her like a monkey. She says, you'd better, fool."

Our pace quickens. We're like first-graders straining to hear the day's installment of "Jack Tales."

"I'm taking things off as fast as I can. Jacket, shirt, pants - the polyester is flying, baby. But I slow down around my hard-on. Don't want to unzip on that thing. This ain't no time for sick bay."

The troops want more, but Robison clams up until we're 10 minutes closer to our final resting place. So this is how it's going to be. He's going to make us earn it.

"She gets me in the toilet and puts rubbing alcohol on my tool," he continues. "Real slow like it's some kind of ritual or something. I'm wanting to fuck, but she goes over and over on that thing."

Back in the Jeep. Another purposeful pause. We bust a gut to get to the next checkpoint.

"We screw like ABC Wide World of Sports," Robison continues. "Up one side of the bed and down the other. I doze off for a few minutes and then she's gone. I'm cool. I'll just get back in line, right? But then I can't find my underpants. I look under the bed. Under the stereo. Under the cans of pinto beans. I mean, I looked for them underpants. Nothing. They're gone, man."

Another round of silence. The Jeep stops at the top of a steep hill. No matter. We're practically climbing over each other to get to the top. How is Story Time going to turn out?

"I give up after a while and pull my trousers up without 'em," Robison says. "I go back in the bar and see a buddy of mine. I tell him about fucking this bitch, and then not being able to find an important clothing item.

"He starts laughing and tells me it was Wanda. I ask how does he know? He says she's damn near famous. She waits until you're either asleep or passed out and then she steals your underwear. Some people collect rocks. She collects drawers.

"Buddy says Wanda has more than 400 pairs. Keeps the things in big trunks in her bedroom closet. She let him see 'em once. Guy said he's never seen so many bloomers. Said it was like like being at the factory outlet store."

Kipler believes she keeps the souvenirs in case the tax man is in the back of the line.

"Probably flunked bookkeeping in high school, so she's got to keep the math simple. After each trick, she makes off with the guy's underwear. At the end of the fiscal year, all she has to do is count soiled Jockey shorts."

I have a completely different take on the situation. She's only a parttime prostitute. Her real job is that of entrepreneur. The Soviet Union drops the bomb. The Midwest is little more than soot and ashes. Naked guys are stumbling around in the streets. She sells the underwear on the black market. Makes a killing.

What's this? Robison's driver does something even better than stopping. He turns off the motor.

We have arrived at the Army's KOA.

But nobody left the light on for us.

Visibility is about 12 inches. I only know I have feet because they hurt. I can't see them. The guy across from me could be Peavey. Could be Nixon.

Robison explains the rules for our slumber party. In a few minutes, he will turn on the floodlights for 30 seconds so we can get our bearings. Then they will go out as we don't want to give away our position. There's that darn enemy again. Conversation is to be at a minimum. Moving around is to be at a minimum. If he hears any bitching about being forced to march halfway to Arkansas in the middle of the night, he is going to kick our goddamn ass.

The juice comes on. We can see scores of cathole-trenches from previous cycles. And the corroded tops of C-ration tins. And toilet paper that may biodegrade one of these days but not in my lifetime. We pair off with our shelter-half buddies and empty our packs before lights out.

I beat the tent stakes into the ground while Skebo uses his entrenching tool to carve out a toilet. Together we pull back, tie off and fasten until we have erected a temporary housing unit that may or may not stand up if a 3-year-old girl brushes up against it.

He tries to sleep. I try to sleep.

It doesn't happen.

For one thing, we're both filthy. The sandman won't come if he has to wade through an expeditionary force of crud.

And we keep hearing noises like there's a herd of wild animals a few feet away who are celebrating their fall festival.

Polecats for sure. And snakes. Poisonous ones, probably. And wolves.

And bears, who are pissed we brought M&Ms and didn't give them any.

One night watchman won't be enough to ward off the beasts. We'll both have to stay up.

On the march, Skebo talked of slow-cooking sorghum, and drinking peyote tea, and getting plugged into a gig with the brush crew.

Ah, yes. Life on the Farm. That's what will get us through the night.

"Rugged capitalism came to be exploitative, you know that, don't you?" Skebo says sagely. "The government started to push everybody's buttons. The idle rich started to take over. The village is an alternative to all that."

So who's your leader?

"David. Groovy guy. Looks a little like Santa Claus. Everybody in the settlement gets $10 a week spending money. He never goes through more than a few cents. Gives it all to the children."

The roots trace back to Venice Beach in California in 1968, Skebo says. Seekers of all kinds - war protesters, rock 'n' rollers, environmentalists, radical politicians and even a few praise-God worshipers - started hanging out together. David was the only one who could pull everybody together. He could hum Grateful Dead lyrics. He could fix the generator. He could preach about man's inner soul. If a child had an earache, he knew to get some amoxicillin. If somebody acted out, he could call him an ego-mongering jerk-off.

My friend manages to get somewhere near the lotus position - God, he should charge for this - and continues.

"A core group formed. It wasn't that they were followers so much as David was the leader. They were after something different. Peace and love, yeah, that was cool, but they wanted more than that. They wanted to prove to Republican America that they could live together in community. Self-sufficient. Beholden to no one.

"So David finds 2,000 acres in rural North Carolina. Cheap acres. Acres nobody else wanted. Went before the yokel powers that be and assured them that just because he has a beard, that doesn't mean he's crazy. Put his VW van down as collateral and the Farm was born.

"The man started a sawmill and eventually landed enough accounts until it was making $2 million a year. This is the same guy who only has one pair of shoes. Takes a four-mile walk every day and kicks at the pebbles in the road like a little kid."

David's slogan, Skebo continues, is "We Be Brethren." Some members never finished high school. Others have college degrees. Some have televisions in their living quarters. Others consider them the most worthless of inventions. The people who clean up at the bakery are no less important than the teachers at the village school. Everybody's the same.

Skebo says David believes that denominations aren't the answer. The secret is you make the Jews like the atheists and the Baptists cut vegetables together with the Catholics. There's no regular worship service, just a Sunday night gathering. You can attend, Skebo says, or get high. Quietly.

The lotus is loosening. His knees are clicking like he's just rolled 500 dice.

"Do you know what we call each other?"

I go with "hippies."

He shakes his head.

"Voluntary peasants. The outside world is stressful. Trying to achieve wealth. Power. Status. Inside the village, there's none of that. You're wearing a dirty T-shirt and jeans. The guy working next to you at the cannery is wearing a dirty T-shirt and jeans. The woman we call Bank Lady because she pays all the bills goes barefoot. There's nobody to impress. No social ladder to climb. No Joneses to keep up with."

I can't believe he answered the Army's call. He could have hidden out at the Farm. Nobody would have ever found him.

"I told David about the Army. I figured he'd think of a way for me to blow it off. He trail-bossed a herd of settlers from California to the wilds of North Carolina. He can beat one person's Army rap, right?

"David asked if I signed up for the military. I said, well, yeah. Then he asked if it was my own free will. I told him it was either join the reserves or go to Vietnam. That's not the point, David said. Nobody forced you to put your name on the piece of paper. I told him, well, no.

"I thought he just wanted to know all the facts. Then he'd throw the whole weight of the Farm behind my getting out of the service.

"Boy, was I wrong. I forgot the big three with David: Harmony, collectivism, honesty. His verdict was in. I told the Pentagon I was coming

Sept. 3. I would arrive at the appointed time.

"I whined, but David said I had made a covenant and I had to stick to it. A few days later, a bunch of us were replacing my canvas roof with a tin one. David walked by. Naturally, he grabbed a tool and joined in. I still had some grump in me. I told David I'd go to the Army, but I don't have to be good at it."

"This big grin came over his face and he said he would expect no less of me."

So when the DIs jump in your shit, I conclude, you're just following your master's teachings.

Skebo bows and starts in on a Hershey bar.

Just then there's a rustling on our, well, porch.

"Uh, can I come in?"

It's Carouthers.

"The doorman is temporarily indisposed," Skebo replies. "You may let yourself in."

He takes a seat in the corner next to the stacked rifles. There's more than a hint of reefer in his exhale. And why not? The Army is engaged in the most non-Negro thing in the entire world: Camping out.

Carouthers grabs Skebo's entrenching tool and twirls it like a baton.

"Still scared of me, ain't 'cha?"

If our heads bobbed any more, they'd come off. Baptists can backslide. So can big black men.

"Like I could kill you or something."

Carouthers lays the thing softly next to my air mattress as he would a funeral wreath.

"Well, it's bullshit."

What's bullshit?

"Me."

He asks if we remember when he told us about cutting the honky's hand.

Skebo and I reply that we never close our eyes in the room without wondering if they've invented hand-reattachment surgery.

"Well, it didn't happen."

You mean you didn't try to cut off a white man's wrist for feeling your forehead?

"Shit, no. I was scared coming to Fort Wood and ..."

"You? Afraid?" I interrupt. "Somebody who could beat the crap out of the Green Bay Packers?"

He puts his head down.

"That's not me. That's just the me I wanted you to believe."

Our jaws have dropped until they're in our chest cavities.

"I ain't no tough guy. I ain't no fighter. I work at the chicken restaurant and then I go home to Mama. The only thing I told you cottontails that was right was about the wrestling. Anything about whipping somebody's ass was just an act."

Skebo and I don't know what to say. All that with the tent stake. All that about us thinking we'd just give him the room and live out in the hall where it's safe.

"You know how some animals puff themselves up to look big and bad? Well, meet Mr. Blowfish."

So everything has been a mirage. The knife. The menacing glances. The cracker factory.

"Yeah."

No black judge letting you off with a wave and a grin?

" 'Specially no black judge. Where I'm from, they barely let a black person in the courtroom. No way they let him sit up front."

I'm delighted to receive this new evidence and am ready to drop the matter. Unless there's a major upset, I will leave this place with two hands.

But, naturally, Skebo presses for an explanation. Why tell us now? he wants to know. Indeed, why tell us at all?

"I don't want to be the buck nigger no more," Carouthers says. "People looking at me and backing up. Like right now. I'm tired of being something I ain't. It's like the queer who's lived his whole life hiding being queer. Then one day he steps up for what he is. He tells everybody around him to deal with it."

Carouthers reviews what he has just said and looks at us sternly.

"Don't you be calling me no queer."

He has our assurances.

"Better go back to my tent now."

Skebo has one last thought.

"That word you used to call us. You know."

"Motherfucker?"

"Yeah. You say it with such power, such conviction, that's it's almost an art form. I feel a sense of history here."

"What do you mean, history?" Carouthers wants to know.

"That after all these weeks we may never get to hear it again. How about once more - just for old time's sake?"

Carouthers is confused. First we didn't want him to and now we do.

"You mean say that you're motherfuckers?"

"Not just say it," Skebo explains. "Feel it."

"But you're not," Carouthers says. "I thought we cleared that up."

I find myself urging Skebo on. It's almost midnight and we're beyond exhausted. Carouthers' incantation might be just what we need to turn off our motors.

"If that's what you want," Carouthers says. "OK, you're both motherfuckers."

"No, no," I say. "You've got to project. You've got to reach down inside yourself."

Suddenly Skebo grabs a tent stake and charges toward him.

"Project this, motherfucker," Carouthers booms as his elbow loses itself in my friend's midsection.

I applaud the performance. So does Skebo as soon as he's able to breathe.

"Are you all right?" Carouthers wants to know.

"It's an old trick of the director's trade, my man. Do whatever it takes to trigger the right emotions."

"But are you hurt?"

"Forget hurt," Skebo says, coughing. "That was a fortissimo motherfucker, quite possibly your best yet. I knew I could bring it out of you."

I concur. It was a motherfucker for the ages.

"Aw, shit," Carouthers says, embarrassed.

"Two more Caucasians, right?" Skebo chimes in.

"Aw, shit."

Morning comes pouring through the top of the tent that we failed to fasten to the best of our abilities because there were spiders on it. The sun lights up our filthy faces and then commences to stabbing our eyes out. We surrender unconditionally. It'll take time to fetch the white flag and do the paperwork. Should be good for two more hours' sleep.

And it is.

The morning is decidedly low-key. The DIs must be having coffee at Denny's. We awake on our own. Wonder where all the polecats went on our own.

There's a chaplain if we want one, and guys we don't know taking pictures of our tents and our stiff-backed attempts to exit them. Skebo says it's for the cycle book we can buy after we graduate basic. There's Pulitzer potential with my cat-hole trench, but they probably aren't into nature scenes.

Litton makes the rounds, shaking hands and slapping backs like he's the dean of alumni relations. Robison tells anyone who asks that we've been a half-decent cycle.

There's a session of dismounted drill, but the cadre doesn't seem to care and we definitely don't. Same way with map-reading. It's like we're walking our dogs around the course. The only sense of urgency is when DI Hicks threatens to piss in Peavey's helmet liner, but uses the bushes at the last instant.

We march back to the barracks with the intensity of first-graders going to the pumpkin patch. It's like, "Right, right, your military right, oh, never mind."

Then a Jeep pulls up alongside and Haddox pops out of the Omar Bradley seat. Bravo, Charlie, Delta and Echo Platoons can leave. All he wants is Alpha.

This isn't good. This isn't good at all.

"You like to laugh, don't you?" Haddox screams. "Well, we're gonna laugh 'em up."

He calls Kippler front and center.

"Ever give head to an M16, boy?"

Kippler keeps quiet. He's too scared not to. This isn't the Army. This is Haddox getting us alone. Getting even.

"Drop your pants."

Kippler hesitates.

"I said drop 'em, motherfucker."

Fatigues and underwear hit the ground.

"Now put your hand on your pecker."

Kippler does.

"Now start shaking it."

Only minor compliance.

"You know you've been waiting to beat off. Now you've got a crowd. Go to it, goddammit."

Then he orders Kippler to take out his weapon.

The troop is crying. He knows what's coming.

"Now put that prissy little mouth of yours on the barrel."

Kippler starts to say something, but only a whimper comes out.

Haddox gets in his face.

"Come on, boy. Ain't got no guardian angel now. What wise-ass shit you got to say?"

Just then we hear flying feet on the troop trail. The dust clears. It's Waldsburger on the dead run. Panting, he calls Haddox aside and whispers something in his ear. As he talks, he signals with the back of his hand to Kippler that it's OK to put his pants back on.

"Uh, something important has come up," Haddox announces. "You troops can carry on."

He gets in the Jeep and hollers at the driver to get the hell back to the bivouac site.

Waldsburger calls us to attention. The incident with Kippler is over, he says. Alpha Platoon will pretend it never happened. Alpha Platoon is not to mock Kippler in any way or hold him in any less standing for what happened.

After a firm, "Is that clear?" we resume the march. Kippler asks for, and receives, permission to get back on his own.

The walk to the barracks is a whispered exchange of ideas on what just happened.

"That was sick," Skebo says.

Total agreement except for General.

"Little fucker had it coming," General responds.

I say Haddox has gone wacko.

General replies that Haddox is more of a man than I'd be even if I was given the nut juice from every masculine person in North America.

Skebo calls General a Nixon-loving slimeball. General calls Skebo a fat man at the circus. We arrive at the barracks in perfect step. Maybe we should have insults instead of cadence.

Skebo and I remain on the front stoop. I've got two letters to write and he doesn't want to leak sweat onto our freshly buffed floor.

Waldsburger waits until the other troops have left.

"Wanna go get a beer?"

We don't know what to say.

"Forget that DI shit. I've checked out."

Skebo jumps up like he's got another 10 miles in him. This is the ultimate sociological experiment. Raising a beaker with a Smokey the Bear hat.

We climb in Waldsburger's Camaro that's parked by the dining hall.

"Don't mind the mess," he says. "Got kicked out of my apartment for playing music too loud."

There's enough dirt inside for a rodeo. The debris begins with back issues of Rolling Stone thrown all over the place, and builds to a crescendo with piles of civilian clothes that have set up their own government in the back seat.

Skebo and I look at each other. This isn't adding up. A DI in disarray. A DI who reads a cool publication. A DI expelled. And for tunes, not for staging paramilitary maneuvers in his living room.

I kept getting pelted by pants every time he comes to a stop. A belt nails me behind the ear hard enough to break the skin. Injured by laundry. Good thing I'm not shipping out overseas.

It's the first time I've been back to the NCO Club since that night with Ya when we crowded around the Vietnam guy who couldn't add up his bar tab, but could kill gooks in geometric progression.

The beer comes within seconds from a young woman with a nervous face. It's not hard to see why. She doesn't know which of us are new hires and which ones spent the last 12 months walking point in Tay Ninh and have pressure cookers for brains. We could wait patiently for our orders to be filled, or we could stare at our watches until the allotted 30 seconds went off, go berserk at the piss-pour way GIs are treated on their time off and proceed to gun down the wait staff. She must deliver each pitcher like it's her last on Earth.

We ask Waldsburger a polite question about which album he was listening to when he got tossed out before getting to the matter at hand.

What did you tell Haddox back there to get him off Kippler?

"That somebody nailed a Tampon box to the wall of the bivouac latrine and printed his name on it."

Was this true?

"No. I made it up."

But why do you care what Haddox does to Kippler? It's no shine off your brass.

"Because it's too easy for people like us to take advantage of people like you."

Time for some expert analysis by my friend.

"Let me see if I've got this straight," Skebo says. "Haddox went to 'Nam, saw all the bad stuff and that's why he is the way he is."

Waldsburger grins.

"Haddox never went to Vietnam."

That can't be right. Haddox took out 17 fire bases while sucking the gangrene out of his arm and hollering if that's all they've got, they don't have the right to call themselves the enemy.

"He wanted to go. Bad. But they wouldn't let him," Waldsburger says.

Maybe a bunch of his brothers went and the Army didn't want to risk him, too.

"No, I heard that they graded him way down on one of their tests. Stamped on the sheet of paper that he's unfit for combat."

Psychological profile?

"Yeah, maybe something like that."

What about the wild-eyed GI we saw in this very room? Freud would have a field day. They let him go to Vietnam.

"What can I tell you?" Waldsburger says. "Haddox must have been worse. He doesn't say and we don't ask. He wants to be an island, we let him be an island."

Pause.

"But I was there."

Waldsburger sees the "No way, you're still rational" in our eyes.

He shows the underside of his right arm. The fleshy part looks like he tried to hammer a nail through it.

"Small-arms fire outside Cu Chi. I screamed like I had been shot in the face. They poured some hydrogen peroxide on it and stitched me up. Sergeant called me a sissy and made me burn the shit that night."

Oh, the new phrases we keep learning.

"The latrines in our base camp were 55-gallon drums cut in half. Every few days you had to carry the things outside and light them with diesel fuel to get the crap out. Naturally, you had maggots in the tubs and they made a high-pitched squeaking noise while they burn up. That was something to hear."

Skebo and I put aside our cheeseburgers. No use for them now.

So what's Vietnam like?

The Viet Cong eat rice balls all the time. Keep 'em around their neck in a plastic bag. Three bags in all. AK-47 rounds in the one. Marijuana in the other. Charlie whiffs a lot of dope."

What was your MOS?

"Infantry. Just another grunt in the grass. Real simple routine. Take a big orange malaria pill every Monday night and shoot anything we see in thong sandals and black pajamas. One night my buddy and I came back from daytime patrol and there was a VC's body beside one of our perimeter's trip wires. We decided to cut off his head, put it on a stick and leave the thing where the bad guys could see it. Like maybe that would make them leave us alone."

Did it work?

"Hell, no. Every time there's going to be a big fight, the gooks' officers make them dig mass graves. Everything they do depends on speed. You die and get dumped in the hole you dug the night before. If that's a part of your routine every other week or so, you ain't gonna get bent out of shape at seeing a head on a post."

But you were in Vietnam and he wasn't. You should be like Haddox and he should be like you.

"Lots of guys came home the way I did. You've seen all the violent acts you ever want to see. Now you're into gentle. Birds, a painting, a nice stand of flowers - that's what I like to look at. I see a momma robin in her nest and I'll stare for 10 minutes. Never was like that before."

But you don't talk about it.

"Not on the Army's time I don't, but that part of my life is over. I'm taking college courses by mail. Get out in 14 months. Might be your boss one of these days."

Why drink with a couple of ignorant-ass trainees?

"The Doors. The not-liking-this shit. The innocence. Yeah, that's it. You guys have never seen a cut-off head and you never will. The things you want to talk about helps me forget."

Haddox is wrong. We do have a guardian angel.

The beer is starting to kick in. I want to get this out while I can still form syllables and before they have to carry me back to the Camaro as they would an upright freezer.

"I can say it now and it doesn't mean anything because you're here and I'm here," I tell Waldsburger. "Time has to pass. I have to get where I'm going in life. Be a writer. Have people I don't know call to say they like what I put in the newspaper. Then I'll find you, wherever you are, and say thanks. You were a human being to me when you didn't have to be. I'll never forget that as long as I live."

I look the DI square in the eye.

"We'll sit at a table like this again. Ten years. Twenty years. Whatever. I'll tell about the grenade range. You'll remember Haddox almost getting decapitated by the Dumpster. We'll put our arms around each other and laugh our asses off."

Waldsburger gets up to piss.

"Won't do you any good to try to hide," I holler after him. "I'll hunt you down."

I have announced my intentions at a sufficient decibel level that everybody in the place is looking at me. The beer and I don't care.

"You got that? I WILL BE at your doorstep."

Waldsburger winks at me.

A homing signal for the ages.

CHAPTER 8

"Ready on the left. Ready on the right. Ready on the firing line."

Yeah, I guess. Let's get it over with.

Assorted crackles, and then the loudspeaker in the cadre tower is back and running.

"You are here because you failed to successfully complete the record-fire phase of your rifle training."

Like tell me something I don't know.

"We are administering a makeup test on the record-fire phase of your rifle training."

Why doesn't he quit reading off the sheet and just say that Peavey, me and 11 other bolos from Alpha Company are spending their Saturday morning at range 235 while everybody else is off-duty. DI Hicks had a name for us while we were getting trucked out here: The guns of Navarone.

"To review what will take place." Crackle.

We don't need a review. We can't shoot. It's that simple.

"You will fire at silhouette targets from 100 feet, 200 feet and 300 feet. You will fire from the prone unsupported position and the prone supported position using sandbags."

Yeah, yeah, we've heard it before.

"The targets will pop up in random order up and down your firing lane. They will only stay up a brief time. You are credited with a kill if any part of the round penetrates the target. Your total will be electronically tabulated in the control tower."

Crackle. "What the -" crackle. "Goddamn -" Crackle. "Why isn't this working?"

Crackle. "There, that's better." Crackle.

You have to score 54 out of 100 shots to pass. I was 25 out of 45 on the first phase which wasn't that far below the company average. But yesterday was like I had never seen a target before. I bombed away to the tune of 16 of 45. I was way off on all the 300-feet silhouettes and only scored a few hits from 200. If your combined total is less than 50 percent, they let you fire the second part again.

Crackle. "Can anybody here -" Crackle. "Fix this stupid -" Crackle. "Aw - " Crackle. "Fuck it."

The last 10 rounds of BRM are at the night-fire range. Twenty-five meter targets, just like with zeroing. Tracer rounds are sprinkled in. The idea is to carefully watch where these go so you can better aim the others.

What we keep hearing is that it's all but impossible to hit more than one or two. You'd better be right at 54 before you get out there.

Right now I'm sitting on 41. I've got to push my numbers up so there's not so much pressure on night fire.

So, yes, I'm nervous.

Lack of advice isn't a problem.

Ya told me to aim low and maybe the round will skip up and hit the silhouette. Fire high and it's all over.

Nordquist told me not waste rounds on the 300-feet Charlies. Just pretend to fire and squeeze off the extra rounds on the closer-in targets. Never mind that they tell you at least four times an hour not to do this or they'll kick your goddamn ass.

Rodriguez suggested I aim at the control tower. Skip the rest of the show and go straight to the lightning round.

I run down my checklist.

The front sight is your friend. Do not abandon your friend at your time of need.

Do not sweat profusely. Your trigger finger has enough enemies already.

Do not get in a hurry. Think before you fire. And breathe. And pray. And be ready to swear to the range cadre that the target malfunctioned, and how can I be expected to hit what's still in the ground?

Do not let the size 24 steel helmet interfere with your marksmanship. Look at it this way. It's plenty roomy in case you get good enough to have a big head.

Don't think about bolt slider group. Don't think about cyclical rate of fire. Just think about bullets going through a quarter-inch-thick soldiers with sufficient accuracy that you can get on a bus and ride out of here.

We hear a medieval clanging from the tower, the signal that the targets have broken from the gate.

A 300-foot silhouette jumps up like a prairie dog. It wiggles with the wind and then goes back into its hole before I can get off a shot. Damn, this is going to be just like yesterday.

Then I hear an official-sounding voice behind me.

"Look to your right at 200 feet."

The M16 and I obey. The almost-an-enemy springs to life. Because I've had an extra couple of seconds to hone in on it, I make the kill.

I start to turn around to thank my benefactor.

"Keep your eyes front. This ain't exactly legal. I'm Sgt. Gulletz with the cadre here. Waldsburger is my buddy. He told me you might need a little help."

Which would be telling me in advance where the malnourished soldiers are going to expose themselves.

I get early-warning notice on a 300-footer and actually hit it - my first time at that distance. I start to go into a dance, but having something on your head that weighs as much as an end table pretty much knocks the glee factor out the window.

"Extreme left at 100 feet," my tutor whispers.

Nailed it.

"Straight ahead at 200 just to the left of the bush."

Gotcha.

"Hundred feet. Dirt mound on top of the hill at 10 o'clock."

One and done.

God, divine intervention is good. Keep this up and I'm the Cordite Kid.

Which, of course, doesn't happen.

Of all the orders to obey at the range, "Cease fire" is at the top of the list. Especially with bolos. Might as well try to earn extra credit for being good listeners.

But Peavey shoots not just once but twice after the command. It's almost as if he did it on purpose. The cadre has ignored him for almost an hour. Can't have that, so he takes a couple of unauthorized plugs at the cloud cover.

The DIs jump him faster than white-hatted Texans on Jack Ruby. Pissed beyond belief, the loudspeaker guy orders Peavey off the range. Naturally, Gulletz is ordered to provide the escort service, which has the effect of setting fire to my security blanket.

I think of grace under pressure. Hemingway. The '69 Mets. Osgood in an ice storm with a mini-refrigerator strapped to his ass.

I can rise to the occasion. I can mount a comeback. I can cast my steely gaze at the targets and cause them to go down.

Bullshit.

The steel helmet falls over my eyes. I miss a 200 trying to put it back on.

A 300 pops up. I aim, breathe, pray and watch the round go into orbit.

I return to old habits. Sweating on the butt plate. Doing the cool jerk on the trigger. Having a front sight for decorative purposes only.

I hit most of the 100s, but they're just sprinkled in to give the troops hope. If you want to return to civilian life, you have to hit the ones that are placed halfway to the Emerald City.

Which I don't. No need for Dorothy and Toto to duck and cover.

The loudspeaker guy gets the scorecards from the control tower and passes them out up and down the line. He's decidedly downbeat, as if one day we'll all be in-country together and his life will depend on whether we can hit the broad side of a VC.

I scan my results. Twenty-six of 45. A distinct improvement, but I still need three at night-fire.

Depression sets in. Gulletz pointed the way to a half dozen hits I probably wouldn't have made. What am I going to do in the middle of the night?

Maybe I can put a flashlight on the front sight. Might as well use the thing for something.

When I get back to the barracks, I see Skebo under the horizontal bars. He's bending over, tamping the soil, fishing something out of his pockets and then bending and tamping again.

"What are you doing?" I ask.

"Planting sweet potatoes."

I cannot believe this.

"Might be a bumper crop," he says. "Never can tell."

"Is late October the season to plant sweet potatoes, and is Central Missouri the place to plant them?" I ask.

"Don't know. Hope so."

"So why are you doing the Farmer Brown thing?"

"For the next cycle. Help their morale."

I don't follow.

"The DI has them out here doing bars just like Haddox did with us, when all of a sudden some smart guy sees the sprouts. He's freaked at first, but then he understands."

I'm glad he understands because I don't.

"Remember early on how we thought they'd keep us jumping 24 hours a day and we wouldn't have even an instant to ourselves? Well, that was crap, right? We've had some kick-back time, especially after the fourth week."

Go on.

"Think how much it would have meant to us if we could have had proof that every week of basic wasn't going to be as bad as the first?"

The anxiety would have gone down 150 percent. Go on.

"OK, so the next basic training bunch sees sweet potatoes growing on a military reservation. They know that at least one wise-ass troop had enough time on his hands to engage in some Ag Studies 101."

Skebo bends and tamps.

"And they'll know if that jack-off had a few hours to himself, so will they. I won't be at the barracks to tell 'em, so I'll do the next best thing.

Maybe put down some tomatoes, too. Give 'em a vegetable medley."

General walks by. He's been in commando mode since yesterday when Haddox said he was the only troop in Alpha Platoon who knows his ass from his dick.

He sees Skebo hunkered down with a spade in his hands.

"What the fuck are you doing?"

"Digging," Skebo replies, not looking up.

"You're not supposed to do that. You're supposed to soldier."

General says this in the manner of a 6-foot, 2-inch, 210-pound second-grader about to tattletale to his teacher.

Skebo ignores him and turns up more topsoil.

General plants his right foot in Skebo's furrow.

"I said the Army don't want you digging up its land."

Then the next foot.

"Put it back, goddammit."

Skebo says something about how it's too late for that, and he'll have to wait for the harvest.

General keeps moving his boots closer and closer to the planter until the inevitable happens. A clump of Skebo's dirt comes to rest on his shoelaces.

Which General reacts to by pushing Skebo against the brick wall. Hard.

Skebo goes into the worst Ali shuffle I've ever seen, motoring in circles and hollering ringside commentary that he heard years ago on the Gillette Friday Night Fights.

General watches in bewilderment for maybe two seconds before moving in for the kill.

But what's this?

One troop after another steps in front of Skebo. Ya. Nordquist. Rodriguez. Carouthers. Me. Even Peavey.

General will have to whip us first.

A second line of defense forms around Skebo's exterior perimeter. And a third. Soon almost all the men of Alpha Platoon form a phalanx around the Curly Joe of a prizefighter.

My friend has stood up for us, entertained us, instructed us, written letters for us, led us and fed us. No way are we going to let him go down.

General tries to advance, but we send him flying.

"What's the matter with you fucks?" he hollers. "Why are you covering up for this weak piece of shit?"

Earlier in the cycle, some of the troops would have rallied to General's side. RAs, mostly. Guys who by the nature of their enlistments take this more seriously. Guys who burned the shine in on their boots back at the reception center. Guys who couldn't wait to be issued their field gear. Guys who wear fatigues on weekends when they don't have to. Guys who give the finger to trainees in other platoons when we're in assembly because they get caught up in the rivalry the DIs try to promote.

General was their guy, their Haddox in acceptable doses. They paid attention to the stupid signs he put on the bulletin board about loose lips and ships. They watched him go around with hair the length of an ink speck and followed suit.

But we've been together for almost two months. Gotten to know each other. Traded KP with each other. Sat for hours together at the end of the day trying to get our M16s clean enough that Armorer Fickey will consent to putting them back in his toyhouse. NGs and ERs know where RAs are coming from. RAs know NGs and ERs are chickenshit, but they give us credit for admitting it.

We've developed our own code of conduct.

Do what you have to do to pass basic, but nothing extra. Don't give yourself an easier path by making it harder on someone else. If the troop besides you comes up short, prop him up and hope the cadre doesn't notice.

The troops saw what Haddox did to Kippler on the march back from bivouac, and they know who sold him out.

General breached the code. His punishment? Standing alone at the showdown at the sweet potato patch.

"Let the tub of lard fight me," General shouts, showing his ass more and more with each syllable. "I'll shove his face into his underpants."

Thirty-plus troops start striding as one. General continues screaming, but must do it in reverse as the sheer weight of our bodies drives him back across the street. He's been banished. He can eat with us. March with us.

Even holler "short" with us.

But the trainee is from henceforth an interloper. One of us on duty-roster paper only. The only thing he can call friend is his GI Joe.

His sphere of influence has been reduced to the man inside his clothes. The NGs and ERs voted him out a long time ago. The RAs waited until today to cast their ballots.

We get back to Skebo and report that the danger has passed, and he can quit his pretend-duking.

I watch my friend personally thank every man who ran interference for him. This is why everybody likes him so much. There's no false bravado, no "I could have handled General by myself, but thanks for the group effort." We saved his ass and he's not afraid to admit it.

I think back to Gaines at the reception center, the black kid who came out here in bedroom slippers, the only footwear he had. The only half-decent thing about the Army is that it forces us hoity-toity college boys to see how the other half lives. Because my draft lottery number wasn't 300, I know that bedroom slippers can not only leave the house but the state.

And I probably never would have met someone like Skebo. That rare hombre who shrugs his shoulders and says, yeah, I'm vulnerable. I'm not strong. I'm not tough. I had hair down to my ass and wish I still did. I'm going to need all the help I can get to make it through this thing, and I don't care who knows it.

Walking up the stairs, he is razzed for being fat, for being sloppy and for finishing behind Mary Poppins in the competition for trainee of the cycle.

He just smiles. The sweet potatoes are in the ground, that's the most important thing. His legacy is in the loam.

Oct. 21, 1971

Dear Mr. Wesley,
    I was thrilled beyond belief to get your letter. Yes, I will come to work at the Bluefield Daily Telegraph in three months after I finish advanced individual training on how to change typewriter ribbons, or whatever they teach you in accounts payable school. Yes, I agree to the salary of $90 a week. Yes, I agree to be a

deskman trainee.

I want you to know that every Sunday I walk to Walker Service Club and read all the newspapers. St. Louis, Chicago. Oklahoma City. Even if they're torn. Even if they're a week late.

I may be a business major, but I understand if you want to write good words, you need to read good words.

I told the guys back at the dorm that the day is coming when they will have to pay to read what I've written. Maybe just a nickel, but they'll have to pay.

I told them it won't always be as convenient as me walking in their room, handing over my three-page article and standing over them with my guffaw meter.

They'll have to go to the store, or put the coin in a rack.

And there I'll be in that day's edition with a story that came out of my typewriter. Maybe on the front page, but more likely on page 22 above the Gold Bond Cream ad.

But that's OK. I'll work my way up. What we observer-types lack in the social gadfly department, we make up for in busting our tails.

One of these days, Mr. Wesley, I'll have my own column. Oh, it'll take a while. Maybe a long while. I'll have to learn to make stories true to life and not funny all the time. I'll have to learn to put hop in my sentences like my idol, Jim Bishop. I'll have to get better at trying that much harder when people say I stink.

I think I've already made progress on the latter. My steel helmet is at least 10 sizes too big. Guess what I do when I get the rejection notices from the big-city newspapers? That's right. Scotch-Tape them to my cranium protection.

A few more letters and the thing will almost fit.

Thank you, again. You won't regret your decision.

Oct. 24, 1971

Dear Kathy,

Thanks for sending the panties. It meant a great deal. Some things a man just can't put into words. Suffice to say I put them in my ditty bag and refer to them often.

No surprise, I passed the PT requirements for graduation. Ran the mile in 5:50 and was beaten only by Hercules. Did 48 bent-leg sit-ups in a minute which placed in the top 10. Was so-so in the inverted crawl and the run, dodge and jump. Barely got the minimum in the parallel bars and Haddox ragged me for having goddamn noodles for biceps.

The first part of next week is reserved for what they call the G-3 proficiency test. Can I pretend to splint a broken leg? Can I read a map? Can I remember what was said in all the stupid classes while I was trying not to fall asleep?

Yes, yes, and hell, yes. If I can get a "B" in money and banking, I can nail any test they have out here.

The night-fire range will be my Super Bowl, Kathy. Ask your dad. Big football game. Played in late January. The pressure is on. Will I knock down enough targets in the blackness to move on to cash-flow school? Or will I shoot like I have so far and get an extra helping of basic training?

I'm not having any trouble with morning inspections.

For one thing, they're not as important as they used to be. Some training days last from 10 minutes after the lights come on to 10 minutes before they go out again. There simply isn't time to create display cases with our footlockers and bunks and they know it.

When there is time in the schedule for polishing, folding and arranging things just right, I get help from Carouthers. I know it sounds funny, but it's like our quality time together. We talk about race relations and housing discrimination and civil rights legislation. By the time we get to the freedom riders, my shit is not only with the program, it's riding herd.

We have off-post passes tonight, but I won't be going anywhere. There's enough depression already in the civilian population. They don't need to see me and get worse.

That's all I have.

See you more or less soon.

"Let's go to Four Corners," Skebo says.

Can't, I reply. My top hat and tails are in the laundry.

"I'm serious," he goes on. "This might be the only chance we ever have to see a living, breathing whorehouse. Pretty soon we'll just be able to read about them in the history books."

I tell him I'll wait until it goes on display at the Smithsonian. Take the wife and kids. Be the highlight of our vacation.

"You're afraid."

Not true, I lie. My day started earlier than yours. I boloed and somehow you didn't. I'm tired, that's all.

"You think the girls aren't tired, too? You think they haven't had a long day? They're probably on their fourth tube of lip gloss. You try making yourself alluring a dozen times a day."

Then you go, I suggest. Allure them once for me.

Skebo shakes his head.

"Won't work. You're a little hesitant, I'm a little hesitant. Together, we'll be twice as bold as we'd be alone. I might end up writing a paper on the experience. You never know."

Look, I tell him, I don't want to screw.

That didn't come out right.

Them. I don't want to screw one of them.

"You think I do?" Skebo replies. "My sex drive and the state of Missouri have irreconcilable differences. We're just going out there to learn."

Learn what?

"Are the chicks into mutual funds? Would they consider doing a Maidenform easy-on, easy-off commercial? Do any of them have the personalized license plate, 'I Hump'? There's probably never been a Legal Pad out there except to keep score. Should blow a few minds."

I have to agree. His paper will either be a raving success, or they'll make him join Sociologists Anonymous.

"You might even write a column about the place." Pause for effect. "That is, if you ever learn how."

My friend is beginning to piss me off, which, I suspect is the desired effect.

I can go to Four Corners any time I want to, I blurt out, and be 10 times cooler than you.

"Oh, yeah?"

Yeah.

And that's why the two of us are in the back seat of a cab speeding toward the front gate.

Driver: "Where to?"

Skebo and I look at each other like two schoolboys with zits on parade and a dozen Playboys under our bed.

Driver: "C'mon, don't make me guess."

Skebo: "Uh, Four Corners."

Driver: "Popular destination."

Me, not wanting him to get the wrong idea. "Oh, no, it's not what you think. We're on a fact-finding mission."

Driver: "Yeah, to see how big their pussies are."

Skebo, academically: "No, to see what motivates the women to pursue this line of work and to see if they can be retrained."

Driver: "Bullshit."

Me, trying to put the matter into proper perspective: "Besides, these women are in the big leagues of their profession. We're just in rookie ball. Wouldn't be fair to us or them."

Driver, throwing up his hands: "No wonder we're losing the fucking war."

I'm surprised when we arrive. It's a simple block building with trailers in the rear and a nice stand of trees in front of the parking lot.

Nothing that screams out sex or sin or even moonlight madness.

Traditionalist that I am, I'm expecting red lights and the sound of a player piano filtering through a velvet vestibule with Trudy and Mary Beth going back and forth on the porch swing.

Instead, there's a blaring "Me and Bobby McGee" from a cheap-sounding jukebox, a creakier screen door than on the Friendy Market back home and some 280-pound security guy telling us to quit staring our goddamn eyes out.

Inside, there's a liquor store, a row of pool tables and two dozen or so women playing touchy-feely with the clientele.

It's like there's an unwritten rule. If you're standing by the pool tables, you're up for grabs.

Literally.

If you and your boner remain seated in the back of the room, the babes look at you funny like how could you bench yourself at a time like this, but they respect your right to keep your pants on.

I watch a guy much uglier than me being led away by an over-Revloned brunette with a dress that barely covers her personal region and fingernails that could cut brush out on the highway.

Part of me wants to get in the game. It's been too many months and there's no wooing and cooing and do you come here often? You just flash your 15 bucks and resin up your bow.

But the rest of me - the pencil-behind-the-ear part - says, whoa, baby. Could be disease. Could be an embarrassing failure to perform. Maybe I need at least a hint of romance. Maybe I'll run up against a broken barrette and beefstick breath and be unable to open my briefcase.

I see at least six women looking at me like I never got looked at in college. Rolling their lips. Rolling their tongues. Hissing like a viper and I'm the little rabbit.

At first, I feel flattered. I didn't score the title-clinching touchdown. I wasn't elected president of the fraternity. I didn't endow a toilet seat, much less a chair.

And these chicks want me anyway.

But then whorehouse reality sets in.

I look at their hosiery that bullets couldn't penetrate, and the caked-on rouge that could conceal leprosy, and how they can hustle a guy from the pool tables to their trailers faster than the cashier at the Piggley Wiggly can ring up a frozen dinner.

They know - or at least suspect - that I have a pecker. That alone makes me a preferred customer.

A crisis develops: Do I stay, or do I do what shy guys everywhere have done for generations when the chips are down?

Pretend we've forgotten something and hightail it out of the room as fast as we can.

I'm in the parking lot in less than five seconds. I take refuge behind a Pinto off to the side where a wooden fence separates Four Corners from the lucky property owner next door.

I have to go back inside. Skebo will blab it to the whole platoon if I don't. But I can wait long enough that the chicks will have fresh visions of sugarplums and forget they ever saw me.

I'm prepared to pretend I've passed out, but no one comes near. I watch as more cabs pull up and troops rush inside in such numbers that the screen door sounds like a drum roll.

Why can't I be like them? Why do I always have to lag back? Why am I always on the outside looking in?

But never mind that right now. I hatch a plan. The best plan of all. A get-out-of-here-without-embarrassing-myself plan.

I'll swagger through the door like there's a blackjack between my legs and I'm about to declare martial law with every babe in the place. But what's this? An appendicitis attack. I can't pleasure a trailer park full of women if I'm in unbearable pain. They'll carry me out, but just as they're about to throw me in the back of the Jeep, I'll conduct a laying on of the hands and declare a miraculous recovery. Everybody in the makeshift medical team will praise the Lord all the way back to the barracks and I'm home-free.

Gathering all the fortitude that's inside me to get, I make my return. The security guard grunts in non-recognition, a good sign. I look to the pool tables, expecting to see the girls whisper to themselves, "Psst, there's the Thing From The Parking Lot. Let's laugh hysterically at his total inability to be a man."

But they're grabbing at the second wave of troops and don't even look my way. They wouldn't know me from vegetation.

Skebo is jabbering with a guy I don't know. It's as if my roommate doesn't even know I left.

I don't need my appendix for this caper, much less for it to burst.

"Uh, sorry about taking off like that," I say, sitting down. "Big commotion outside. Bunch of non-coms thought we were being attacked, but it was just a meteor shower."

"Do you know who this is?" Skebo asks breathlessly.

I look at the straight-arrow in his late 20s who looks like a cross between a potentate and a Ruritan.

"He's a cop. Plainclothes."

Then why doesn't he arrest somebody? It's the easiest multiple choice. All of the above.

"He's staking the place out. Just looking around. Like us."

Well, what of it?

"Don't you see? This is your big chance."

I don't follow.

An exasperated look comes over Skebo's face as he pulls me aside.

"Do I have to do everything for you?" he whispers. "Do you want to be a newspaperman?"

Yes.

"And what is it that newspapermen do?"

Uh, type.

"They interview people, dumb ass. We're sitting with a guy who arrests whores and dukes it out with pimps. Don't you think that's interesting? Wouldn't you like to find out more?"

Yeah, but...

I look at the lawman. He's obviously been around a lot of idiots. He's smiling.

"You have no idea what to ask, do you?" Shebo says.

I feel lower than groundhog shit.

"You want me to do it for you, don't you?"

I nod like Goofy on little blue pills.

"Geez, all right."

Skebo looks at the guy he's only known for a few minutes and Jim Bishops him.

"Is Four Corners the only brothel in these parts?"

"Pretty much. You used to have Ozark Ikes, the Black & White and the Red Door, but they're out of business. There're a couple of rinky-dink operations, but this is the only one that brings 'em in by the carload." Pause. "Like with you boys."

I wince. We're researchers. What do we have to do? Wear a sign?

"What happened to the other establishments?" Skebo asks.

"Shootings, competition for territory, competition for the girls."

"Is coming here something you usually do on Saturday night?"

"Yeah, I want 'em to see my face. Let 'em know I ain't been run off."

"Have you ever had a gun pulled on you working the whorehouse beat?"

"Hell, yes. One time the bastards put a $10,000 contract out on me. Never got scared 'cept on the Fourth of July. Every time something went boom, I checked myself for holes."

"Are the girls local?"

"A few, but mostly they come down from St. Louis and and Chicago. Work a few payday weekends and then go back."

"How often do you guys raid this place?"

"At least once a month. Take the GIs back to the post in a paddy wagon. Run the girls in on $500 fines, but the pimps bail 'em out and they're back in the trailers in less than two hours."

"So you're not exactly a popular person around here."

"Fuck, no. The worst time was when the MPs and the cops were gonna hit Four Corners at the same time. Communications screw-up and the MPs are 30 minutes late. Me and another officer are standing in against eight or 10 bad guys. We had to fight our way out. I blew a shell from a 12-gauge shotgun through the roof, but that didn't even slow 'em down. They beat the living shit out of us. I broke a rib and was spitting out teeth. Had to go to the hospital.

"They ain't gonna be here much longer, though. Won't be in business. Attorney-General's on their ass. FBI's on their ass. CID's on their ass. There won't even be a mattress they can call their own. You boys better have your fun now. Army's getting ready to put Four Corners officially off limits. Never mind jumping a whore. Just walk inside to take a load off and it's an Article 16."

"Have you ever had it out with the people who own Four Corners?" Skebo wants to know.

"Never see 'em. It's like they're invisible. You can get a search warrant and go room to room, but all you ever get are pimps and pussy. We keep hearing that it's organized crime. Mob boys out of Kansas City. They set up whorehouses outside military bases the way McDonald's hands out franchises."

The cop looks at his watch.

"Better go find some lawbreakers who don't use their dicks."

He makes a little hole with the thumb and forefinger of his left hand and brings his other middle finger through it. The grin gets more salacious with every upward thrust.

"You boys go ahead and get you some. Just wait 'til I'm gone."

I start to tell the man we're not Action Jacksons, but Skebo waves me off.

"Thanks for talking to us, sir," he says officially. "You've certainly served to enhance the moment."

I look at Skebo like he's crazy. There isn't going to be any moment.

"Shut up," Skebo says under his breath as he waves goodbye. "A news source is like a customer. He's always right."

The lawman purposely bumps into the security guard on the way out, slams the screen door extra hard and he's gone.

I'm ready to leave, too. It's been quite a night. We've seen women more aggressive than defensive backs, talked with the Eliot Ness of the anti-whore movement and contributed to the GNP of mob rule.

But Skebo will not be moved.

"Can't go back yet."

Why not?

"Oh, I can. You're the one who has more to do."

More what?

"This observer thing. You keep hiding behind it. When are you going to do something on your own?"

I don't have an answer. The pitcher of beer I inhaled while the town cop held forth has taken away any chance of a snappy rejoinder. And there's something else. He's right.

"You've got to put yourself in jeopardy. Cut loose from that safety net."

I slip through the Blue Ribbon haze long enough to ask myself loudly why I should listen to this guy. So what if I look through the rear window the rest of my life? Why should he care?

"Challenge yourself," Skebo goes on. "Come face to face with whatever it is you're afraid of."

"Getting caught," I mumble. "I hate getting caught."

"Why?" Skebo asks.

"Being embarrassed. Being stared at. Being put on display."

My friend is trying to help me. My friend also has an uncanny knack for doing the right things. Why should I fight him? Maybe he can bring me out of the wilderness.

"You don't have to be like that," Skebo says gently. "You can change if you want to. Do you want to?"

I just sit there the way I did when my father enrolled me in business. It's my way of saying, OK, do me.

He looks behind the bar at enough half-pints to take out an entire battalion.

And he looks at my footwear - calf-high cowboy boots that I bought because it doesn't matter what color socks you wear under them and my grandparents gave me lots of pink ones.

"Big boots, aren't they?"

"So?"

"Who's the CQ tonight?" Skebo asks.

"Haddox," I reply.

"Perfect."

His eyes light up.

"What's the rule they hammer into us above all others?"

"Don't sneak liquor on post," I tell him.

"Under penalty of what?"

"The DIs don't say and we never ask because they'll presume guilt. Probably somewhere between 50 lashes and the penitentiary."

Skebo grins.

I see where this is going.

"No damn way. Out of the question. I'm not doing it."

Skebo does his business at the cash register. Gin, tequila, vodka, two bourbons and a Cutty Sark.

"We can mix and match. Extended cocktail hour. Maybe invite the buffing machine."

"You're not getting the picture," I tell him. "I'm not a rum-runner."

He jams three half-pints into my left boot and three into my right. I take a step and it's like the Tin Man without oil.

Skebo turns into the fiery football coach who's down 28 points at halftime.

"You WILL get this contraband to A-2-2. You WILL get past the CQ. You WILL get six troops off. And I'm not going to help you."

With that, he bolts out the door and flags a cab. By the time the haze lifts, I'm sitting on the stoop wearing my own personal crime scene.

Tough love.

Until now I've only read about it.

Let's see. I could crawl in a ditch and die. First person to find me gets a free stupor.

I could stay at Four Corners until closing time and ask for a ride back to the base. They'd take me halfway to Kansas City, rob me, stab me and leave me to decompose until I fit right in with what grows under the guardrail.

Or I could put on my grownup training wheels and chart my own course.

I take stock of the situation.

Most of the beer has worn off. That's good.

I clank when I walk. Bad.

Some of the smuggling tales my mother told me at bedtime are coming back. Good.

Those stupid stories always kept me awake for hours. Bad.

The strip is winding down. What was a swirl of neon has been reduced to the occasional glow from a distant instrument panel. Even the tattoo parlor across the street has turned on its night light.

I reject the idea of a ride in a cab or any other conveyance. The MPs at the main gate have been known to shine lights on late-arrivals in back seats, and I've never done well with shined lights. Tonight, I'm wearing guilt like an Indian headdress. I'd crack before their high-beams even got to the upholstery.

Nope, I'll have to slink my way back.

I look around one of the private parking lots just outside the base. Too many floodlights. Too much fence. Too much chained-up dog.

I explore the rear of a service station. If I stack enough pallets, I might be able to scale the barbed wire.

Then I remember nimbleness lost. I move only slightly better than Frankenstein climbing the National Monument. There will be no leaps on my great return. No bounds.

But what's this way off to the right? Why, a subdivision for the unfortunate shits who vowed loyalty to this place and were rewarded with pea-green split-levels.

There's a fence, but just high enough for home-run distance at a Little League field. No checkpoints. No back-porch lights. No snarling animals on patrol. Just a Lawn Boy soaking up dew and a couple of squeaky kids' toys by a swing set. If I step on them, I deserve the stockade.

I advance to the basketball goal in the side yard. This is the closest I'll ever come to walking point. No calling in artillery. No calling in reinforcements. Just the very real chance I'll be aimed at by the non-com of the house who got up to go to the bathroom and saw an unidentified small forward cowering under the rim.

A baby cries, and I dive to the ground. There's a crash against my right shinbone as if the timpani player tried to make up for missing his first cue by doubling up on the second. All the liquor bottles on that side of my leg crack open. Shards of glass slice a path to my ankle on a swift current of 86-proof. It feels like a punch bowl disintegrated and the embarrassed hostess dumped the works into my sock.

I go into my best low-crawl. Dear God, please make Mr. and Mrs. E-5 tell their toddler to suck it up. Please let them look upon prowlers as friends they haven't met yet.

A minute passes. Then another. I don't dare move. This isn't just National Rifle Association territory. This is where they go to train. Blades of wet grass poke around inside my nose, probing for a weakness, but my septum will not be moved. It is the performance of a lifetime.

I'm 30 feet from the street. Thirty feet from being able to claim that I'm taking a 2 a.m. constitutional on broken glass so I can practice pain management.

I look for living-room lights to be turned on. For curtains to spread apart. For front doors to burst open.

They've got to hear me. Try as I might, I'm breathing like a water buffalo.

And they've got to see me. Six-foot earthworms aren't native to these parts.

Nothing. Just a bunch of birds pissed that they've being driven to the power line a full six hours ahead of schedule.

I've made it. All I have to do is hoof the three miles back to the barracks with a right foot that feels like I'm walking on a broken window.

But after what I've been through, limping is a cinch. There are no whores to hide from. No cops to interview. No mob boys to die for.

I've gotten past a mom, a baby, a Lawn Boy and a bladder-deficient NCO. I'd click my heels if I had enough morphine.

Subterfuge, I am thine. The hell with inventory-control school. Let's change my AIT to something where they give you top-secret briefings and little cyanide pills.

Blood has soaked through my boot, and it smells as if a distillery has been built on my ankles and the works piped up my leg.

One whiff and Haddox will know I not only showered in the stuff, I used it as body oil.

Skebo thinks I'll walk meekly into the CQ and say, hey Sarge, ever seen a moving violation of the Army's liquor policy? Well, I walk, I talk, I crawl on my belly like a reptile.

Well, it isn't going to happen. I've come too far to fail now. By God, six troops are going to drink a toast to 2 a.m., even if one of their number has more foreign bodies in him than a Sergio Leone film.

I stop at a Pepsi machine, drop 15 cents into the slot and pour the contents into the inflamed boot. It sends my sock over the flood line, but never mind that. Haddox will smell soda pop instead of speakeasy and let me pass.

I get to the company area and see Skebo and Carouthers looking out the window. If Haddox hassles me, I'll tell him I've been at a wine-tasting at the Book Lovers Club and somebody read a couple of extraordinary paragraphs and the Chablis started flying. I'm not really gassed, just in metaphorical high spirits.

Timidly, as is my way, I tiptoe in the ÇQ.

Haddox is reading a fuck book.

"Who the hell are you? It's after-hours. Company personnel only."

I cannot believe this. I've trained seven weeks under this guy. Been told I'm a dickhead by this guy. Been esophagus to esophagus with this guy. Had my bunk almost ripped apart by this guy.

And he doesn't have any idea who I am.

My prophecy from the beginning of the cycle has been fulfilled. I'm mere days from getting out of this place and he wouldn't know me from Alan Ginsberg's poetry pal.

"Uh, my buddy in A-2-2 lost his billfold at the PX and I'm bringing it back to him."

He turns the page.

"Can I give it to him?"

"What?"

The man's a complete idiot. Until now, I've only heard about people who have the cerebellum of a rotten orange. He suspects nothing. He's too busy hoping there's a color picture.

"The wallet. You know, his money."

"I don't give a shit."

Between the Pepsi and the fair maiden's flesh heaving under the stud's stiletto of a prick, I have MacArthured myself.

I trickle up the stairs. So does the blood. If there's an inquiry, I'll say it was an unsuccessful transplant. They tried to give me some heart for this place, but my body rejected it.

I no sooner reach the top step and Carouthers makes a substantial withdrawal from my good leg. The man's cat-quick. I don't even break stride.

"Good stuff, man," Carouthers says, pulling on the tequila.

I explain there was an accident in transit, but that's what happens when you don't insure delivery with shin guards.

"I'm happy you got here with what you did," Carouthers says. "Skebo didn't give you a chance in hell. Said we'd have to go back to Four Corners and scrape your ass off the side of the road."

"Where is that porky bastard?"

Carouthers points to the bathroom where in front of Stall 2 Skebo has assumed the worst lotus position of the cycle.

"Ah, sir, if I could interrupt your meditation a minute, I made it and you said I couldn't. How do you feel now, oh exalted one?"

"Wise," he says, burping. "Very wise. For once, you acted instead of reacted. Forgive me the military analogy, but you climbed over the wall with the first wave instead of waiting for the women and children. I knew you could do it."

"Then why did you tell Carouthers I'd need a rescue mission?"

"Simple. I threw out bad vibes so your karma would trump it. Your spirit heard me say we'd have to throw you in the back of a truck and you said, nope, ain't gonna happen. You fed off the doubt and it made you stronger. All part of my master plan."

Shit. Even drunk, the guy is dead-on.

I bow obedience. What else can I do? He's the Gandhi of the platoon. Just let him drop 130 pounds and give him a cane.

Skebo begins the slow process of trying to get to his feet. I'd like to watch, but I need to coagulate.

"We sure proved one thing tonight," Skebo says.

He stops halfway to rest.

"That your boots can do more than walk."

CHAPTER 9

Ya comes running into the room holding a copy of *Sports Illustrated*.

"It's him, it's him," he hollers, pointing to an article halfway through the magazine.

The story is about highly touted high school football players from the class of 1967 who signed college scholarships, but didn't make it to the end for one reason or another.

Several coaches and athletic directors are interviewed about the alarmingly high percentage. The article concludes with a "Where Are They Now?" chart that tracks dozens of grid prospects who never had occasion to rent that cap and gown.

Listed toward the bottom is Wilson Andrews, the guy we've been calling Hercules. I follow his name across the page.

"Position - Fullback."

"Strengths - Power. Size. Intelligence."

"College - University of Tennessee."

"Career highlights - Had promising freshman season."

"Academic proficiency - Flunked out."

"Current whereabouts - Last seen on back of garbage truck."

We run a fly pattern to Hercules' room and show him the story.

"Oh, shit," he says, putting down the Brasso. He scans it and takes on the countenance of a bed-wetter forced to appear before the House

Unsanitary Activities Commission.

"Are you the same Wilson?" we ask.

"Yes."

"Is the chart accurate?"

Word gets out that Hercules is on the griddle. Half the platoon fans out on either side of the door until they look like a glee club.

He doesn't say anything.

"It's all right," Skebo says, gently. "We just want to know, that's all."

"I was good in high school, but not that good," Hercules testifies. "I'd run over you from three yards out and score the touchdown, but the guy Tennessee really wanted was our halfback. Fastest football player I've ever played with. And the toughest. Tackling him was like trying to grab hold of a Roto-Rooter. I blocked for him. We were a helluva combination. Only lost two games in three years.

"College recruiters called me a couple of times a week, but they camped out on Quinton's doorstep. We were best friends. Even double-dated together. He'd never seen a white couple make out before and I'd never seen blacks. Did it in shifts so we could look on.

"He decided he wouldn't go to a college unless they took me, too. The day before the college SATs, he got a concussion on a pass play over the middle. Spent the night in the emergency room. Proctor passes out the test booklet and his head is pounding so hard he can barely think straight, much less get the answers right.

"I scored an 1140, plenty enough for UT. Quinton came up way short. He had to throw up halfway through the verbal and didn't even have time to finish.

"The football staff heard about his test score and panicked that they were going to lose one of their top recruits. A few days passed and the phone rings. It's one of the coaches. He's got this deal for me. I take another SAT, only this time I sign up as Quinton. Said it was no big deal. Happens all the time.

"My gut told me this was wrong and I could get in trouble, so I told the man no. Then he got mad and said they were only interested in giving me a scholarship because me and Quinton were tight. Said if I turned him down, I wouldn't get a scholarship from UT or anybody else. 'We'll put the word out on you, son', he told me."

"So what did you do?" I ask.

"What any kid who wanted to play big-time football would. I gave in. Took the test again in two weeks. Got an 1190. Quinton joked about how he beat me.

"So he got his scholarship and I got mine. Everything was cool for a while. I made second-string on the freshman team and Quinton ran back punts and kickoffs.

"Then he fell in with a different crowd and we didn't see much of each other. He started partying more and going to class less. The desire that he had in high school was gone. He became an OK player, nothing more. Hanging out at the right places became more important than the game.

"The coaches realized Quinton wasn't going to be an Earth-shaker on the field. If he transferred, or if he quit, it wouldn't be a big blow to the program. And they sure as hell weren't going to keep a scholarship for his friend from high school.

"So I get called in to the office. Damn near a platoon of coaches in front of me. One after another they accuse me of taking the SAT for him. I say that's what they told me to do. They say I did it to cheat for my buddy. My word against theirs.

"I'll never forget it. Long brown table. Carpet like a putting green. Big paintings on the wall. It was like I was at a State Department briefing, except they were telling me I had broken an NCAA rule and they were booting me out of school. To make it look good, they signed me up for a full load of classes next semester. When I didn't show up, it went in the books that I flunked out."

"What about Quinton? Didn't he stand up for you?" Skebo asks.

"He couldn't do anything. His scholarship was hanging by a thread. We were just a couple of kids and those guys could have their way with the president of the university. He had no shot. I never blamed him."

"Shit, man," says Carouthers, who knows a thing or two about injustice.

"That wasn't all. If I talked, they had this English lit major who was prepared to swear I had sex with her against her will. All we ever did was meet in the library a few times. Always her idea, too. If I wasn't such a rube, I would have known she was a plant. I'll tell you this. The CIA has nothing on Division 1 coaches. They'll do whatever it takes."

"So what did you do?" I ask.

"You mean after lying and telling my family I couldn't cut it with the books? And then lying and telling the local sports reporters?"

"Yeah, after that."

"Got a job on my home town's garbage truck. I figured life doesn't get any more anonymous than watching a bunch of maggots bench-press a hamburger bun. Kind of enjoyed it, really. Hell of a lot less stress than trying to remember which formation to be in on second down and eight. Street department gave me a free jacket, free work gloves and weekends off. That's a lot more than the university gave me. Draft came up and here I am."

Choirmaster Skebo steps up.

"You didn't have to be so secretive with us. There aren't any reporters out here."

He looks at me.

"Except maybe this guy, but he's not ready to interview people yet. If you were a goal post he might be able to pull it off."

I love the way my friend builds my confidence.

"Maybe I was too paranoid, but put yourself in my shoes," Hercules says. "The same coaches are still on the sidelines and the girl is still in school. How long is the statute of limitations on trumped-up morals charges? You find out and tell me. Right now, the way I feel is if I don't get any questions, I don't have to make up any answers. I loved it when you guys called me Hercules. It was like finding a perfect hiding place. Then this."

He throws the magazine on the floor.

"You're trapped, aren't you?" I ask.

"That's a fair assessment. Goes something like this: Employer looks at my file and says, hmm, good student in high school. Earned a college scholarship. Made A's and B's as a freshman. Then a 0.0 GPA sophomore year. Hmm, obvious lack of motivation. But wait, let's have the guy explain why all of a sudden he couldn't even make a "D." Hmm, he clams up. OK, that's the way the kid wants it. Let's give the job to somebody else."

"So what's your plan?" Skebo wants to know.

"Finish basic. Go to infantry school. Go to Vietnam. Can't start over here. Maybe I can there."

He's interrupted by the loudest whistle we've heard since the reception center. What's going on? It's Sunday night. Graduation in six days. Supposed to be downhill from here.

But no.

"Fall out, goddammit."

It's Haddox.

We race down the stairs and dress-right-dress like we've been doing it all our lives. Forty sets of boots click as one.

Wait a minute. Where are the other four platoons? If this is going to be a group function, let's mail out all the invitations.

Just us.

"Robison says you've been a good cycle," he rants. "Litton says so. Probably the goddamn colonel at battalion thinks so. Fuck 'em. I think you're a bunch of pricks."

The words are the same that he's spewed for as long as we've known him, but the presentation is different. His belt is flapping almost to his hip. One pant leg is tucked neatly inside his boot as per regulations, but the other is flying free. His insignia is nowhere to be seen. He's not as much wearing his Smokey hat as he is cocking it.

"Son of a bitch is drunk," Carouthers whispers.

Keeping us at attention, Haddox walks through the ranks. Ya's chin isn't high enough. The DI comes under it hard with the side of his hand. We can hear teeth chattering.

He breaks the guidon over his knee and tells Nordquist he couldn't lead piss to the stream.

"Where's that fat fuck who's always taking up for everybody?"

"Here, drill sergeant."

Skebo takes two steps forward. Boldly, almost triumphantly. It's as if he knows all this crap is winding down and he needs one more war story to tell his grandchildren.

Haddox staggers in front of him.

"You know what you are, don't you?"

"No, drill sergeant. What am I?"

"A prick with a big boil on the end of it. Know how to get rid of it?"

"No, drill sergeant."

Haddox puts his hands inside Skebo's belt, steps on his toes and lifts up as hard as he can.

It's hard to imagine a more painful sub-orbital flight. Skebo hits the ground like a construction accident.

Several seconds pass as he assesses the damage to his balls.

"Permission to relieve myself, drill sergeant," Skebo groans.

"Permission granted, ass-face."

Skebo crawls into the barracks.

"Fat man ain't the worst troop of this outfit. Peavey ain't the worst troop."

Haddox is balancing himself on what's left of the guidon. Using it as a half-crutch, half-pointer, the DI locates his quarry.

Kippler.

He holds out the stick.

"Wanna suck on it? You know, like last time."

The platoon seizes its breath. Kippler has barely spoken since that afternoon at the rifle range when Waldsburger rescued him from having to go down on his weapon of choice.

"Actually, drill sergeant, I didn't suck on it. Sucking is like this."

He makes like a trout out of water.

"What I did was more like this."

He moves his mouth back and forth like an asthmatic during a smog alert.

"Finding the correct nomenclature isn't easy. You could call it sniffing. You could even call it coughing. But sucking? No. Afraid not."

As in previous such performances, Kippler is worthy of a Broadway opening. Too bad there's just a row of street lights with moths flying underneath. There should be spotlights. And curtain calls. And standing ovations.

This is the part in the show where Haddox steps away. Cussing and throwing things, to be sure, but realizing he's not going to win. Kippler's too good. Too nonplussed. Too much the debate champion. Just let it go and pick on somebody the next time who isn't going to be on the Supreme Court before he's 40.

But tonight Haddox is writing a new ending.

"See how high I'm stepping," the DI screams, raising his knees to mock height. "I'm wading through all your bullshit."

The man is close enough that Kippler's nose is almost pressed against his chest.

"You think I'm stupid, don't you, motherfucker? You think you can talk college to the ignorant drill sergeant, and you can laugh your ass off. Well, who's laughing now?"

Haddox is really roaring. Lights are coming on all over the quad.

The little troop just stands there.

The silence makes Haddox madder. He needs a line to play off. Fluffy pillow, maybe. Or disappearing endoplasm.

But Kippler gives him nothing. Eyes straight. Shoulders back. A Munchkin Patton.

"Fuck you," Haddox says.

Not even a quiver.

The DI pushes him.

"I said, fuck you, goddammit."

Kipppler falls back a full four feet. He rights himself and gets back to attention.

Haddox can't stand it. He wants sass, not rigid compliance.

The DI shoves Kippler again.

"Fuck your momma."

Suddenly Kippler lowers his shoulder and mounts a ground offensive on the DI's civilian leg. Limited warfare. One shinbone and one shinbone only.

A more surprise attack has never been launched in the annals of military history. Haddox does the one-step fandango for a second or two before the leg buckles and he falls back on the concrete. He screams in pain. We've been wondering what the man's weak spot is. Now we know. He has your grandfather's coccyx.

Haddox pounds the ground with his hands. With a temporarily paralyzed ass, that's all he can beat up. He's like a spider with a squished center. The appendages move, but they don't know why.

His vocal cords are unaffected, however.

"You little motherfucker," he shouts. "You're dead. You got that?"

Kippler returns to attention. The bowling over of the DI was a now-you-see-it, now-you-don't.

Haddox tries to stand, but it's not going to happen.

"Only one thing gonna save your life. Blow me. In front of all your peckerhead buddies. Right here, right now."

He tries to loosen his belt, but the harder he tugs the tighter it gets.

"Report for duty, pretty boy. Bring your pussy mouth front and center. That's an order, private."

Kippler stays where he is, but Haddox doesn't notice. He's too busy trying to pull his pants down with his thumbs.

Suddenly, a deuce-and-a-half rumbles down Caisson Avenue. It careens over the curb and jerks to a halt in front of our horizontal bars.

A bunch of guys jump out the back. Their leading man races to Haddox and says a call came in that a trainee was being sexually abused at A-2-2, and your pants pulled down to your knees with your cock hanging out is more than enough grounds for suspicion, and your sorry ass will be herewith removed to the stockade.

"Skebo," Rodriguez concludes. "From the CQ."

The DI screams that they're all communist bastard motherfuckers, but his words hold no sway. He kicks one guy and head-butts another, but is quickly subdued and thrown in the back of the truck in the manner of a mail sack. The driver throws it in reverse, there's a screech of tires and a thud signifying a shifting of the weight of the sack, and they're gone.

Three minutes, tops. The MPs aren't that good. It takes them that long to find their shiny helmets.

Must be covert ops. A special squad dedicated to goodness and mercy.

Whoever they are, I'm spellbound. It's my first palace coup.

Waldsburger is probably at a weiner roast somewhere. That means Nordquist is in charge.

"Uh, stand down. Or stand up. I don't care."

We don't know what to say to Kippler. This is his greatest moment.

Hell, our greatest moment. But he knows what we saw that day at the rifle range. The one time he didn't have all the right words. The one time he broke down.

There's tremendous awkwardness, which can only be warded off by tremendous sensitivity.

Which we, being a bunch of guys, cannot muster. The backdrop of blow job is too much to overcome. We think where his throat almost was, and we'd no sooner get near it than a radiation leak.

"Uh, ah, good job there," Peavey mumbles, making absolutely no eye contact and making sure not to touch him.

We almost treat it like a bereavement - filing past Kippler like he's stretched out with $100 worth of flowers on either side of his ears.

We even refer to the troop in the past tense.

"God, he was good," Hercules says as he walks by the bier.

"The man couldn't have done more for morale unless he airlifted us out of this place," I chime in, paying my respects.

We turn to leave, wakes not being a required part of our training.

"Wait, wait, don't you want to know how I did it?" Kippler calls out.

Are you kidding? We're dying to find out. We just need some kind of sign from Kippler that he's OK with what we saw.

"I'm not damn dead, you know."

That's what we were looking for. We crowd around in eager anticipation for the return-from-exile story that will knock Napoleon on his ass.

"I was on my high school's wrestling team and ..."

We get back on our feet. I mean, shit, if he's going to lie to us.

"It's true, it's true," Kippler insists. "Dad made me go out for a sport because he wanted to make me more well-rounded. I picked wrestling because I knew where their locker room was."

The troops keep walking, still not hearing anything we can believe.

"But the guys on the team asked me to leave after two weeks."

We about-face in perfect understanding. Kippler has his audience back.

"We were practicing takedowns one day when the coach asked if we wanted to learn to break somebody's leg. It was like asking a bunch of welders if they'd like to see an acetylene torch. I thought he was kidding. This was wrestling. Break our ears off maybe.

"But the coach gets into his crouch like this."

Kippler gives his best impression of a geriatric sumo wrestler.

"Then the man charges against this kid's unsuspecting leg. He's holding it and saying, 'Boys, this thing is as stiff as the stakes on one of my tomato plants. You put that kind of pressure on an unsuspecting opponent and he can only do one of two things. Fall down or...' "

Kippler snaps a twig's worth of air.

We get the picture. Excruciating pain and a six-inch scar that he'll have for the rest of his life.

"Haddox is pushing me and I know it isn't going to stop. I can keep standing there and he'll have me backed up to Interstate 40 by morning."

Pause for dramatic effect.

"Or I could take decisive action."

Kippler has us eating out of his hand. Toppling a DI. To the Vietnam generation, this is our Objective Burma.

"I knew all this was patently illegal. Drill sergeants aren't supposed to discuss dicks other than clinically as in what happens to them in the event of chemical attack.

"DIs aren't supposed to mention blowing, and sucking isn't even on the chart. I felt I had a pretty solid case should it get to evidentiary proceedings.

"Haddox stumbled a little when he pushed me that last time. I looked at his leg and that's when I thought of the coach's special takedown. Prior to that, the only thing I could remember about wrestling had been the guys giving me a pink belly for what they said was general principles.

"I got a mental picture of what I was going to do, did the sign of the cross and went at him with all I had."

He takes our questions.

"So you decided on a quick strike."

"Exactly. I knew if my response lasted for any length of time, it would be considered retaliatory in nature, and the onus could shift back on me."

"Can you quit using such big fucking words?"

"Sorry."

"You had to realize that tackling a DI has probably never been done before, not even at Valley Forge and those guys were starving."

"I considered that, yes. I also considered performing fellatio on something that's gas-operated and air-cooled."

"How did it feel having Haddox's leg in your hands?"

"Like I was president of the United States."

"How did you feel when the shithead got hauled off to jail?"

"That he was going to a better place."

Long silence. There has to be some mention of what happened at the rifle range. The platoon needs closure. Kippler's throat needs closure.

"It was OK back there," Skebo says diplomatically. "You were under a great deal of pressure. Anybody here would have, you know, gotten emotional."

Kippler rises to his full height, which is just barely being able to stand up at the five-foot mark at the pool.

"What do you mean, gotten emotional?"

"You know, crying and all."

"I wasn't crying."

"But we could see the tears. A few more minutes and you would have been at flood stage."

"Clearly, you have a problem with facial moisture," Kippler replies. "There's tears and there's sweat. It was a hot day. I was perspiring."

"You were whimpering. I saw it. Everybody saw it."

"Define whimpering."

"Sniffing," Skebo says. "You were doing a lot of sniffing."

"That's because there were a lot of smells in the air that afternoon. Dry-rotted pistol belts, as I recall. And sodden ammo pouches. My brain was saying, hey, this stuff stinks really bad. The information went out to my sensory receptors. Result: Sniffing."

Kippler's shaky this time. Sniffing, hell. Haddox finally beat him. We want Skebo to administer the verbal haymaker that will catch the troop in a lie.

It doesn't come.

"You're right, now that I think of it," Skebo says, backing down.

"Sweating. You were definitely sweating. I could tell by the salt formations."

We can't believe this. Let's inject some truth serum here.

"Can't you see how much this means to him?" Skebo tells us under his breath. "He's not going to win in the gym. He's not going to win on the field. Throwing words around is the only time he's somebody."

So what can we do?

"Let him carry the day," Skebo whispers.

"But he was crying and he won't admit it," Rodriguez says.

"Crying, shit," Ya adds. "It would have taken a horse blanket to dry his eyes."

"Let him walk away with his pride," Skebo says. "What's it going to hurt? We can count the hours until we're out of here. Tell it to your moms and dads and girlfriends, but don't tell it to him."

We follow our spiritual leader and murmur to Kippler that we must have been mistaken, too. Haddox was being his big turd self just as the relative humidity shot past 95 percent. You tried to wipe your brow, but sweat beads came tumbling down like Victoria Falls. It's amazing you didn't lose consciousness.

As always, Kippler has the last word.

"Must be this rare Ozark air."

I'm still laughing as we climb into the cattle car for night fire. Might as well laugh. They ran out of things for us to do so we spent the last two hours looking at gangrenous limbs. If my legs ever look like that, I hope they do more than shoot film of it.

And now I'm getting ready to fire bullets more important, at least in my opinion, than any shot at the Alamo.

And thanks to the moon pulling all the covers over its head, the aiming will take place in total darkness. We motor past the quick-fire range. There's more light inside one of Bela Lugosi's capes.

Ten shots into the blackness. I need three if I want to change addresses.

I try to intellectualize the situation.

The Armed Services of this great nation isn't going to hold three lousy rounds against me. My paperwork has been processed. All our paperwork has been processed. Graduation is tomorrow. They need to know who's going to be passing in front of the colonel's reviewing stand and who isn't. I've made it this far. They won't deny me now. The results are already in. I've passed.

But there's another scenario I can't shake.

The screws must maintain discipline. Must maintain standards. Must not let anyone off easy.

Can't shoot? Can't go home. If we make an exception for one, we'd have to make exceptions for all the dickheads.

You want a free ride? No way, pal. Hit the prescribed number of targets or else we'll be requesting the pleasure of your company at the next cycle.

The truck stops. It's so dark the cadre guy has our driver aim his headlights so we'll know where to go.

I trudge up the hill like a cow going to the meat-packing plant. It'll be another eight weeks before I see Kathy. Another eight weeks before my parents can say I graduated something other than college.

We file by the corporal of the bullets who passes out the 10-round clips with assorted tracer rounds. Because he can't see anything either, he touches us on our shoulders first before working his way down to our hands.

DI Cannon announces over the PA that DI Hicks, a former sharpshooter with Special Services, will show us how it's done.

Hicks assumes the prone-supported position, props the M16 on the sandbag and looks out at the 25-meter target that's disguised as a black cat.

The orange tracer whistles 10 feet over the silhouette.

"Having made visual contact, the shooter will now make the proper adjustments," the PA drones.

Another shot rings out.

Cadre guy No. 2 walks out halfway with a flashlight. He hollers back that the target is still standing.

Hicks fires off another tracer. It misses by the length of a mobile home.

"Fuck," Hicks says.

Another shot. Another go-around with the flashlight. Another no-kill.

A fresh tracer rushes to daylight. We watch it hit the dirt 15 feet in front of the silhouette and careen over its head.

"Bad hop," Skibo whispers.

Hicks squeezes off five more shots. The flashlight holder signals there is no need to call the half-soldier's next of kin.

"Fuck."

Hicks, an expert at this shit, has gone 0 for 10. What possible hope is there for me?

None, I conclude.

Just forget the whole thing and tell Kathy to send more panties. Take me to the reception center so I can meet the next batch of troops. May as well get to know each other. Let them see my ammo pouch. Be a great icebreaker.

But the PA system won't let me leave until the last act is in the books.

"Alpha Company, fall out left to right to the rear-numbered stakes."

We can't even see our knuckles, much less the feet of the guys in front of us. Some of us fall onto gravel that's been sharpened and left here by skilled craftsmen.

The tower is a distant planet. There's no permanent party to usher us to our spots as in previous bolt-carrier engagements. They're drinking coffee by the butt cans. It's late and they miss their fuck books.

I assign myself the final post. Peavey is beside me, but for all they know it could be Kissinger.

Naturally, somebody's steel pot falls off. It sounds like incoming. We wait for a DI to holler that somebody's going to get his goddamn ass kicked.

Nothing.

What is this? Free day?

There is no last-second pep talk. No, let's shoot one for the Gipper.

Our supervisory personnel are here in insignia only. It's as if they're as tired of the training as we are. It's as if we aren't the only ones who are short.

"Got to piss," Peavy declares.

He lets fly downwind of the sandbags. It sounds like someone turned on the tap.

This is a major rules violation. We're not supposed to urinate except inside factory-approved housing.

Peavey starts out cautiously with two fingers against his tool and playing it off to the side.

This is unbelievable. His stream is coming down in sheets. Even if they can't see what he's is doing, they can hear it.

Nothing.

Emboldened, the troop grabs hold with both hands like he's a fire hose and his mechanism is raging out of control.

Forget the Bill of Rights.

This is freedom.

I join him.

We who are about to be recycled deserve empty bladders.

There are no clear mountain streams at this shit pit. We'll have to settle for gurgling piss.

A sharp piece of gravel bites my ankle. The pugil-stick swinger deep inside me comes alive long enough to cuss out the night-fire permanent party for not policing their area.

The words bounce harmlessly off the rear-numbered stakes. But an idea is born, suckled by the night.

We have a disinterested cadre that can't see and can't hear.

We have rules that have been rules for almost two months that suddenly aren't rules any more.

And, Lord knows, we have a last stand of gravel - enough to raise welts on a division of enemy. That half-soldier 25 meters away doesn't have a chance. Any penetration is a hit, right? Bullet, act of God, stone -what does it matter?

I stuff the 10-round clip into my field jacket. Won't need it.

"Alpha Company, assume the firing position. The targets will stay up three seconds for each round. If you do not make contact, they will go down briefly and then reappear for Shot No. 2 and so on until you're fired all 10 rounds. Everybody got that?"

I pay no attention. I'm too busy gathering gravel.

"Alpha Company, lock and load."

I arm my right hand. I arm my left hand. Normally, I'm not ambidextrous, but this is war.

"Alpha Company, sight your target and commence firing."

I throw for all I'm worth. Fully grown stones. Pebbles. Boot residue. Anything that will render the silhouette unconscious.

There's a hail of gunfire up and down the line.

And a sound from my end like a rain cloud formed above the target and let out the briefest of storms.

The troops reload.

I re-rock.

The signal is given. They shoot. I hurl everything within hailing distance of my sandbags. I don't care about molecular structure. If the ground creature has mass, I fling it the 25 meters.

I'm throwing Chapstick, clumps of grass and an empty tin of shoe polish. Got to pass rifle training. Got to graduate.

Guys beside me are doing like they've been taught. Breathing calmly. Squeezing the trigger calmly.

The hell with that.

I'm throwing gumballs, packs of shoelaces and fingernail clippers. Anything for a knock-down. Anything to get out of here.

The whistle blows.

"Cease fire, Alpha Company. You ain't hitting nothing anyway."

I put down my Fig Newtons from Skebo's kitchen. This shows how desperate I am. I'm prepared to launch a basic food group.

We march back to the black hole of a control tower where we stand at parade rest and wait for our scores to come down the pike.

I try to relax. I did all I could do. Let fly more than 200 pieces of matter. Even discounting for windage and panic, at least some of them had to hit home.

Litton is given the figures. A hand comes over his mouth. He cannot believe what he is reading.

The captain summons his minions. Can this be right? Was there a recount?

We hear their whispered replies. Yes, it's true, they tell him. Unbelievable as it may seem.

"The night-fire results were generally poor," Litton announces. "Apparently, most of you had difficulty seeing the targets."

He looks skyward. There's greater visibility inside dog hockey.

"But one trainee put that behind him. One trainee didn't let the conditions affect his concentration. One trainee shot like it was broad daylight."

General. The big shit.

"This troop has not exactly been Mr. Success these past eight weeks. Hasn't shot well. Hasn't done well in morning inspections. In fact, he's been about this far from being a fuckup."

He puts his hands up by his crotch a dick-length apart. Ah, yes, peckers. Once again the Pentagon's measuring stick.

"But when the pressure was on, this man rose to the occasion. This man said, goddammit, I'm going to do what nobody expected me to do."

Litton is fired up. His adam's-apple hair is waving like a wheat field.

"This man came out here and shot the shit out of the targets. A perfect score. Ten out of 10. The next closest guy only got half that many.

"I want everybody to see what can happen when you apply every inch of your being into something."

I'm stuffing Fig Newtons back into my field jacket when he shouts out my name.

My body goes into emergency shutdown. This is praise. I am not programmed for praise.

"Alpha Company, attention," Litton orders. "Pay the proper respect to one of your own."

I can't walk. That would require presence of mind. I waddle.

"What do you say to somebody who lit up night-fire?" the captain screams. "C'mon, what do you say?"

Alpha Company applauds. A couple guys go retro and let out huzzahs.

Jesus, they actually think I gunpowdered the silhouettes. They don't know that I all I did was reroute a quarry's worth of fill.

I have no idea how you're supposed to act when you've been voted King of the Muzzle Velocity Court. I take a couple steps forward, tip my hat like Arnie walking to the 18th green at Pebble Beach and return to formation.

Litton will have none of that.

"Don't be so modest. Get to the head of the platoon. I want to shake your hand."

He pumps like there's oil at my elbow. I'm hoping Fig Newton particles don't come off.

"Hicks couldn't hit shit tonight and he was a goddamn superstar at Quantico. We've got us a trainee who leaves him crapping in the wind."

What can I say? I can throw like the Seventh Cavalry can ride.

"Ten out of 10 in this slop. Shit, that's the Olympic team, son. You know them interlocking rings? Shoot 'em right off."

Litton insists that I tell the men how I did it.

All I can think of are sports cliches.

"I made every round count. I shot like there was no tomorrow. You've got to dance with the rifle that brung you."

Not all the troops are buying it.

"Dumb bastard finally remembered to use his front sight," somebody hollers.

But never mind that.

I'm going to depart these premises. Passed rifle fire. Passed PT. Passed the classroom crap.

It's in the books. Basic training and I are no longer one.

I find Skebo the instant he finds me.

"How did you do it?" he says.

I pretend to blow smoke off the barrel.

"Just good shooting, Tex."

Some things you don't tell.

We hug. One hundred ninety eight men are picking up brass and ammo and two are in each other's arms.

"We made it," Skebo screams.

"We didn't die," I holler.

"I get to go back to the Farm."

"I get to see Kathy's legs."

DI Cannon walks by.

"This ain't no goddamn love-in."

But his heart isn't in it. He knows this shit is over. The last "You WILL do this" on their list was night fire.

"Aw, fuck," he says. "Carry on."

They load us on the cattle car like always, but this is not like always.

We're beating our steel helmets on the roof like we're coming back to the fieldhouse after winning the big football game.

"I don't want to be no airborne ranger," Nordquist, the team captain, sings.

"I don't want no life of danger," Rodriguez joins in.

The junior Echo Platoon DI is assigned to our truck. This exuberance is completely unauthorized. Nowhere in the field manuals does it say troops can damn near beat a hole in the Army's rolling stock while desecrating the Mekong River and all its tributaries.

But he says nothing. And even laughs. God, when it's over out here, it's really over.

Somebody asks the DI if there were any BRM bolos after night-fire.

"About a dozen. The other trucks will be pulling out soon. One'll stay behind for them."

We're just wondering. These guys couldn't hit the targets before. It's even darker now. What could possibly save them from a repeat performance?

He looks at his watch and yawns.

"Dawn."

I think back to the first night I sat in one of these things with Boil on my lap. I was convinced we were beginning the Bataan Death March, and they were giving us a break by letting us ride.

Something crazy has happened.

I have a sense of accomplishment for this place.

For the first time in my life I've done a hard thing.

The screaming. The marching. The shooting.

The going-to-bed dirty. The going-to-bed knowing I've screwed something up and they just haven't told me yet. The going-to-bed hoping nobody has shit on the toilet seat so my first duty of the next day won't be the worst.

No matter how stupid the past eight weeks have been.

No matter how irrelevent to how I will spend the rest of my existence.

I got to the end. I'll get to see the colonel's stupid dog.

Fair and square.

More or less.

While I have not earned the Army's seal of excellence, I can fully accept its checkmark.

The growing glimmer that is the writer inside me - OK, OK, deep inside - knows I needed this.

If your job is performing exploratory surgery on the human condition, you must have life's experiences and I had precious few before shipping out here.

It's like God said, hey, I could give you a 321 draft lottery number and you'd never know an operations shack. Never know bolt sliders come in groups. But it wouldn't be in your best interests. Trust me on this, kid. You'll scream and cuss your No. 71, but it's all going to work out in the end.

Keep hanging out with those college buddies of yours, God continued, and you would never meet a Haddox. Never see whores on parade. Never trade rocks for bullets.

I've shown you a brand new world, He said. Peavey. The grenade range. The gas chamber. The importance of Brasso to the national defense. The cauldrons of plenty at the mess hall. The Little Vietnam at the NCO Club.

You'll harken back to this world when you go to work at the newspaper, God went on, even if it's just to laugh like hell in some beer joint at 2 o'clock in the morning. You'll write about what you went through. Won't have a choice. The words will stage a revolution inside your psyche until you put them on paper. Send me some bylines. I maintain the world's largest clip file.

Someone points out that West Pointers celebrate graduation by tossing their hats high in the air.

We throw our steel pots inside the cattle car. They bounce perilously in the manner of small cannonballs. Several troops narrowly escape injury.

It's hilarious.

Thanks, God.

An M&M wrapper is attached to the guidon.

"Long may it wave on high," a troop calls out.

"Now we've finally got something we can follow," another guy says.

It's like this all the way back to the barracks. A hay ride without the scratching.

Nobody wants to go to bed. We exchange addresses, pictures and souvenir items from the PX.

It's almost time to leave, but there's a hitch in our step. You'll write, won't you? Or call. We've been through too much together. Can't let it end in some mindless formation by the horizontal bars.

Many of the RAs are trying on their Class A uniforms for tomorrow's gala. They're shining their low quarters, polishing their buttons and ironing their shirts, making sure their rank is properly displayed nearer the shoulder than the elbow. They march in place and practice what to do when Litton hollers, "Eyes right."

Few NGs and ERs are in this camp. We'll dress like D-minus students. Proud of every uncreased pleat. Proud of every rumpled shirttail. It's our fashion statement. We could open a Goodwill Store.

The RAs don't rag us for being sloppy. We don't run them down for standing straight and tall.

We're like an old married couple. Being together all this time, anything that comes up between us is an "Oh, pshaw, never you mind."

They understand our perspective.

The several liberal arts profs who gave extra credit to students who participated in protest marches. The petitions passed out before Chaucer class calling for Nixon to quit. The midnight peace rally on the drillfield that drew more than 6,000 students, so many that they had to get extra candles from the Episcopal Church.

We understand their background.

They had peer groups who believed Vietnam was about honor and glory like all the other great wars. The school of thought pushed upon them that they're going to be factory workers for the rest of their lives anyway, so why not join the Army, see the world and kill a few gooks before settling in with that lathe. And the reality that the Army, whatever else it might be, is a job where otherwise there might not be one. Three hots a day, a bunk and a uniform for every hanger in your closet.

Carouthers is primping like he's going to the Percy Sledge concert and it's 60 percent off if you're green.

I watch.

Not scared like I used to be.

But hoping he doesn't get killed.

"You're going to Vietnam and I'm going to a typewriter."

Carouthers doesn't know what to say. He can only react to inequity, not explain it.

"But you can make it. The tour of duty is only 12 months. You can stand on your head that long. Be back cooking chicken before you know it."

"Don't know about that, man. Lot of shit can happen in the jungle."

The same awkwardness swirls as when Ya and I visited this subject.

Carouthers didn't have a well-placed, well-spoken someone to get him in the reserves or National Guard.

So he wins a free trip to Vietnam.

My dad worked the phones harder than Alexander Graham Bell.

And I'll get no closer to Saigon than Rand-McNally.

Living or dying. Decision by pedigree.

Carouthers gives me one of those soul handshakes with knuckles and fingertips.

"I'll get through it, cottontail. You just make sure you find all the typewriter keys."

"Meeting you has been one of the most significant occurrences in my life," I say.

"Aw, shit."

He fingers the side of his forehead and grimaces.

"Fell against the vending machine at the PX. Hurts like hell. Big knot. Wanna feel?"

Now it's my turn.

"Aw, shit."

Skebo is rubbing his foot. It seems a steel pot came down for a landing.

"Cheeseburgers," he says. "Yeah, that's it. Cheeseburgers."

Say what?

"When you come back to Fort Leonard Wood in 20 years, what's the thing you'll most want to do?"

"Moot point. Won't happen," I reply. "Not only will I never return to this military installation, I shall never again darken the state of Missouri. If my plane's flight plan calls for a fly-over, I'll have the pilot let me off."

"You'll be back. We'll all be back. Stroke our chins, push the ear hair back in and tell the grandchildren how rough we had it back in 1971."

I shake my head vigorously.

"Not me. When I ride out that front gate, I'm gone. I don't care if there's a gold rush outside the main PX."

"Yeah, yeah, we'll see about that," Skebo says. "Me, I want to get a big bag of cheeseburgers, lean against the Dumpster and watch troops train. They're running and grunting and sweating. I don't have to do any of it. Just stand there and chew.

"What a beautiful moment. Don't have to fall in. Don't have to dress-right-dress. Don't have to holler that stupid cadence about the pretty girl huffing weed in the latrine.

"Be like the spectator at the 50-yard line. Only thing missing is a seat cushion, a flask and a program. I'd drive 400 miles for that. What am I saying? I'd drive 1,000 miles. Just to see one troop with galoshes banging against his ass. Just to see one KP fall exhausted against a vat of lima beans. Make the whole trip worthwhile."

"I'm still not coming back of my own free will," I say, "but if the world got turned upside down and I landed here, I'd go out to the rifle range, wait until nobody is looking and steal a silhouette. Throw it in the back seat with the kids.

"The target was my sworn enemy for eight weeks and now I'll consort with it in my den. Rig the apparatus to register a kill when I lob a beer bottle."

I watch my friend toss bags of potato chips to everyone who sticks his head in the door.

We'll ship out in 12 hours. Probably never see each other again.

"Thanks for helping me get through this," I tell him.

Skebo puts a flip-flop against the ceiling, takes out a pen and outlines the edges.

"For the next training cycle," he explains. "In case the sweet potatoes don't come up."

"Pay attention, dammit. It was enough hell getting through basic with a buddy. I don't even want to think about going it alone."

He grabs a mop handle, holds the shaggy end against the back of his head and pretends to be road guard - a tie-dyed flashback from that first morning.

"Be serious. You counseled me and you dared me. You were somebody I could talk to. Somebody we all could talk to."

Skebo takes the handle and attempts to flog his private region. He misses every time.

"Just like I thought," he says in Haddox-speak. "Can't hit your dick with a stick."

He's not going to let me declare Skebo Appreciation Day. I can't pass out the plaque if I'm too busy laughing.

A bunch of troops come in the room. They want my friend to reprise the Apperson shitpaper-on-the-pillow incident.

He obliges.

"Yeah, but there's a whole half turd on there!" Skebo shouts, feigning horror.

Thunderous applause.

"Do your getting ready to fight with General," somebody asks.

"No, no, do the hiring Kippler to fold your socks," somebody else requests.

Guys being guys, this is their way of saying goodbye.

I slip away and take a seat in the hall.

Rodriguez has fashioned his pistol belt into a soccer ball. His team asks me to move so he can take a penalty kick.

I remember another time I was asked to resettle. Eight weeks ago. A lifetime.

The housing unit that I thought was mine had already been assigned to four other sorry asses, and I would have to move the fuck.

I sat on this same floor and cried. Scared. Confused. I needed a cheat sheet just to breathe. Moving the fuck was out of the question.

Well, I've done all right.

Didn't turn into a casserole, as Carl predicted.

Didn't have to suck anything.

Only had to rake up the one rubber.

Shot better than a fox terrier.

Didn't have a lawn mower taken to my balls.

Didn't have to low-crawl to eternity.

Didn't have to be ball-checker.

Didn't get killed by the buffing machine.

Skebo is finishing his encore presentation about how the arresting officers at the Ellipse took one look at him and realized they needed to start lifting weights.

"Do you think we'll make it out of this place?" I holler.

"Yeah," he shouts back. "But we'll need a victory lap."

Printed in the United States
91814LV00006B/106/A